Critical Praise for Nina Revoyr

for *Wingshooters*

- A *Booklist* Editors' Choice
- Finalist for Southern California Independent Bookseller Association's Fiction Award
- Winner of the Midwest Booksellers Choice Award
- Winner of the first annual Indie Booksellers Choice Award
- Selected for IndieBound's Indie Next List, "Great Reads from Booksellers You Trust"
- Featured in *O, The Oprah Magazine*'s Reading Room section as one of *10 Titles to Pick Up Now*

"Revoyr does a remarkable job of conveying [protagonist] Michelle's lost innocence and fear through this accomplished story of family and the dangers of complacency in the face of questionable justice."
—*Publishers Weekly* (starred review)

"Revoyr writes rhapsodically of . . . the natural world and charts, with rising intensity, her resilient narrator's painful awakening to human failings and senseless violence. In this shattering northern variation on *To Kill a Mockingbird*, Revoyr drives to the very heart of tragic ignorance, unreason, and savagery."   —*Booklist* (starred review)

"Hauntingly provocative . . . an excellent choice for book discussion groups."   —*Library Journal*

"Gripping and insightful."   —*Kirkus Reviews*

for *Southland*

- A *Los Angeles Times* Best Seller
- Winner: Lambda Literary Award
- Winner: Ferro-Grumley Literary Award
- Winner: American Library Association's Stonewall Honor Award
- Finalist: Edgar Award
- A Book Sense 76 Pick
- Selected for the *Los Angeles Times'* Best Books of 2003 list

"Fascinating and heartbreaking . . . an essential part of LA history."
—*LA Weekly*

"The plot line of *Southland* is the stuff of a James Ellroy or a Walter Mosley novel ... But the climax fairly glows with the good-heartedness that Revoyr displays from the very first page."   —*Los Angeles Times*

"Compelling ... never lacking in vivid detail and authentic atmosphere, the novel cements Revoyr's reputation as one of the freshest young chroniclers of life in LA."   —*Publishers Weekly*

"If Oprah still had her book club, this novel likely would be at the top of her list ... With prose that is beautiful, precise, but never pretentious ..."
—*Booklist* (starred review)

"... an ambitious and absorbing book that works on many levels: as a social and political history of Los Angeles, as the story of a young woman discovering and coming to terms with her cultural heritage, as a multigenerational and multiracial family saga, and as a solid detective story."   —*Denver Post*

"Subtle, effective ... [with] a satisfyingly unpredictable climax."
—*Washington Post*

for *The Age of Dreaming*

- Finalist: *Los Angeles Times* Book Prize

"Rare indeed is a novel this deeply pleasurable and significant."
—*Booklist* (starred review)

"Reminiscent of Paul Auster's *The Book of Illusions* in its concoction of spurious Hollywood history and its star's filmography ... ingenious ... hums with the excitement of Hollywood's pioneer era."
—*San Francisco Chronicle*

"Fast-moving, riveting, unpredictable, and profound; highly recommended."   —*Library Journal*

"Revoyr conveys in a lucid, precise and period appropriate prose ... a pulse-quickening, deliciously ironic serving of Hollywood noir."
—*Kirkus Reviews*

"It's an enormously satisfying novel."   —*Publishers Weekly*

"[Nina Revoyr is] an empathetic chronicler of the dispossessed outsider in LA."   —*Los Angeles Times*

LOST CANYON

A NOVEL

BY

NINA REVOYR

Published by Akashic Books
©2015 Nina Revoyr

Lost Canyon map by Courtney Menard

Hardcover ISBN: 978-1-61775-353-4
Paperback ISBN: 978-1-61775-354-1
Library of Congress Control Number: 2014955092

Akashic Books
Twitter: @AkashicBooks
Facebook: AkashicBooks
info@akashicbooks.com
www.akashicbooks.com

Felicia

You cannot stay on the summit forever; you have to come down again. So why bother in the first place? Just this: What is above knows what is below, but what is below does not know what is above. One climbs, one sees. One descends, one sees no longer, but one has seen. There is an art of conducting oneself in the lower regions by the memory of what one saw higher up. When one can no longer see, one can at least still know.

—René Daumel, *Mount Analogue*

The body is the one thing you can't fake; it's just got to be there.

—James Dickey, *Deliverance*

Chapter One
Gwen

The picture opened on Gwen's computer, revealing a lake framed by pine trees, a backdrop of snow-covered peaks. A small stream flowed from the lake and when she looked very close, Gwen could almost see the water moving, the clouds drifting over the mountains. She imagined herself in the scene—the warm sun on her skin, the smell of pine—and felt her breathing slow, her shoulders ease. Just for a moment she forgot where she was—in a dingy building on 103rd Street in Watts.

Tracy's e-mail had come with the subject line, *Cloud Lakes Trip: Last-Minute Details!* Although Gwen was about to step out of the office, she couldn't resist checking the message. Besides the photo, there was a bullet-point list of food and supplies, plus directions to Tracy's house. Gwen glanced at the list and looked back at the picture; then she picked up the phone.

"Tracy Cole," came the voice on the other end. As always, she sounded focused and busy. Gwen could imagine her in her workout gear, standing arrow-straight behind the counter at the gym.

"Hey, Tracy, it's Gwen."

"Hey!" Tracy's voice was friendlier now, although she still sounded poised for action—ready to run a marathon, or break up a mugging, or hang glide off a cliff near the coast. "You got my e-mail?"

"I did, thanks," said Gwen. "It looks like I still need a few things. A sleeping pad, extra batteries. An extra fuel canister. How much is all of this going to weigh?"

"Maybe thirty-five pounds. A piece of cake. You're not having second thoughts, are you?"

"No," Gwen assured her, although she was. What had she gotten herself into? Gwen was a city girl, born and bred—she knew chain-link fences and concrete better than rivers and trees. And she spent most of her time in South LA, where she worked for an organization that provided counseling and after-school programs for low-income kids. Although Gwen had started hiking a year and a half ago, it had all been short and local—she'd never hiked a trail more than five or six miles long, and she'd never spent the night in a tent. This trip would be unlike anything she'd ever done before—a four-day, three-night trip into the Sierra backcountry, a real wilderness experience. She imagined how the pack was going to feel on her shoulders—like carrying a child piggyback, and never putting him down. But she needed this; she needed to do something different, to see a world that was not shaped by people. "I'm just not sure about carrying all that weight," she said.

"You'll be all right. Just load your pack up the next few nights and walk around the block."

"Okay," Gwen said doubtfully. She imagined the stares she'd get from neighbors. Backpacking had never been a part of her world. Most people she knew would think of it—if they thought of it at all—as an activity for tree-hugging granola types with excess time and money. It definitely wasn't anything that black people did—especially not women.

Besides, all of this was easy for Tracy to say. Tracy was

strong and fit—a combination of the Japanese sleek of her mother and the Idaho mountain man stock of her father. She'd been a star soccer player, an alternate for the US national team, and had followed that up with a slew of outdoor pursuits—rock climbing, mountain biking, snowboarding—that, in Gwen's opinion, bordered on extreme. Now she was a trainer at SportZone, a physical therapy center and gym run out of a converted warehouse downtown, and she also had private clients on the side. Gwen had met her while doing physical therapy for a hyperextended knee, which she'd hurt during a volleyball game at the company picnic. Once she graduated from PT, she'd joined the fitness classes on the other side of the gym, and Tracy was the teacher.

"You know, I have an extra sleeping pad," Tracy said now. This trip to Cloud Lakes had, of course, been her idea. "Don't buy one. And I've got fuel and most of the group gear too. Is there anything else you need?"

"No, I think I'm okay." Gwen appreciated the offer, though. She'd borrowed the backpack and a sleeping bag from someone at work—but she'd still had to buy a headlamp, a rain jacket, and some lightweight pants, not to mention a sturdy pair of hiking shoes. She wouldn't be able to pay off her credit card bill that month, but one month of overage wouldn't kill her. Much worse, she knew, would be to stay in the office all summer.

"Well, all right then!" Tracy said cheerfully. "I'll see you at nine on Thursday at my place. It's going to be beautiful, Gwen. Classic Sierra backcountry. Trust me. You're not going to believe it."

"I'm excited," Gwen said. But she was nervous too. "Hey, who are the others again?"

"They're all clients. A couple of married stock-fund managers, the Pattersons. Todd Harris, the lawyer. And Oscar Barajas, the real estate guy."

"Don't I know Oscar?"

"Yeah, he comes to my Tuesday morning class."

Gwen was quiet for a minute and Tracy broke in again.

"Don't worry! They're nice people. I wouldn't subject you, or me for that matter, to spending four days with a bunch of assholes."

"Okay, okay," Gwen said, laughing. "I'll see you on Thursday."

After she hung up, she sat thinking for a moment. What would she have to talk about with a lawyer and two finance people? But she shook these doubts off. She needed a change of scene, a mind-frame adjustment. There'd been a lot weighing on her this last year, ever since the loss of Robert, a kid from one of her groups. Thank God for this trip. Thank God for Tracy, who made Gwen get out and do things that she would never have done on her own.

Gwen had never really been into exercise. But as she'd lifted barbells and hoisted medicine balls and trudged up the stair machine in Tracy's class, she was amazed at how much stronger she felt. Muscles she didn't even know she had grew sore, and then firm. Her excess pounds fell away. For the first time in her life, her body didn't feel like an encumbrance, or an enemy. And when Tracy invited her to join her twice-monthly hikes in the local mountains, Gwen had jumped at the chance. She'd been on a few hikes with the kids from work, but this was different. There was something about Tracy's energy, her lust for adventure and her solid belief that any new skill or pursuit could be mastered, that appealed to Gwen. She had needed that kind of optimism, especially this last year. She hoped that some of it might rub off on her.

Gwen grabbed her purse, stepped out of her office, and headed toward the entrance. The building had originally been a hospital for the mentally ill, and that's what it still felt like. The offices, converted from bedrooms, were windowless and claustrophobic. Half the overhead lights were burned out and the rest flickered unreliably. As Gwen passed through the front lobby, she saw the crack in the ceiling that was the shape of a lightning bolt; one good shaking from an earthquake might bring the whole place down.

She walked out to her car, a ten-year-old Honda. The weather was cool and overcast even though it was summer; she thought, not for the first time, that June Gloom was especially gloomy in South LA. She drove east on 103rd Street past the old train station, past the apartments for low-income seniors, barely glancing at the Watts Towers to the right, whose curling, colorful spires usually cheered her. Beyond Wilmington the broad street narrowed as it entered an area of small, rundown bungalows and apartment buildings, which faced the public housing projects across the street.

At Lincoln High School, she showed her ID to the security guard, who waved her into the lot. Then she walked across the concrete playground and into the ancient high school, which looked like a 1920s Department of Water and Power building that hadn't been painted since it was built. She made her way down a long hallway, past a custodial crew scrubbing curse words off the walls and graffiti from the lockers, and into the administrative office. There, she was pulled into an inner office while the secretary dug up the papers she needed to sign—the new memorandum of understanding between her agency and the school, program completion forms for some of her kids.

As she went back out to the waiting room, a group of students arrived to sign up for summer school. Two of them were black, the rest Latino, reflecting the change in the neighborhood. Just a few years ago, Watts had still been mostly African American. But last semester, in Gwen's youth leadership group at this school, she'd been the only black person in the room.

"Hey, Ms. Foster!" one of the kids called out. It was a student from the job readiness program that was run by her colleague Devon. "It's Sylvia," the girl said. "Sylvia Morales."

"Oh, hi!" Gwen answered, summoning the upbeat, caring energy she always tried to have with the kids. "I didn't realize you went here. You're a junior now, right?"

"Gonna be a senior next year," said Sylvia. She was a stocky girl, 5'8" or so, and she carried herself with a confidence that belied her surroundings. "I can't wait to get *out* of this mess."

"Are you coming to Devon's group at the office this summer?"

"No . . ." Sylvia said, and now she glanced back at two other kids, another Latina and a black girl, both standing with their arms crossed and looking away like there was something else they'd rather be doing. "Actually, Lupita and Dawn and I were hoping to be in one of *your* groups. Sandra was in your leadership group this year—Sandra Gutierrez—and she told us we should join it for sure."

"That would be great!" Gwen said, pleased in spite of herself. "Hi, Lupita. Hi, Dawn. I'm Gwen. It's wonderful to meet you. I look forward to getting to know you next fall."

And just like that, facades began to crumble. Lupita blushed and mumbled hello, and Dawn met Gwen's eyes and smiled big.

"Just talk to your resource coordinator," Gwen continued. "Or better yet, stop by our office and sign up with the receptionist."

"Will you be around on Thursday?" Sylvia asked. "We could come by after school."

"Actually, no. I'm taking a little vacation."

"Really? Devon said you're always at work."

"Only most of the time," Gwen said, smiling. "But yeah, I'll be gone for a couple of days. I wanted to get away."

"Get away from all this?" Sylvia asked, striking a pose like a game show assistant. With the sweep of her arms she took in the office, the school, the neighborhood.

Gwen laughed and promised to see the girls the following week, and to save them spots in one of her groups. Now she remembered hearing about Sylvia from both Devon and Sandra, who'd been one of her hardest cases this year. These teens seemed so tough on the surface, but softened when you took the time to see them. Bright kids, all of them, full of potential, and as she walked back to her car, she felt cheered.

But as Gwen drove back toward the office by a different route, she remembered what those kids walked back into. This neighborhood felt like a bombed-out city, deserted after a war. Trash was piled everywhere. There were broken TVs and discarded tires, old mattresses, dirty clothes. Greasy food wrappers balled in gutters or fluttered away down the street. Doors and windows were covered with iron bars and particle board. The threat of crime hung in the air like a layer of smog; just last week there'd been a lockdown at the office because of a nearby shooting, and the week before, a man on a bicycle had held up two of her colleagues as they left a client's apartment. Inglewood, where Gwen lived, had its own share of troubles. But here, it felt like there were no rules at all. You always had to be on guard working in this neighborhood. You had to be prepared for the worst.

And yet, that was exactly why Gwen liked working in Watts—because the kids here had so much stacked against them. When she kept a young boy from joining a gang; when a girl she worked with made it to college, Gwen felt a huge sense of triumph and vindication. She'd had a rocky road herself when it came to school and family. No one had really expected anything from her, and no one expected anything good from the kids she helped. They were kids that other people thought expendable.

She turned onto a street that led into the housing project where Robert and his family had lived. It was a labyrinth of two-story bungalows that might have once been green. As always, she was struck by the desolation. On the dead grass between the units were old sinks and barbecue grills, piles of rusted bike and auto parts. Laundry waved from clothes lines, colorful items that stood out against the gray sky, like flags hung in surrender. A few proud residents struggled mightily against their surroundings—their entryways were swept clean, with maybe a potted plant or two—but this couldn't make up for the heavy gates over the doors, the paint flaking off the walls, the chunks of roof that collapsed with each rain. Once she had to stop for a legless woman in a wheelchair. Twice she slammed her brakes to avoid a loose dog. There were kids everywhere—youths circling on bikes, toddlers sitting on stoops with their mothers or grandmothers, a group of middle school kids throwing around a football. A dozen little ones waited in line for the single swing on an otherwise broken play set.

Gwen wove her way through the development, looking but not stopping when she passed the row where Robert had lived. Once he had been one of those kids, sitting on his stoop. Now he was gone, and she couldn't bear to look for very long at the place where he should have been, but wasn't.

Gwen loved her job, but lately she'd been feeling overwhelmed. It seemed like no matter what they did, no matter how many kids they helped, there were always others, so many others, who couldn't be reached. It was like trying to rescue people from a flood or tsunami—you might be able to pluck one or two out of the swirling waters, but hundreds more got swept away right in front of you.

And the neighborhood itself didn't help. In this community, it was hard for Gwen and her colleagues to preach about the promised land of college and a well-paying career, to instill that kind of faith, when no one in most of these kids' everyday experience had ever laid eyes on it or breathed its different air. There was no way a kid could walk into that school, or through Gwen's office building, or down these streets, and feel anything but second-rate. Now Gwen was starting to feel that way too.

Just as she turned into her parking lot, her cell phone rang. She picked it up and saw the caller ID— Alene Richardson—and let it ring one more time before she answered.

"Hi, Mom."

"Oh, hello, Gwen," her mother said, sounding distracted, as if Gwen had been the one to call her. "Are you at work?"

"Yes." Where else would she be?

"Good, good. I was just calling to remind you that Dana's birthday is on Friday."

"Yes, Mom, I know. I sent her a card today."

"Oh, wonderful! Thank you. You know how lonely your sister gets up there at school. It's good for her to hear from her family."

Gwen tried to quell her irritation. Her sister, she knew, was just fine. Twelve years younger than Gwen, she was now a first-year student at the Stanford Graduate School of Business. Dana had been raised in a totally different era of their mother's life. She'd grown up in the house in Ladera Heights that had just been a stopping point for Gwen; had been lavished with clothes and trips and extracurricular activities; had been part of Jack & Jill, a young women's leadership group at church, the AKAs at Berkeley. Now, at twenty-four, Dana's birthday was still celebrated with as much fanfare as if she were a child. Yet there had been years in Gwen's own childhood, when she lived with her great-aunt, that Alene had forgotten Gwen's birthday altogether.

"I'm not going to be able to call her on Friday, though, Mom," Gwen said. "But I mentioned that in the card."

"Why not?"

"I'm going on my backpacking trip this weekend. Remember?"

A tense silence. Then a sigh. "Yes, now I recall. You're really going to do that, Gwendolyn?"

"Yes, Mother, I'm really going to do that."

"It just sounds so . . . *uncivilized*. I mean, how will you *bathe*? How will you . . . use the *restroom*? Where will you *sleep*—on the ground?"

Gwen didn't answer, partly because she wondered

these things herself. She stared out past the fence that en-
closed the property and over toward the railroad tracks,
where a mangy brown dog picked hungrily through a
mountain of trash.

"I just don't know how you got this idea in the first
place," Alene continued. "It's not the kind of thing we've
ever done."

Gwen thought wryly that her mother had little idea of
what she'd done, but she kept this observation to herself.
"Chris and Terry Nelson went on backpacking trips every
summer," she said, remembering her mother's neighbors.

"Yes, but they're boys," Alene replied. She didn't add—
although Gwen knew she thought—*and white.* "And speaking of boys, are there any men going with you?"

"Yes, three men."

"Couldn't one of them carry your things?"

"No, Mom. They'll have their own backpacks."

"Well I don't know what kind of man would let a woman
carry so much weight."

She stayed silent, waiting for her mother to launch
into a lecture about Gwen's nonexistent love life, but she
didn't.

"And is a hotel too expensive?" Alene asked. "Is that
why you're sleeping outside?"

"It's not that. We *want* to be outdoors."

"I really wish you'd do something that would pay you
a decent salary."

And here we go, Gwen thought. Out of nowhere. "I *like*
my job, Mom."

"You've done your part giving back, don't you think? I
just worry about you in that dangerous area, with all those
desperate people. You could always go to business school

at night, you know. Or even law school. Stuart and I could help you."

"Thanks. Listen, I have to go. I'll give you a call before I leave." Gwen hung up, took a deep breath, and got out of the car.

She never failed to rile her, Gwen's mother. In the space of five minutes, Alene had managed to denigrate both the white people whose unclean habits Gwen appeared to be emulating, and the black and Latino kids with whom she worked.

Gwen was born when her mother was seventeen. Although no one ever talked about it, it was believed that her father had been the vice-principal at Alene's school. Alene had dropped out, fallen into the grip of alcohol and God knew what else, and eventually disappeared, so from the time Gwen was three until just after she turned twelve, she had lived with her great-aunt Emmaline in Inglewood. It was Emmaline, a retired mail carrier, who'd come up with Gwen's name, in honor of the famous poet. And it was Emmaline who'd passed on family stories—of Gwen's great-grandfather who'd left Alabama for Chicago in the early 1900s; of her ancestor Phillis, who'd escaped from slavery in Tennessee and fled up to Ohio, where she'd given birth to Emmaline's grandmother. For much of her childhood Gwen only saw her mother two or three times a year, and sometimes not at all.

When Emmaline passed away, Gwen lived with two foster families—first the Grandersons, a black family in Culver City, and then the Weisses, a Jewish family in the Valley. Both families had been kind to her, but by the time Gwen was fifteen, all she wanted was to live with someone who wasn't paid to take care of her.

And then, almost miraculously, Alene reappeared. She'd sobered up, earned her GED, gone to college. She'd eventually gotten a master's degree and started a job with a food company. She'd married Stuart Robinson, whom she'd met at their church, and given birth to another child. When Gwen went to live with them soon after her fifteenth birthday, the Alene she met was so different from the one who had left her that it was almost like she'd been placed with another foster family. Her own experience had made Gwen shy away from the idea of having children. There were enough kids in the world already, she thought, too many of them unwanted.

After telling the receptionist that the girls from Lincoln might drop by, Gwen made her way back to her office. She called up the image of the lake on her computer again and tried to recapture her sense of calm. But the scene was flat now; it had lost all its power. Damn her mother, she thought. Damn her for so swiftly poisoning even this.

She brought her mind back to where she was, the office where she spent so much time that she sometimes inadvertently called it "home." On the walls there were pictures of her colleagues at various work events, a certificate naming her employee of the year, a framed commendation from the city councilman for her outstanding work with youth. On her bulletin board, there were photos of kids who'd been in her groups, and school portraits of some of her colleagues' children.

At the corner of the board, closest to her, was a picture of Robert. He was posing on a rock high up on a hiking trail with all of LA spread out behind him. His hands were on his hips and his chin was raised at a jaunty angle, as if he were a conquering hero. He looked beautiful and ridiculous, pleased with himself and with the world. Gwen had taken this picture two weeks before he died.

Robert had been in seventh grade when Gwen first met him; he'd been referred by a therapist at his school. A tall, gangly kid, he'd shown up for group sessions in threadbare clothes, with holes in his worn-out sneakers. But he was unfailingly polite, and he always seemed to speak in complete paragraphs, using words—*sustainable, honor-bound, erudite, Darwinian*—that were almost comically formal. When Gwen finally asked him what had brought him to group, he answered only, "I was suspended for fighting."

She couldn't fathom the idea that this gentle kid was a fighter, and so she tracked down the school therapist. That was how she learned that Robert and his little brother Isaac had bounced around to several homes as their mother fled an abusive relationship. Robert had seen the man hold a gun to his mother's head; he'd watched him break her arm. He'd gotten into several fights at his new school, the therapist said, while standing up for girls when boys harassed them.

Robert had always been a good student, so he didn't need help with academics. But he was awkward and shy and down on himself, so Gwen connected him with other activities—Devon's job prep group, a digital media class, and a group that went on outings, like that hike in the local mountains. He stayed in her youth leadership group through middle school and high school, where he got mostly As and a couple of Bs. In his senior year he applied to UCLA, and when his acceptance letter arrived, there'd been an impromptu celebration at her office—cupcakes and soda and teary speeches from the staff, Robert grinning and embarrassed at the attention. He seemed like the ultimate success story—a black boy from Watts who'd grown up in extreme poverty, and who had made it to a top-notch university.

Then Robert showed up to group one day with a fresh black eye. He wouldn't talk about what happened. But Trey, another student, told her that some boys had started bugging him again, a couple of the same ones from back in seventh grade. Robert was skinny and nerdy, too into his books—he thought he was something special. He didn't try to get with girls; there must have been something wrong with him. Gwen went to talk to the principal but he just smiled and nodded absently; he was new to the area, from Maine or Maryland, and he said the boys should "work it out themselves."

A few days later the boys cornered Robert in the locker room. They stripped off his clothes, knocked him around, and left him there, naked. There was speculation that more might have happened but no one knew for sure. When the school staff questioned Robert, he just shook his head, refusing to talk.

Gwen tried to get him to open up, to no avail. He'll tell us when he's ready, she'd thought. He was subdued for several weeks, but then he seemed to turn a corner, and everyone was cautiously relieved. This was a terrible thing, but he'd been through worse, and he'd get past it; he always did. As the school year wound down he grew more cheerful again; he almost seemed at peace. He was talking about plans for the summer, and they'd even gone on that wonderful hike. That was why everyone had been so stunned when Robert hanged himself.

It had happened a little more than a year ago, the second week of June, and Gwen still felt completely undone.

All these months later, she still asked that question that people ask and never get an answer to: *Why?* And even more, particular to her: *How could I not have known?* It was easy to say in retrospect that she had always sensed Robert's sadness; that there was a stillness in him that she couldn't touch or understand. And maybe, with his recent troubles, that sadness had tipped over into despair. But mostly what she remembered was his hopefulness. She couldn't believe that he was not coming back; she kept expecting him to walk through the door of her office.

But then she did believe it, and she believed it still. Robert was gone and he wasn't returning; he'd chosen to take his life. And besides the feeling of loss that still threatened to swallow her whole, Gwen couldn't get over the fact that she hadn't done more to help. She should have made him tell her what had happened; she should have forced that principal to do his job. She should have told Robert that no matter how bad things seemed now, they'd get better; the trouble would pass.

Gwen looked back at the picture and her eyes filled with tears. Robert had overcome so much, and he had everything going for him—good grades, the toughness to survive a difficult home life, a future that was bright and limitless. If *he* couldn't find a reason to keep going, what hope was there for the other kids she worked with? Why did she even bother? Why risk her own safety every day for the sake of kids and families who were so deeply mired in problems that they were never going to get better? She didn't know what to do anymore with her helplessness, her grief. Now her eyes returned to the picture of the lake. Yes, she thought as she looked at it. Yes, she needed to get away from all this.

Chapter Two
Oscar

Oscar Barajas turned left onto York and immediately ran into stopped traffic. There was a line of it, both ways, bumper to bumper, inching slowly through the main corridor of Highland Park.

"Shit," he said softly, and then he remembered Lily, his four-year-old daughter, who was sitting in back. He glanced up at the rearview mirror but she was staring out the window and hadn't heard him.

"Papá, can I have a SPAM musubi?" she asked, pointing at the Hawaiian barbecue place that had recently sprung up, along with a Starbucks and a CVS, in what had once been a stretch of dilapidated houses and trash-filled empty lots.

"No, mija. Not today. Grandma's probably made you dinner. We can get some when I pick you up on Monday, okay? I promise."

"Oh-kay," Lily answered, with an exaggerated shrug. Oscar smiled. She was damned cute, his daughter. His mother doted on her too, and he was grateful to her for watching Lily while he went on his backpacking trip, especially since his ex, Tammy—no surprise—had refused to take her for more than her required time. He just wouldn't tell his mother that Lily liked SPAM—and red curry from the local Thai place, and of course her mother's phở—as much as she did her grandmother's enchiladas.

He inched forward, past the sunglasses store and the graphics shop run out of small converted houses, the check-cashing place, the liquor stores, the hole-in-the-wall taquerías. He couldn't believe the traffic. When had it gotten to be like this? Five years ago, York had been a drive-through street, a barrio artery, that no one but locals ever stopped on. It was gritty, rough, dirty, all the doors and windows covered with bars, a place where members of the Avenues gang strutted openly down the sidewalk, tagging storefronts and walls in broad daylight. But then real estate had boomed, the Northeast had been "discovered," and white yuppies who'd been priced out of the Westside came flooding into the hills of Glassell Park and Mount Washington, the quiet streets of Eagle Rock, some even venturing into the flats of Highland Park. Now, young professionals and fedora-wearing hipsters, many in the entertainment industry, were living side by side with Mexican families who'd been there for generations, and with Chevy-driving, blue-collar whites. And a whole new crop of restaurants, shops, and businesses had sprung up in unexpected places, like hearty plants blossoming in what had long been arid, inhospitable soil. Eagle Rock and Colorado boulevards, once full of car repair shops and storefront churches, now boasted several *Los Angeles Times* and *LA Weekly*–sanctioned eating establishments, including a sushi joint run out of a converted auto body shop and the best cupcake place in the city.

But the most surprising transformation had been on York itself, which one of Oscar's realtor colleagues—before the boom—had half-jokingly referred to as "Mexico." Oscar had come here often when he was a kid, to pick up milk from his mother at the corner bodega or to visit his buddy

Reynaldo at the bike repair shop, and the conversations, the store signs, the music wafting through the air, were all in Spanish. It had stayed that way for years.

The first sign of change had been the hipster bar, called simply The Highland. Oscar was driving down York late one Friday a few years ago, heading home from a family-run Mexican place that had been there all his life, and was surprised to see dozens of white people in their twenties and thirties milling around on the sidewalk. At first he thought he'd had too much to drink. But no, they were really there, in front of a brand-new establishment. He peered in through the floor-to-ceiling windows and saw at least a hundred people, an L-shaped bar, and a huge screen airing an old black-and-white movie. The beers were all microbrew, he found when he went in, the salads watercress and arugula. After The Highland came a coffee shop, a few more restaurants, a wine bar, a pilates studio. But while these places gained a foothold, the advance stopped there—the rest of the block remained stubbornly barrio, and really, Oscar was glad; it was hard to see such drastic change hit so close to home, especially since people he'd known for years were getting priced out of the neighborhood.

He had profited, too, from the real estate boom. Truthfully, it had made him. In his early- and midtwenties he had worked for his uncle David, building driveways and brick patios and retaining walls, trying to stabilize all the properties in those unstable hills. But he'd grown tired of the physical work and of spending days in the sun, and ten years ago, at age twenty-seven, he'd gotten his real estate license, just before property values went through the roof and the feeding frenzy began. Little two-bedroom bungalows that had fetched $150,000 before the boom were suddenly selling for five or six hundred thousand, anything three bedrooms or more was up to a million, all this in neighborhoods that were never mentioned—at the time—in any guidebook description of the city. Empty land was going too, to developers building on spec. Sounds of construction echoed through the once-quiet canyons.

At the height of the market, Oscar was making thirty-five, forty grand a month. He bought a BMW, a Rolex, and a four-bedroom house in the hills of Glassell Park. He bought a small Craftsman bungalow for his mother too, down in Highland Park near the apartment building where he and his sister had grown up. And there were women, lots of them, of every color and creed, single women and lonely married women who showed up for open houses and lingered after everyone else had left. He'd dated other agents too, including Lily's mom, Tammy Ng, who'd represented a buyer to his seller during a particularly drawn-out transaction in Eagle Rock.

But the housing frenzy had come to a halt five years ago. Not sudden, not screeching, but gradual, first fewer clients and properties on the market for weeks, even months, and then the prices started to fall. By the time Oscar realized what was happening, he'd sunk a couple hundred thousand into a string of five houses built on spec in a canyon in Mount Washington. Finished three years ago, the houses stood empty, the gas and electric never hooked up, the connecting road from the main street never completed. All through the hills, houses stood half-built, foundations or retaining walls or septic tank pipes sticking out of the ground, like the remnants of a ghost town that had never been a real one. Now, Oscar was lucky to move a house every other month. Now, his savings were almost gone, and he was barely making his mortgage. He'd defaulted on the loan for the spec houses and the bank had taken them over, but that was the extent of the damage. Thank God he'd put down half the price of his house, and paid his mother's place off in full.

He turned right onto Avenue 50, which had a new coffee shop on the corner, empty now, at six p.m., as the artists and hipsters who filled it during the day moved a few doors down to The Highland. Two blocks later it was left on Baltimore, past his old elementary school and then to his mother's place. It was cute, her house, a two-bedroom bungalow placed well above the street, a single-car garage at street level. Oscar had cleared a little seating area on top of the garage, but his mother preferred to sit on the patio, under the overhanging roof, where she could look out at her yard and keep an eye on the neighborhood. She'd lived alone since Oscar's father died when he was nineteen, and he tried to see her at least once a week. His sister, who worked as an insurance claims adjuster down in Tustin, didn't make it over as much.

"Grandma! Grandma!" Lily cried out excitedly, as they pulled up in front of the house. From next door, he could hear the strains of music, people laughing on their patio. It was a gorgeous night—warm, but with a breeze, the scent of jasmine and oleander in the air, the clouds turning pink over the San Gabriel Mountains. The night-blooming cactus was preparing to flower, elegant green and purple fingers holding a single white orb, like a hand gently offering an ornament. He reached up to pull the string that undid the gate latch, wishing again that his mother would let him put a lock on it. There'd been a couple of break-ins recently, and the block was home to several members of the

Avenues, who'd linger on the sidewalks or drive slowly down the street to remind everyone of their presence. Lily scrambled up the stairs ahead of him and straight to the front porch, where his mother was sitting in her usual spot, in a cheap metal-framed chair with a faded blue cushion.

"Buenas noches, mija!" she exclaimed, arms open wide, and Lily ran straight into them. "Hi, mijo," she said to Oscar, smiling, and as he mounted the patio stairs, he said, "Hola, Mom. Did you just get home?"

She was still dressed for work, in the gray blouse and skirt issued to the female catering staff at the Hilton Pasadena. Her hair was tucked into a ponytail, with a couple of strands loose. She looked tired, and it pained him to see her this way, pained him that she worked this job at all. He didn't like that she was on her feet all day, setting up tables and clearing plates, being ignored or worse, yelled at, by the kinds of people who go to hotels for conferences. He didn't like that people called her by her first name, Dulce, which was printed on the name tag the staff were all required to wear.

"Yes," she replied. "There was a conference today, nine hundred people, continental breakfast, lunch, and afternoon snack. It kept us busy. Ay, I'm tired."

"I'm sorry. We could have come later, Mom."

She waved him off. "No, no, it's fine, Oscar. Besides, our little girl here needs to eat."

"Oh, I should have *brought* something," he said. "You've been working all day. You shouldn't have to cook."

Again his mother waved him off. "Ay, mijo, it's no big deal. I made some enchiladas last night. All I have to do is warm them up."

They moved inside, and his mother disappeared into her room, returning in loose pants, a button-down shirt, and sandals. She slid the baking pan of enchiladas into the oven, while Lily went to the cabinet in the living room where her toys were stored and pulled out several dolls. Oscar sat in the dining room where he could keep an eye on Lily in the living room and on his mother straight ahead in the kitchen.

"So . . . you can drop Lily off at day care any time after seven a.m.," he said. "And then pick her up—"

"After four thirty. I know, Oscar. I promise it will be fine. I did raise you and Sylvia, you know."

"Sorry. I've never been out of touch for this long. I guess I'm a little nervous."

"Well, don't be nervous about us, mijo. I'm more nervous about your trip. Why are you going off so far away, into the mountains? What will you eat? And who are these people you're going with? Is this one of those groups from the Internet?"

"I *like* the mountains, Mom. You know that. And no, it's not a Meetup group. It's people from my gym." Two of them were, anyway: Tracy, who taught his fitness class, and whom he'd represented when she bought her house; and Gwen, who he sometimes saw on Tuesday mornings. Another regular at the gym, a high school football coach named Eric, had laughed at the thought of Oscar making the trip. "You won't last one night in the wilderness, pretty boy," he'd said. Eric's disdain was half the reason he'd decided to go.

He didn't answer his mother's question about what they would eat—freeze-dried meals, jerky, and trail mix would be totally foreign to her; would not even qualify as

real food. And he agreed, because one thing he *wasn't* excited about was his supply of "dinners"—beef Stroganoff
and chicken and rice and salmon with pasta—all light, colorless, and desiccated as a block of Top Ramen, in plastic
packages with pictures of landscapes that tried to divert
your attention from the strange matter inside to the pretty
places where you'd be consuming them. But he did like
the mountains, and for that he could thank Eduardo, his
college roommate from Cal State Northridge. Eduardo was
a former Boy Scout who loved the outdoors, and who'd
taken him hiking in Griffith Park and up in the San Gabriels. Once they even went over to Mount Baldy in winter, and he'd been amazed by the pine trees with their
snow-laden branches, how they folded in on themselves,
bent over like praying nuns.

"But aren't there bears in those mountains?" his mother
asked.

"I don't know. Maybe."

This last exchange brought Lily running in from the
living room. "You're going to see bears, Daddy? I want to
see a bear!"

Oscar scooped his daughter up and sat her on his lap.
"I probably *won't* see them, mija. I hope not, anyway. But
we'll go see some at the zoo sometime, okay?"

This didn't seem to convince her. But she was quickly
distracted as soon as her grandmother took the enchiladas
from the oven. They sat and ate at the dining room table
by the window looking out at the mountains, now hulking
shapes against the darkening sky. Lily chattered on with
her grandmother in English and Spanish, with a word
or two of Vietnamese sprinkled in. And Oscar's mind
wandered—to last-minute preparations, to his girlfriend

Claudia, and finally to the conversation he'd had with his uncle earlier in the week.

Oscar had worked for his uncle for three years. Their jobs had familiarized him with the neighborhoods where he later sold and bought houses; had given him the eye to see what improvements a property might need, and how much those changes were likely to cost. When the market collapsed, his uncle's business still managed to thrive, as people hunkered down and improved what they'd originally thought of as "starter" homes. Now, David was sixty-three and getting tired. He'd first called Oscar a couple of months ago: would Oscar be interested in coming back and taking over? David would still handle the business end, at least for a while—negotiate with contractors, help to choose and plan jobs. But the actual projects, the day-to-day site work, would be Oscar's.

At first Oscar had said no. Going back to his uncle's company would feel like a step back, a step down. He couldn't stand the idea of wearing workingman clothes again. He couldn't stand the idea of someone treating him like a laborer. But as the weeks went by and he watched his savings drop, he thought about his daughter. Real estate was hit or miss, and he was missing more than hitting these days. By the time the market rose again, he might go bankrupt, and then where would he be? His uncle's company wasn't glamorous, but it was profitable and dependable. He knew that David must have had some sense of his troubles; everyone knew about the empty houses on Vallejo. When his uncle had called again a couple of days ago, this time Oscar listened.

After they finished dinner, Oscar went back out to the car and brought in the rest of Lily's things—her pink suitcase full of clothes for the rest of the week, her Hello Kitty backpack. Then his mother handed him a plastic container of leftover enchiladas.

"Mom, I can't take these, I'm *leaving* tomorrow. You and Lily can eat them."

"We have plenty, Oscar. And maybe you'll want a midnight snack or something to eat in the car."

He knew it was no use arguing. He put the container down on the table and gave his mother a hug. "I'll see you on Monday."

Then he turned to his daughter, whose big brown eyes gazed up at him totally without guile. It made his heart melt. He'd never expected to be a father, had been surprised when Tammy, his decidedly unserious girlfriend, broke the news that she was pregnant. Initially he'd been furious and resentful, and even after Lily was born, he'd been ambivalent about his new role as dad. But now he couldn't imagine his life without his daughter. He knelt down and hugged her tight, feeling her spindly arms around his neck. "Bye, mija. I won't be gone long. You listen to Grandma Dulce and pay attention in school, okay?"

"Okay, Papá," she said gravely. This self-possession just made him feel worse for leaving her.

"I'll try to call you tomorrow from the campground, all right?"

"Okay, Papá," she said again.

And then he left and walked outside and down the front stairs, turning once to see his mother and daughter waving at him from the doorway. He waved back, taking one last look at his girl, a knot forming in his stomach as he turned away.

He took backstreets to El Paso, over to Division, and

then left up into the hills, Glassell Park on his right side, the fancier Mount Washington on his left. He avoided the street that would have taken him past his unfinished properties. Other houses he'd either helped buy or sell were sprinkled along the streets he drove: the two-bedroom, one-bath on Division, the three-bedroom with den and mountain view on Panamint. Ten years ago, when he'd bought here, the streets were quiet, and the cars parked on them were Hondas, Fords, Toyotas. Now every other car was a Volvo or BMW. He knew it was good for property values, this influx of money, but something solid and familiar was lost too. The first yuppies who'd moved in, maybe eight or ten years ago, had treated the old-time Latino families, blue-collar whites, and elderly gays with respect. The newer ones— well, they behaved differently. They complained about the bright paint on houses owned by Mexican families who'd been there fifty years. They didn't pick up after their dogs. They sometimes turned their heads when Oscar and Lily went out for walks. Just that morning, on his daily run, Oscar had said "Good morning" to a thirty-something woman who was out walking with her toddler. She looked at him with what might have been fear or disdain, pulled her child close, and didn't reply.

Oscar turned onto his street, pressed the button on the garage door opener tucked above the sun visor, and pulled into the safe cavern of his garage. It was good to be home. His house was folded into the hill, with the garage at street level, the living room, kitchen, and two bedrooms above, and the master bedroom and bathroom perched like a ship's lookout on top of everything else, with a bank of windows facing the mountains. He'd been lucky to buy this place when he had, in 2003; now, even after the bubble had burst, it was worth almost twice what he'd paid for it. And he was proud to live in Glassell Park. Not like the other realtors who tried to expand the boundaries of Mount Washington. Not like the owners of the property that had just been featured in the *Los Angeles Times*, in an article titled, *Mount Washington Eclectic*—even though the house was only three doors down from Oscar's.

He made his way to the main level, where he put the enchiladas in the fridge and checked his messages. Only one, from Claudia, saying that she hadn't called his cell because she knew he was at his mom's.

He smiled. She was like that, Claudia. He wasn't used to the women he dated being so thoughtful and low-key. It was easy to take her for granted, and he did so now—not calling her back as he got his gear and clothes together.

There wasn't much to do, actually. Since he hadn't had any showings that day, he'd been home in the afternoon, and had already packed most of his gear—filling up the bulky, old-school backpack, borrowed from Eduardo, organizing his food. His bags of jerky and trail mix and freeze-dried meals were all stuffed into his pack. He double-checked to make sure he had the new items he'd splurged on—a headlamp, a GPS device, lightweight collapsible plates. Then he decided to throw together a small duffel for the first night, when they'd be staying at a campground. He packed sneakers and extra jeans, a heavier jacket. But soon he was done, his two bags ready by the door.

He opened a beer and stepped onto the patio, gazing out at the lights of Eagle Rock and Pasadena. It was a cool night, but clear, early summer in LA; the head and taillights of the cars on the 134 looked like stars moving sideways across the sky. For the first time in ages, he felt truly alone, felt what it was like to be by himself, and to *be* himself, Oscar Barajas, not a father or son or boyfriend at this particular moment, just a man, about to spend four days away from everything he knew. Fuck Coach Eric, he thought. Fuck anyone who didn't think he could do this.

It was after ten, and he knew that Claudia would be in bed—she worked the early shift as a pediatric nurse at Kaiser on Sunset—so he texted her goodnight and said he'd call her in the morning. Then he went to bed, leaving the sliding glass door to the deck open to get some fresh air.

He awoke around three thirty a.m., groggily, not sure what had disturbed him, until the sound from his dream continued as he opened his eyes. It was a car horn, going off for several seconds. He heard the horn, and then the silence—and then another horn, held slightly shorter, answering back. He lay fully awake now, and it happened again—one car horn, followed seconds later by the other. And again, and again, and now he was annoyed. Really? he thought. At three thirty a.m. on a Wednesday night? The sounds could have been from people leaving The Eastside, another new hipster bar down on Verdugo. He got up and closed the door to the deck but still he could hear them—one horn rich and sonorous, almost like a trumpet, the other one higher and flatter. The sounds would vary in length and in the time lapsed between them, so when the first horn sounded he couldn't relax until the second one completed the exchange. Sometimes the answer came right away, sometimes it took five or ten seconds. There was no pattern he could expect and tune out. Again he cursed the newcomers, the hipsters who'd invaded this part of town and showed so little regard for those who'd always lived here, working people. Now it was four a.m. and he was getting up at six.

But then he thought of the Great Horned Owls that appeared every winter, one that took up residence in a tree across the street, its mate on a telephone pole just down the hill. They'd start at dusk, the black silhouette of the male almost eye level from his bedroom deck, leaning forward and spreading his wings as he released his call, the four-syllable appeal to his smaller intended. It would be followed, soon after, by the answer from down the street, and the two owls could go on like this, calling and answering, for hours. He and Lily would step out on the deck and watch them sometimes, to witness the conversation, the courting. One night they came out and saw not one silhouette but two—the owls perched on the branch just inches apart, quiet now in their togetherness.

The thought of the owls calmed Oscar—if he could sleep through them, he could sleep through this. Besides, maybe there was something kind of sweet about this exchange. However awkwardly, however inconsiderately, people were reaching out to one another—sending a call into the world and getting a response. On a night when he'd felt so alone, he suddenly wasn't lonely. He closed his eyes and drifted off to sleep.

CHAPTER THREE
TODD

Todd Harris woke up before the alarm sounded and listened to the quiet. He loved these few minutes at the start of the day—before he showered and dressed for work, before the chaos of breakfast with children. Often it was still dark—he usually woke before six—and he felt like the only person in the world, or one of two. He reached out for his wife, Kelly, but she wasn't there. He could tell from the empty coolness of the sheets that she'd already been gone for some time.

During the first few years of their marriage, they always woke together. Even after Joey was born, they'd lie in bed in the morning, talking about their plans for the day. Often, morning was when they'd make love, the sense of peace and connection sustaining them through the day. And they'd lie together at night too, reading or talking, the bed a refuge from the constant motion of their lives. When Brooke came along three years later, things started to change. They'd fall asleep as soon as they went to bed, and Kelly would be up before him in the morning. It was easy to blame these changes on exhaustion, on the kids, but Todd knew it was more than that. Even with all the time they spent together, they had somehow lost touch.

Todd sat up, swung his feet over the side of the bed, and thought about work. He was a partner at Harrington

& Fletcher, one of the top law firms in the city. He worked on corporate antitrust and licensing cases, and there was never a shortage of companies that wanted other companies to stay out of their field, not compete for their customers, or not exist at all. Just two weeks ago he'd helped negotiate a $300 million settlement on behalf of DataSense, a software company in Silicon Valley, bringing the firm—and himself—a big payout. Now he was working on a couple of smaller licensing issues, including one on behalf of the Colsons, his clients from hell. But then he noticed his backpack in the corner and remembered that he wasn't going to the office. Suddenly everything shifted and he thought: I don't have to put on a suit today. He felt tremendous pleasure at this fact.

He stood up, slid into his slippers, and walked over to the window. He looked at the empty cat hammock there, half expecting to see Roger, his cantankerous gray tabby. But they'd had to put Roger down last month, and he felt again the twinge of sadness. He opened the curtains and looked out into their yard, just revealing itself in the first light of morning. It was gorgeous here in June, the jasmine white and pristine, the lantana delicate and purple against the thick green shrubs. A hundred feet in front of him was the giant oak with the kids' treehouse, which was as big as his first apartment. They lived in Brentwood, close enough to the ocean for the overcast skies of June Gloom to last all day and into evening, yet what they lost in sun they gained in landscape, their yard and garden much more lush than those of properties farther inland. But the thick grass, the sculpted rosebushes, the native poppies and Mexican sage and primrose didn't happen by accident; their gardener came twice a week, and it showed.

It also cost. The gardener, the tree trimmer, the house-keeper, the cook, the nannies for Brooke and Joey, all of it took money. Not to mention the obligations of the house itself—upkeep, taxes, insurance. They had a four-bedroom Spanish-style traditional, with a spacious living room that opened out onto a half-acre lot, even a wet bar in the basement where he and Kelly had once made cocktails, when having their own place had still been a novelty and pleasure. Even though the house had been a wedding gift from Kelly's parents, the expenses were a lot to manage. And then there were other things—the kids' tuition, and fees for their summer activities. Membership dues for the Ocean Club and the country club and the women's auxiliary that Kelly belonged to, not to mention her clothing and accessories, their evenings out and the charity events, their always clean luxury cars. Todd was doing well at work, making more money than he could ever have dreamed of as a boy in Wisconsin, before his father died and his mother met John Ingram and they moved to California, and he traded the woods and lakes and marshes for the beach. And yet somehow, paying for everything was still a struggle. Kelly didn't seem to comprehend that money was something that Todd *earned*, something he had to work for; in her experience, money simply accumulated. It boggled Todd's mind that his father-in-law, who lived solely off investments, made several times as much money each year as Todd did.

He took a quick shower—a quiet, less amusing process now that Roger the cat wasn't sitting on the edge of the tub to supervise—and shaved, examining himself in the mirror. He didn't look bad for forty. He had a full head of dirty-blond hair, just a touch of gray at the temples; his face was tan, with a few wrinkles at his eyes and brow.

He was pretty fit too, thanks to weekend runs and his sessions with Tracy, although he had a stubborn bit of gut he
couldn't seem to get rid of, no matter how many crunches
he did. All in all, though, he couldn't complain.

Todd put on khaki shorts and a green striped polo
shirt. He hoisted his big backpack onto his shoulders and
maneuvered downstairs, setting it down in the front hall,
next to his duffel. Then he went into the kitchen, where
both Joey and Brooke were sitting at the kitchen table,
working on bowls of Cheerios with bananas. It was just
before seven.

"Good morning, Daddy!" Brooke cried out enthusiasti-
cally, her face lighting up, spoon waving in the air.

"Hi, Dad," said Joey, more shyly.

"Hey, kids," he replied, kissing his squealing daughter
on the forehead and rubbing his son's hair. "Good morning."

Kelly had been facing away from them, putting the
milk back in the refrigerator; now she turned and smiled.
"Good morning, honey," she said, meeting his eyes. There
was nothing unpleasant or angry in her look, she seemed
genuinely pleased that he was there. But there was something impersonal about it, like a reaction she might have to
a good deed done by a stranger—approving, but somehow
removed.

"Good morning," he answered. "Thanks for getting
them fed."

"There's coffee here for you. And I could put in some
toast. Do you want Cheerios instead?"

"Toast is good."

"Are you going to work like that, Daddy?" Brooke asked
loudly, pointing at his shorts.

He turned in mock confusion. "Like what?"

"Like *that!*" she repeated, waving her finger back and forth. She hiccupped, then giggled, covering her mouth.

"Well," he said, taking the chair next to her, "I decided that I like wearing shorts better than wearing suits. Do you think anyone will notice?"

"Really?" Joey asked, glancing up from the comic book he was reading.

Todd nodded, looking from one of them to the other. "No."

Kelly placed a cup of coffee in front of him and then went back to the toaster. "Actually, Daddy's going out of town," she said.

"Where are you going?" Joey asked now, and there was an edge to his voice. When he was four or five, his father's travels—usually work trips—hadn't fazed him. Now, at seven, he was suddenly more attuned and more anxious.

"I'm going on a backpacking trip. I'm making a big loop through the mountains, and camping out at night."

"You're camping?" Joey said, brightening up. "Like we did last summer?"

The year before, Todd and Joey had gone with a group of other kids and dads to a camp facility in the Malibu Hills. It was pretty cush—they slept on cots in big domed tents, and ate in a mess hall. But it was the closest thing that Joey had had to an outdoor experience.

"Something like that," Todd replied.

"Why, Dad?"

"Well, sometimes I like to go out where it's quiet."

"By yourself?"

"No, I'll have some friends with me."

"All right, you guys," Kelly broke in, hands on hips.

"Time to get ready. We have to leave in twenty minutes. And put your bowls and spoons into the sink so Juanita doesn't have to pick up after you. Go!"

There was the scraping of chairs against the tile floor, the clang of dishes and silverware in the sink, the padding of bare feet out the door and up the stairs. Todd smiled— he had fantastic kids, but he worried about them growing up in such a bubble. They lived in an area so pristine it was like a caricature of a wealthy neighborhood. Some houses, like theirs, were relatively modest; others were mansions locked behind ivy-covered gates. People whispered of neighbors' excesses—the man with the collection of over fifty vintage race cars, the woman who'd spent half a million dollars on her fortieth birthday party, the couple who'd bought the $18 million estate adjoining theirs to create a bigger play yard for their dogs. ("Shih tzus!" Kelly had said, incredulously. "How much space do they *need*?") It all fed into a kind of isolation, a museum-like stillness. You didn't see people out much—the lack of sidewalks discouraged walking. When dogs were walked, it was usually by servants.

And the kids' private school, Northgate, was unquestionably strong in terms of academics. But the campus was as nice as a college, and a private one at that. He worried that the kids were getting coddled and soft: even at the luxurious Malibu camp last summer, Joey had had a tough time sleeping on a canvas cot, sharing tents, using a communal shower. Both kids had squealed in horror whenever Roger brought in a dead mouse. For Todd, who'd grown up roaming the countryside, this was all a bit hard to accept. When he suggested, in front of Kelly's mother, that he take Joey camping "for real," she'd looked down her fine aquiline nose at Todd and said, "No blood of mine sleeps on the ground."

Todd hadn't fully understood at first what kind of family he'd married into. When he'd started dating Kelly back in law school at Stanford, she seemed like the embodiment of his dreams—beautiful, blond, athletic, and from an old Los Angeles family. She had a social grace and confidence that made her irresistible, and he couldn't believe that she would fall for him, *him*—Todd Harris, who, sure, had been a star baseball player at UCLA and was third in his law school class, but was really a blue-collar Midwestern boy at heart. There was no doubt he'd enjoyed all that her family's money had made possible—the kids' schools, ski vacations in Aspen and Sun Valley, and of course their beautiful house. But he hadn't been prepared for the nonstop social obligations, the inane conversations at parties, where the women cooed over each other's outfits and the men bragged about their golf games and stock portfolios. He hadn't expected to be applying for the kids' spots in preschool before they'd even reached their first birthdays. Ten years ago, he'd felt pretty good about his life; he'd thought that if his old friends and relatives in Wisconsin could see him, they'd think he was a pretty big deal. Now he would just be embarrassed.

When the sound of the children's feet stopped, Kelly sat down at the table.

"They sure listen to you," Todd remarked, not knowing what else to say.

Kelly took a long drink from her coffee. "They listen to you too. We're lucky."

"Are you going to be all right with them for a few days?"

She smiled at him and gave him a look he couldn't read. "I always am."

She was still a beautiful woman, his wife. At thirty-nine,

her face had thinned out, which made her cheekbones more prominent, and there were a few lines around her mouth. She was thin and toned, thanks to regular trips to the gym, and her hair was still naturally blond. A bit of the suppleness of her skin around the jaw and neck was gone, but Todd didn't mind these little markers of time passing— he knew he had them too. He much preferred Kelly to age naturally than to resort to the Botox, fillers, and face lifts that made so many of the women they knew look like the walking dead.

"What are you up to today?" he asked.

She sighed. "Well, I'll drop the kids off, and then I'm meeting Leslie for coffee. Then I think we'll go to Saks—I need a new dress for the museum benefit on the twenty-sixth."

"Right," Todd said, remembering. Another event. Another expensive dress.

"Then we'll meet Dana and Adrienne at the Ocean Club for lunch. And after that, it'll be time to get the kids."

She smiled, a formal, distancing smile. Was she really happy with this life of shopping, lunches, and charity events? She'd been an attorney too, a rising star at O'Melveny & Myers. But when Joey was born, she left—just until their son was school-age, she'd said. And then Brooke was born, and she didn't talk of working anymore. They both knew she wasn't going back now.

"Sounds good," Todd said. Then hesitantly, "I'll miss you."

"We'll miss you too," Kelly said breezily. "Joey especially. And what will *you* be doing today?"

"I'm going to meet up with the other people in Mount Washington. Then we'll drive up to the Sierras. There's a campground near the trailhead, so we'll stay there for the night. We'll start our hike in the morning." He considered telling her why he was so excited about the route—the glacier-carved valleys and sparkling rivers, the pristine mountain lakes, the jagged peaks still covered with snow. But he knew it wouldn't mean anything to her.

She took another sip of her coffee. "And who's going again?"

"The Pattersons—you remember them, from the Children's Hospital dinner? And a couple of people I don't know. Some Hispanic real estate guy, and a black woman who works for a nonprofit. We all work out with Tracy, who's arranged the whole thing."

"I do remember the Pattersons. Your trainer, huh? Isn't she kind of attractive?"

"I don't know, I've never noticed. I'm usually too busy crying in pain."

"Hmm. Out there in the wilderness with another woman?"

"Oh, come on, Kelly," he protested. But he was secretly pleased at her jealousy. Normally it didn't occur to her that anyone else might find him attractive. "I don't think of her that way." And neither would Kelly, he knew, if she actually saw her—his wife and all of her too-thin friends would consider Tracy "solid," substantial. He noted that Kelly didn't seem worried about the black woman, and this made him dislike her just a little.

"And *why* are you doing this again? I mean, why don't you just stay in a hotel?" She paused. "I'll bet you're going to stink when you come out."

He laughed, not sure whether to be hurt or amused. "Thanks! It'll be good for me, honey. Good to be out of range for a while. But I'll call you the second I'm out."

"Four days with no phone or Internet?"

"It's kind of the point."

"Well. If the Colsons can live without you for four whole days, then I guess we can too."

He smiled at this reference to his nightmare clients. "Being out of touch with them for a while will be the best vacation I ever had."

"What should I do if they call here?" Kelly asked.

"Tell them they have the wrong number."

"I don't think that will work. They know my voice."

"That's true. Bummer. Tell them I went out to the wilderness. Tell them I got eaten by a bear."

"Okay," she said, smiling. "But don't."

"I won't. I promise."

Fifteen minutes later, he had hugged both his children, kissed his wife goodbye, and watched them drive away.

Todd had met Kelly during their second year of law school. He'd been walking home to his apartment in Palo Alto one Sunday, enjoying the spring air, when he saw an impatient-looking woman standing beside a black BMW. He recognized her from his torts class; he'd often stared at the fine lines of her jaw as Professor Zaslow droned on about unintentional harm. She'd dropped something off at the building next door, it turned out, and now her car wouldn't start. She barely registered Todd as he offered to take a look, and he realized the problem was simple—a dead battery. After trying unsuccessfully to give it a jump with his own car, he drove to an auto supply store and bought her a battery. From there it was easy: disconnect the old battery, put in the new. He sat in the driver's seat and switched on the ignition. The leather was so creamy he thought he might melt into it. He looked at the gorgeous instrument panel, the high-end sound system, and his pulse quickened with excitement. He had no right to be touching such a classy machine. When the car finally started, Kelly sidled over and thanked him, and said, "You know, you look familiar."

"I'm in your torts class," he replied, and now she tilted her head and opened her blue eyes wide, as if seeing him for the first time.

Todd sat at the kitchen table and finished his coffee, listening to the quiet. It was strange, unnerving, the silence of a space that was normally full of life making the space itself feel totally different. He put his cup in the dishwasher and took one final look around—everything was in order—and carried his backpack and duffel out to the car.

Within minutes he was on Sunset heading east. As he saw the buildings of Century City off to his right, he looked up at the one he worked in, feeling a rush of guilty pleasure at driving right past it, like a usually responsible student ditching school. And he loved that he would soon be unreachable to the Colsons.

Skip and Dolly Colson had originally hired the firm five years ago to represent them in a land use deal, and now Todd was lead attorney on one of their business ventures. They had created a watermelon-based sports drink, Suika, that was supposed to provide a jumpstart for intense activity, stave off colds, and slow the aging process. With a major branding effort and marketing push—a Lakers star and Oscar-winning actress were among the celebrity endorsers—Suika was a surprise success, and now the Colsons were trying to take down any drink or food manufacturer that used watermelon in their products. Dolly called Todd at least five times a day, starting before eight a.m., and sent at least a dozen e-mails. If he didn't reply to a message or e-mail within the hour, he'd get a scolding call from Skip.

The Colsons' special brand of attachment had not gone unnoticed by other people at the firm.

"Todd, it's your favorite lady," his assistant, Janet, would warn when Dolly called. Rachel McDermott, a dark-haired, sharp-eyed junior associate, would simply say, "Todd, it's your girlfriend."

Then in January, when he came back from a trip to Aspen with Kelly's family, he'd walked into his office to find an explosion of color: green and pink and orange *While You Were Out* stickies covering the ceiling and the walls, stuck to his desk and computer, his chair and his lamps and the bookcase.

Dolly called, read one of the pink notes, pasted on his phone. *Wants to know who you like in tonight's Lakers–Mavericks game.*

Skip called, said one of the green notes, affixed to his chair. *Had a question about the real benefits of going gluten-free.*

Dolly called. Was curious about your opinion on index funds.

Skip called. Wondering if you can shine his golf clubs.

Dolly dropped by. Saw the picture of the kids on your desk and says you really need to work on another.

Skip called. Says hi. Just feeling lonely.

And on and on, over three hundred of them, all written by hand. He kept turning, seeing new ones, a bit overwhelmed, but happy, touched that his coworkers would tease him about his troubles. When he turned back to the doorway, there were a dozen people standing there, grinning.

"You guys," he said, shaking his head.

Todd inched down Sunset, past the Standard, Chateau Marmont, and finally to La Brea, where he took a left to get up to Franklin. He passed Yamashiro, the Hollywood Bowl, turned north again toward Griffith Park. As he got farther from the Westside, he felt the tension subside, felt his job and the Colsons and even his stale marriage become part of the world he was leaving behind.

He was tired of it—tired of wealthy, entitled clients and of helping people who didn't really need help. He was tired of worrying about his hypertension, which was what had killed his father. He was tired of socializing with women who wore full makeup to retrieve the paper and with men who could recite daily LIBOR rates but couldn't put up drywall. Most of all, he was tired of how he felt about himself for doing what he did, which didn't do a damned thing to make the world a better place.

When he and Joey had stayed at the Malibu campground, he'd spent some time with one of the other dads, Paul Halstead, a former venture capitalist who now ran the Oakwood School, a private high school in Beechwood Canyon. When Todd had told him of his discontent with practicing law, the master's degree in History he got before he went to law school, Paul had asked, "Why don't you become a teacher? I see how you are with kids. And you like history too? Go get a credential. I'd hire you in a heartbeat."

And that had been the seed. Once planted, it had grown stubbornly, despite his attempts to suppress it. It was totally impractical, he knew. His family couldn't afford it. And yet, he found himself looking at credentialing programs, and at Oakwood's website; he was impressed with the fact that 70 percent of the students were on scholarship. He loved the idea of working with kids who just needed a leg up—he might have been one of those kids, until his stepfather came along. And he wanted that ease and air of purpose that Paul Halstead had—the knowledge that he was doing something good.

But he knew that Kelly would never go for it. Give up a partnership in a prestigious law firm—to become a *teacher*? Make a fraction of his current salary? They could manage, he knew. Kelly could always go back to work, or failing that, maybe—although he hated the idea—they could get help from her parents. Or they could just decide to live more simply. Give up the shopping sprees and club memberships and whatever else they spent so much money on.

He knew it would never happen.

But he couldn't get the idea out of his mind. He needed a change—before the Colsons and their like pushed his heart past its breaking point, or slowly crushed his spirit. Before he collapsed under the weight of the utter meaninglessness of the way he spent his days. Something had to change—it just had to. Not only for him, but for the sake of his kids.

He drove past the Griffith Park Observatory and as the street angled down, the hills receded and the San Gabriel Mountains came into view. They were breathtaking. Not majestic and lush like the Sierras, but impressive just the same. For years, he hadn't really registered that there were mountains surrounding the city. Now he could not look away from them. Straight ahead was a cluster of hills— Glassell Park and Mount Washington. Whatever apprehension he'd felt about this trip began to fall away. All he could see now were the mountains in front of him—the San Gabriels, and later today, the Sierras. He didn't know exactly what awaited him this weekend. But he couldn't wait to get there.

Chapter Four
Gwen

Tracy's living room was spare and minimalist, the furniture white and earth-toned; even the landscape photos that hung on the walls were all in black-and-white. The only touch of color came from the magazines on the side table, and from the dozen or so action shots of Tracy that were scattered throughout the room. Gwen had been to Tracy's place twice before to meet for hikes, and it seemed like there were fewer things with each visit. The house looked stripped down to the bare essentials.

Gwen sat rigidly on the edge of the couch and sipped her coffee. She didn't really need the stimulation—she was hyped up, had tossed and turned most of the night with thoughts of rattlesnakes and lightning and bears. In daylight she felt better, although the fears remained. She tried to assuage her guilt for not calling her mother as she'd promised—she'd left a message instead on Alene's voice mail at work—as well as her larger guilt for missing work. This was Thursday, and she normally had two afternoon groups. Most of the kids would be fine skipping a week, but she worried about Sandra Gutierrez. I'll call her on Tuesday, Gwen told herself. I'll touch base with her as soon as I'm back.

"You're going to boil in those jeans."

Gwen jumped. Tracy had come back from the kitchen,

bearing a tray that held a serving dish of sliced fruit and several small plates.

"You scared me!" Gwen said. "I know, but it was cold this morning. And I'm thinking it'll be cooler in the mountains."

"You're right. Although it looks like we're in for good weather. Highs in the seventies, lows in the low to mid-fifties."

Tracy sat in the armchair perpendicular to Gwen and put the plates on the coffee table. She was one of the few women Gwen knew who seemed truly at ease in her body. It had the shaped, chiseled look of someone who worked out hard, and often; and who cared about how she fueled it. Even now, as she was resting, there was something in her posture that suggested energy and movement, like all that muscle was ready to spring. This was part of why Gwen liked being around her—you wanted to know what would happen next, and if lucky, you might be included. Tracy's classes at SportZone were always full, popular with men and women alike. Her allure wasn't really sexual, or at least Gwen didn't think so. Tracy had a fine enough face—high cheekbones, strong nose and lips, bright hazel eyes—and straight black hair she usually wore in a pony-tail. But it didn't quite add up. Some other quality skewed her looks toward severe. Sometimes, when she focused on something and Gwen saw her in profile, Gwen thought that she looked like a wolf.

"Am I going to be warm enough at night?"

"You brought a base layer, right? Plus that down sleeping bag. You'll be fine. That reminds me—I should go get my pack."

Tracy stood up and went into the other room, closing

the door behind her. Gwen looked at the fruit—the perfectly cut wedges of honeydew and watermelon, cantaloupe and mango—and spooned a few pieces onto a plate. It occurred to her that she'd never seen more of Tracy's house than what was visible to her right now—the bright, airy living room, the little bathroom, the kitchen. She had seen the garage where Tracy kept a huge amount of canned and boxed food, containers of water, a generator—but most of the inside seemed off-limits. The door to what she assumed was Tracy's bedroom was always closed, as was the door to the stairs that led to the lower floor. The house looked small from the street—one-story, wood-framed, with a few succulents planted half-heartedly in neat ceramic pots. But from the side you could see that it spilled down the hill, another floor below the first one. Down in the yard there was a separate structure, which Tracy had converted into a gym. How wonderful to be able to decide what to do with your space. Someday, Gwen thought, someday I'll have a place of my own.

Gwen put her plate down, stood up, and walked around, looking absently at the framed action shots. Each of them captured a moment of triumph or drama—Tracy on the summit of a snow-covered peak, ice axe extended above her head; Tracy hanging precipitously off a rock face; Tracy and a dark-haired man in a kayak negotiating rough-looking rapids. She had the same joyous, self-satisfied look in all of them, the kind of expression that Gwen had seen in pictures of hunters displaying their kill. Tracy was alone in some of the photos, in others with the dark-haired man; in two, with a young blond woman. Was the man Tracy's lover? The woman? It was impossible to tell.

Gwen sat back down and picked up the first magazine

on the stack, an issue of *Outside* with a rock climber on the front. The magazine beneath it caught her eye. It was called *Modern Survival*, and on the cover there was a couple in full camouflage gear, the man holding a rifle, the woman a radio. Gwen picked it up carefully and flipped through the pages—there were pictures of people canning food, starting a fire with sticks and flint, of exercises for women to build upper-body strength so they could fire high-caliber assault weapons. *How to Recognize a Bomb Threat*, one article promised. Another was titled, *Pedal Power: Generate Your Own Electricity—With Your Bike!* In the back there were ads for prebuilt emergency shelters, food storage sheds, bullet-proof vests, and boots that could walk through fire. Gwen put the magazine back on the pile and dropped *Outside* on top of it, as if replacing the lid of a container whose contents she wished she hadn't seen.

Just then Tracy returned, carrying her gray and red pack. She set it down next to Gwen's by the door. It looked svelte, no lumpy spots like Gwen's lavender pack, which was so stuffed she thought the seams might burst. Gwen's sleeping bag dangled from the bottom of her pack; Tracy's bag was nowhere in sight.

"That looks very . . . efficient," said Gwen. "You could probably teach me a thing or two about packing."

"We can do a pack check when everyone's here."

Everyone, Gwen knew, had reduced in size—the Pattersons had dropped out at the last minute because the wife was sick. She wasn't sure whether a foursome would be better or worse than the original group of six, but then the doorbell rang, and Tracy was greeting her real estate agent, Oscar Barajas, with a thumping jock-like hug. They sounded like teenage boys: "What's up, Oscar?" "Nothing.

Just getting ready to kick some mountain ass!" And Gwen suddenly felt like the grown-up in the group, worried that she wouldn't fit in. Maybe she should have just driven to Santa Barbara or Palm Springs. Maybe she should have gone to a spa and gotten a massage, a facial or mani-pedi, some pampering. But then Oscar walked over to her, real-estate charming, and extended his hand.

"Nice to see you, Gwen," he said. "I'm glad you decided to come!"

He was a little slick, Oscar. You could see it in his combed-back hair, his soft hands, his well-ironed clothes. Mostly you could see it in his face—handsome, friendly, but controlled. He must have worked hard to be as successful as he was, selling houses in what had long been a Latino neighborhood to nervous whites. Since he was wearing a short-sleeved shirt, she saw what his long-sleeved work shirts concealed—a tattoo of a mountain lion crouching on his right shoulder, the name *Lily* in script across his left bicep. Yes, it must have cost him something to be so agreeable. But she knew he had a little girl and that he took good care of her, and so Gwen was inclined to give him slack.

"My stuff's out in the car," he said now. "Should I bring it in?"

"No, leave it out there," Tracy answered. "Might as well just transfer the bags straight to my car."

He glanced around the room. "Looks good in here."

"Thanks," Tracy said, hands on hips. "A little different than before, isn't it?"

"The family that was here before were pack rats," Oscar explained to Gwen. "It took them so long to clear out of here that we had to delay the closing."

"I keep thinking about them and all their damned *stuff*," Tracy said. "Better to live simple and not accumulate things, you know? You hear about people having to evacuate because of fire and they can't figure out what to take. It's better not to have so much to lose in the first place. I mean, what if something *really* bad happens? What if there's a terrorist attack? Or the economy collapses? Or the Big One finally hits? You've got to be able to pick up and exit, quick."

"Well," Oscar said, "I hadn't thought of all *that*."

"Think about it, buddy. Think about it. And there are limited ways to get out of here, you know? Just last winter I was trying to get back *into* the city, from Sequoia, and the Tejon Pass was closed because of snow. The hotels before the pass all filled up quick, and people were sleeping in their cars, and the restaurants ran out of food and water. I turned around, went back up the 5 and over to the coast, and came down through Santa Barbara. Took nine hours from the Grapevine instead of ninety minutes. But hell, at least I got here."

Gwen wasn't comfortable with the banter, with the talk of crisis and doom. And again she felt bad about missing Sandra Gutierrez in group this week. Sandra had been an A student at King Drew Medical Magnet when suddenly, during her sophomore year, her grades began to plummet. Then it was discovered that she was cutting herself, and no one could figure out why—she had a stable home, a good mom with a steady job; they were generally better off than the other families Gwen worked with.

But then Sandra told her mother that her stepfather had been molesting her, in the evenings while her mother was at work. Her mother had locked the husband out and immediately called the police, and slowly, through intensive therapy and Gwen's leadership group, Sandra had started to pull herself back together. She was a shy girl, soft-eyed and quiet, and when she first came to group, she sat in a folded-in, self-protective way that broke Gwen's heart. Without her mom's steadfast toughness and love, Sandra might not have made it through.

And now she was facing a new challenge—her step-father's trial was starting in a couple of weeks, and Sandra had to testify against him. *That* was a crisis, she wanted to say—facing someone who raped you; having to tell your story in front of strangers. Gwen felt little patience for people who had to invent or imagine disaster.

Now Tracy clapped Oscar on the shoulder again, grinning. "Hey, you want some coffee? Water? Fruit?" She was so pumped up that she was practically jumping in place. Tracy seemed to possess the secret of a fully lived life, and inhabited hers completely. Even her preparedness kick had a kind of enthusiasm mixed in with the worry. The terrorists might come, Tracy's attitude suggested, but she would make quick work of them, and have fun in the process. Gwen was drawn to her in spite of herself.

"I'm good," Oscar said, and then the doorbell rang again.

Tracy was at the door in an instant, pulling it open wide. "Todd!" she exclaimed. "You found us!"

Todd looked like he wasn't quite sure what he had found. He was, Gwen thought, a pretty average-looking white guy. About 5'10", dirty-blond hair, with a broad face that, in another ten years or so, might be described as "meaty." He seemed preppy—Ralph Lauren polo shirt, khaki shorts, expensive leather sandals. But there was something that didn't quite hold together in all of this, as if he was dressing like his successful older brother. And at the moment, he seemed a little confused.

"Hi, Tracy. Yeah, but not without some wrong turns. My GPS sent me up a one-lane dirt road."

"GPS and MapQuest are useless up here," said Oscar, in a litany he must have used a thousand times with clients. "This neighborhood was designed to turn people around. There used to be speakeasies up here during Prohibition. And then it was a communist hangout."

"Todd, this is Oscar Barajas and Gwen Foster," Tracy said, ushering him into the house. "Oscar and Gwen, this is Todd Harris."

Gwen saw something shift in Todd's eyes—an acknowledgment that he was in the minority here. He probably wasn't used to being around people of color—at least, not ones who didn't work for him. She thought of the looks she'd gotten at REI when she'd gone shopping for supplies, and had been the only black person in the store: not hostile, not unwelcoming—in fact, a couple of the clerks were overfriendly—just simply noting the unusual fact of her presence. But Todd shook their hands firmly and met their eyes. "So we're just waiting for the Pattersons?" he asked.

"They're not coming, unfortunately," Tracy said. "Carolyn is sick."

Again, a flicker in the eyes, but he quickly recovered. "*That's* too bad. They're both great people."

"I know. We'll have to manage without them. But in some ways it's easier—now we can take one car."

"Yeah, I guess," Todd said, still not convinced. "Hey, is it okay to leave my car here?"

"Absolutely," Tracy answered, and Gwen had to look

away. What a rarified world Todd lived in if he thought *this* neighborhood was iffy.

After Todd declined the offer of coffee or food, Tracy took everything back to the kitchen and led them all outside. There, they did a pack check, and with Tracy's help, Gwen winnowed down to a single long-sleeved shirt, removed an extra jacket, kept one extra set of socks and underwear instead of two. With the extra space Gwen could fit the sleeping bag inside the pack and pile everything else on top.

Once their packs were reorganized, they loaded up Tracy's Volvo XC60. Gwen watched Todd heave the cooler and packs into the car; she saw Oscar help figure out how to fit everything; she saw Tracy direct the whole process. The back of the SUV was soon full to the roof.

Gwen felt like a neophyte, useless. What had she been thinking? She looked at her own Honda across the street, flanked by the BMW she knew to be Oscar's and the Audi she assumed was Todd's, and had an urge to just make a dash for it, drive away, get out while she still could. She could drive to the office—that's where she really belonged. Not with these people whom she barely knew. Not in the outdoors, in some remote corner of the mountains.

You just can't *do* this, she thought, and the words appeared so fully formed that she realized they came from someone else: Chris, the last man she had dated. Chris was a field deputy for the local city councilman, a charismatic, talkative guy she'd met when he toured the agency. They'd had a whirlwind year of dinners, neighborhood events, Saturday brunches with his politically active family and friends. Gwen had found this all thrilling, until eight months in, Chris began to say that she worked too much, that he didn't like her clothes, that she needed to lose ten pounds. ("What kind of self-respecting black man," remarked Tanisha, her best friend at work, "complains about a black woman's curves?") He hadn't been terribly sympathetic when Robert died, and he'd been dismissive when she'd started going to SportZone. When she told him she aspired to do a really big hike one day, like Half Dome or Whitney, he'd scoffed. "There's no *way* you can do that. That kind of thing's for people who are really in shape."

Gwen was hurt when Chris left her for a Princeton-educated lawyer, but in the wake of Robert's death, all losses were relative. How, she thought, did she manage to attract such jerks? Why did she get involved with men who told her what she couldn't do? Chris's insults stayed with her, though, and she still felt them now.

But then she turned and caught sight of the mountains, the San Gabriels starting to the west and extending to the east, getting taller as they went. There was 10,064-foot Mount Baldy in the distance, and closer, Mount Wilson with its satellite spires, and closer still, Musgrove Point. Last spring, she had hiked to Musgrove Point with Devon and three kids, including Robert. It was the hardest hike she'd ever done. The trail was three miles up, two thousand feet of elevation gain. It was punishing, and Gwen would never have made it if Devon and Robert hadn't pushed her along—cajoling, teasing, encouraging. On the top she'd taken the picture of Robert that now hung on her bulletin board.

They'd stayed an hour up there, eating lunch, taking in the view. From that high up she could see the buildings of downtown, the curve of the coast, the way the ocean hugged the land. How small the problems of people

seemed from this perspective, how miniscule the neighborhoods and buildings. A few hearty wildflowers were
still in bloom, and she was lifted by their beauty. I'm so
happy to be alive, Gwen remembered thinking. She might
have even said it out loud.

Ten days later, Robert was dead, and part of what tor-
tured her in those first confused weeks was that his death
had come so soon after this day, when all the world seemed
well. While she had been exhilarated, he must have been
miserable, already making plans. She would have said so
much more that day if she had suspected what was coming. She hadn't even had a chance to tell him how much he
meant to her.

"Gorgeous, isn't it?" someone said, and Gwen turned
to find Todd standing next to her. She didn't know how
long he'd been there.

"Yes," she replied. "It's amazing how much you can see
from here."

"When I was driving up, I just kept looking from one
view to the next. That's part of why I was late."

"Where do you live?" she asked.

"Over on the Westside. I didn't even know this neighborhood was here."

Gwen felt a twinge of distaste. But this guy, whatever his
limits, was making an effort to be friendly, so she would
try to do the same. For a moment she wondered if she
should have signed on with a professional guiding service,
maybe even for a women-only trek—but the descriptions
she'd found on the Internet had put her off: *Hiking and Jour-
naling for Inner Peace,* one of them said. Another promised,
Find Yourself in Nature! But she wasn't going on this trip to
find herself. She was going to find the mountains.

"Okay, kids. Ready to go?" asked Tracy.

"Let's do it!" said Oscar, grinning.

And then there was the awkwardness of who would sit where, which Todd solved by saying, "Why don't you ladies ride in front?"

They all seemed to understand that, whatever the arrangement, Tracy would be driving. And so the men got in back, Todd directly behind the driver's seat and Oscar behind Gwen. Tracy took a deep breath and smiled, her energy so palpable it seemed to light the whole car.

"Ready, captain?" Oscar asked, and Tracy nodded.

"Ready." She turned the key in the ignition, put the car into gear, and drove off down the hill.

CHAPTER FIVE
OSCAR

As they headed north on the 2, and then west on the 210, Oscar stared at the huge swath of bare brown mountain. Three years ago, the Station Fire had set half the range aflame. During the day, dense smoke formations like nuclear clouds had loomed over the peaks; at night, the dark shapes were lit bright orange. Bears, deer, and mountain lions had fled down from the mountains, some ending up in suburban backyards. When the fire was finally out three weeks later, over 160,000 acres had burned and two firefighters were dead.

"All that damage," Gwen remarked. She was sitting rigidly, fingers drumming her thigh. "It looks like a giant blanket's been draped over the mountains."

"It does," agreed Oscar. A nice woman, and not bad looking, with a pleasant shape, he thought—but she was in way over her head. He'd watched her struggle in Tracy's class with some of the tougher exercises and wasn't sure she could handle this hike.

"They've finally just opened up some more of the trails," Tracy said. "And it's about time too. I mean, Echo Mountain's nice, but it's gotten so crowded. It's like running at the friggin' Rose Bowl." Tracy was driving fast, weaving in and out of traffic. Every few minutes she reached over to take a gulp of coffee from her travel mug.

"The hikes out of Chantry Flats are cool," Oscar said, trying not to glance at the speedometer. Chantry Flats had an old-time pack station, complete with mules, goats, and horses. He liked to take Lily sometimes, to see the animals.

"Mount San Gorgonio is awesome too," Tracy said. "I was just up there last weekend, and there was still snow at the top. Best thing you can do down here to train for altitude."

Now Gwen turned to her. "Train for altitude? How high up are we going?"

Tracy waved her off. "We'll be fine. We'll top out at Green Pass at about 11,500 feet, but not until the last day, so we'll have time to acclimatize."

Something occurred to Oscar. "If there's snow on San Gorgonio, won't there be snow on our route?"

"It'll be fine," Tracy said again. "There wasn't much snow last winter and most of it's probably melted off by now. If not, we'll just make our way over it."

"Is that safe?" Gwen asked.

"Don't worry, it's no big deal. Not like Rainier or even Shasta. You need crampons and ice axes for those, to keep from sliding down a slope or into a crevasse."

"Sounds dangerous," Oscar said.

"That's part of the point, buddy. That's part of the point. Climbs like that, one wrong step and you're toast. You have to focus every second. But there's nothing like a bit of risk to make you feel alive."

This didn't make Oscar feel better, but he decided to let it go. She was right—what was the big deal about a little snow? As they merged onto the 5 north and skirted up between the hills, he felt the first real sense of escaping, a sheer, uncomplicated joy at leaving his job behind. He was heading off to a place where income-to-loan ratios meant nothing, where no one cared about the best way to stage a house for a showing, where no one was even thinking about the steady drop in home values over the last five years, and where he wouldn't see his empty, unfinished houses. In the mountains, he'd have no smartphone, no sharp clothes or fast car to fall back on. He'd have to depend on his endurance and grit, and if he got into a scrape, it would be his own guts and thinking that would have to get him out of it. He could do this, he knew it; he was up for the challenge. Coach Eric from the gym could kiss his ass.

"So, Todd," Oscar said now, "have you hiked or back-packed much?"

Todd looked startled that someone had spoken to him.

"More when I was younger," he managed. "I used to camp with my dad. But not so much as an adult, to tell you the truth. I go for hikes with the kids sometimes out in the Palisades or Malibu."

Of course, Oscar thought. The Westsiders go farther west. This guy was probably soft.

"Most of my workouts these days are with Tracy," Todd continued. "I went to SportZone for physical therapy last year for a shoulder injury, and then they referred me to Tracy. She pushes me hard, but it's all in the gym—I've really missed being outside."

"You're a lawyer?"

"Yeah, a litigator. I work for a great firm, but it's pretty dry to tell you the truth." He sounded self-conscious. "The thing I like most is the pro bono work. I do some volunteer work for a couple of youth organizations."

Gwen turned around in her seat and looked at him. "Really? I work for a youth organization down in South LA."

"Tracy mentioned that. I'd love to hear more about it."

And so Gwen began to tell him about the kids her agency helped, and Todd asked questions that seemed genuine, if clueless. ("But why do the kids join gangs?" "Why don't the families show up for services, if they're free?") Oscar was a little irritated at Gwen—she talked as if Watts were the only tough place in the city. So he spoke up about Highland Park and Cypress Park, the poverty and crime, his own friends who'd been lost to gang violence. He described what had changed and what hadn't in the last few years, the mixed blessing of gentrification. And while this was mostly directed at Gwen, he was annoyed at Todd too, for being so Westside sheltered.

But Oscar decided to go easy on the guy. It didn't make sense to write him off, not yet. Not when they were north of Castaic now. Not when they were actually on their way, and there was so much anticipation in the small shared space that it seemed like the car might lift off the road and fly. Oscar grinned as they passed Pyramid Lake, with its namesake land mass rising out of the water. Then they drove on to Tejon Ranch and down the other side of the mountains, where they were treated to a bird's-eye view of open plains flanked by hills as they arrived at the southern gate of the Central Valley.

Which wasn't, Oscar remembered now, anything to write home about. They passed a clump of gas stations, hotels, and fast-food joints, and stayed on the 99 while most of the traffic veered away on the 5 toward San Francisco. They were entering a different California. Oscar had only driven on the 99 once before, and again he was struck by the contrast between the state's heartland and its cities on the coast. Near Bakersfield they started to see the antiabortion signs, one of which bore an image of an aborted fetus so graphic that Oscar had to look away. Other signs blamed the current drought on the Federal Reserve. All of them towered over a landscape that was stunning in its flatness. Once they passed Bakersfield, they were deep into farmland—fields of onion and alfalfa and groves of olive trees. The vibrant green was dotted here and there with spots of color—farm workers, surely Mexican, toiling in brightly colored clothes in the sweltering summer sun. Late-model cars were parked at the edge of the fields, and some rundown trailers too; the people clumped around them looked so destitute that Oscar felt a lump in his throat. His own grandparents had been migrant workers; they might have worked these very fields. But before he could think too much about the workers, the car was past them.

He saw haphazard stacks of pallets, discarded farm machinery, ads for irrigation systems and pest control. He saw motels that looked like they hadn't had a guest in his lifetime. They passed signs for an Indian casino and a half-built housing development, and trailers and RVs dumped in empty fields. Twice they passed huge cattle pens maybe half a mile square, full of cows jostling each other for food and moving around in their own slop. And the towns, or what were called towns—low-profile clusters of buildings that were all some shade of brown. Near one of them was a billboard boasting, *Guns! Next Exit!* with a silhouette of an assault rifle. Scraps of tire tread and tumbleweeds bumped against the guard rail, and every few miles they passed a gruesome bit of roadkill, a cat and several skunks and a brown, bloated dog. Hanging over everything was a haze of more brown—dust and smog and insecticide and God knew what else. No wonder crystal meth was such a problem here, he thought. As if boredom weren't enough, you could die of ugliness.

And yet, and yet. Out the window, to the right, Oscar saw a line of white against the skyline. "Is that the mountains?" he asked.

The others turned and stared out the window.

"Looks like it!" Gwen said from the front seat.

"That's them!" Tracy confirmed, and as they looked closer, Oscar could see the dark shape of them, the uninterrupted mass, the very tops covered in snow.

"Wow," he said.

"They don't look real," Gwen said. They were so startling, so incongruous with the ugly terrain, that it was as if someone had rolled in the wrong backdrop.

"They're real, all right," said Tracy, grinning. "They're *very* real. And that's where we're headed, kids. Right into the heart of 'em. Right into the heart of it all."

They were quiet for a moment. "How far are we going, again?" Oscar asked. He was so used to letting Tracy take the lead on things that he hadn't paid that much attention to details. But suddenly he felt a flash of concern. The one time they'd had a beer together to celebrate the closing on her house, she'd let slip that she was bored of Sport-Zone, the neglected housewives and the midlife-crisis men who were trying desperately to hold on to their physiques. He had the sense that what qualified as interesting to her might be beyond what the rest of them were up for.

"It's a thirty-mile loop," Tracy answered. "We'll start out near Redwood Station and take the Cloud Lakes trail clockwise."

"I looked at a couple of trip reports online," Todd offered. "It sounds pretty challenging—almost five thousand feet elevation gain."

"Yeah," Tracy said, "it's going to be a butt burner. But this is the real deal, guys. No simulated experience, no obstacle course, no artificial Tough Mudder bullshit."

"Should we think about taking one of the less strenuous trails?" Oscar asked.

"They're *all* going to be strenuous," Tracy said. "Personally, I'd rather do a route that has a bit of challenge. Get away from the day hikers and car campers, you know? But suit yourself." She shrugged. "If you'd rather take one of the easy trails, we can. It just won't be a real wilderness experience."

Annoyance flared up in Oscar's chest. Tracy did this during workouts too, subtly or not so subtly challenging one's bravery or manhood, and his knowing this didn't make it any less effective. He'd signed up for Tracy's class because he'd thought she was cute, but that had worn off fast. He remembered the crazy grin she sometimes got when some poor bastard was pushed so hard he started to retch.

"I'm game," Todd assured her. "I just want to know what we're getting into."

"We'll be fine," Tracy said. "This trail's established and there'll probably be a few other people. It's not like we'll get turned around, and besides, you can't get *that* lost in the Sierras. Walk two or three days, and eventually you'll get out."

"I brought a GPS," said Oscar.

"Cool," Tracy said. "See, Todd? We'll be fine."

"What about bears?" Gwen asked suddenly, and Oscar realized she'd been listening with growing anxiety.

"What about them?"

"Are there bears on this route?"

Tracy smiled. "Yes, but it's nothing to worry about. They just want our food, and as long as we use our bear canisters, they'll generally leave us alone. They're kind of like stray dogs, you know? Just need to be shooed away."

Oscar wondered if Gwen was having the same thought that he was—stray dogs, in his neighborhood, were often of the unneutered pit bull variety.

"I took this trip two years ago where the craziest thing happened," Tracy continued. "I was alone in the back-country north of Kings Canyon, ten or fifteen miles off trail. I was camping at one of those lakes up there that doesn't have a name. One afternoon a huge thunderstorm rolled in, crazy torrential rain, and all the little streams that fed the lake swelled up into rushing waterfalls. There was a big-ass bear across the river from me and I was keeping an eye on him. Then a deer comes tumbling over the falls, legs and head flailing. It fell about two hundred feet. At first I thought I'd imagined it, but then some other debris came over and then the water got real brown, full of mud. A river bank must have given way up there and swept the deer with it. Anyway, I'm looking at this, not believing my eyes—and then the bear stomps over to the river and picks up the deer. He drags the carcass up the side of the mountain. He's got it by the neck and it's broken and limp, and he keeps stepping on it, trying to carry it up. He finally hides it behind a boulder, and then he looks back at *me* as if I'm going to challenge him for it. I'll tell you . . ." She whistled and shook her head. "That was a moment when I felt the power of nature. That was a sight I won't forget."

Everyone was quiet. What was the point of this story,

Oscar wondered, except to freak them the hell out?

They got off at Visalia and took a two-lane road to the north. Here, in the eastern part of the valley, there were hundreds of citrus groves. Lemons and oranges were plump in the trees, in rows that extended to the horizon. Every mile or two, they saw a makeshift fruit stand. The citrus groves were broken up by low, open fields; there were signs for squash and bushels of cucumbers. With the opening up of the landscape, the small quiet roads, Oscar felt more of the city fall away. The old wood-frame houses had tall, square structures behind them that looked like guard towers.

As they approached the junction with the highway that led up to the mountains, there was a cluster of buildings—a diner, flanked on one side by a dozen trailers. Across the narrow two-lane road stood a rectangular brick structure, the Franklin Cash Store.

"Let's stop here," Tracy said. "We can eat and grab some last-minute supplies."

She parked in the dirt lot in front of the diner and they all stumbled out of the car. Gwen put her hands on her hips and leaned back, stretching; Oscar bent to touch his toes; Todd spinwheeled his arms like a batter on deck, loosening up his shoulders. "That was *long*," he remarked.

"Yeah, I know, sorry guys," Tracy said. "I was so pumped up to get here, I lost track of time."

They had lunch in the diner, where the clientele was equally divided between locals—farmers and ranchers—and people headed up to the mountains. When they were finished, they walked across the road and over to the Franklin Cash Store. The building was boxlike, one story. It was painted white, or at least it had been white at one time; age and weather had stripped a layer of paint away. In the window there was a picture of the store in a previous incarnation, when it was the depot of a backwater train station. Tracy pulled the door open, which caused a bell to ring loudly, and they all stepped inside.

The place was chock full of stuff, so crammed with odds and ends that Oscar didn't know where to look. Right in front of them was an old-fashioned punch-button cash register, and all around the store, on a continuous ledge that ran two feet below the ceiling, there were bottles and boxes and tins, everything from Morton's Salt containers to SPAM tins to Hershey's boxes to colored bottles of liquids and medicines that hadn't existed since his grandparents' time. Old street signs were mounted on lateral beams, and there were hand-painted messages on every wall. *Don't forget to be happy*, one of these read. *Never give up or grow up.*

Oscar saw built-in shelves filled with random, haphazardly arranged goods—wooden signs with religious sayings painted on them, hand-knit scarves and socks, weird contraptions made from pieces of farm equipment, stacks of old paperbacks, colored soaps in the shape of feet, a display of local honeys and jams. Glass-fronted cabinets were stuffed with old newspapers and magazines, and flip-flops waved from a circular rack. There was a cluster of metal watering cans beside a bright pink piano decorated with black and white polka dots, and a bench with a leopard-skin cushion. There was an elaborate candleholder with half-burned candles, a pile of straw hats, a stuffed boar head wearing sunglasses, a cloth pig with an arrow through its shoulder. Right beside them a small refrigerator had a handwritten sign that read, *Nightcrawlers and red worms. Fish love 'em!* Straight ahead, on the back wall, was a collection of orange crate labels, and the railroad sign from the picture in the window. To the left, there was an old drugstore counter and a half dozen red-topped stools. A tall woman of indeterminate age stood behind the counter, and two middle-aged men in farm clothes and baseball caps sat facing her, nursing Coors Lights. A yellow sign on the wall behind her read, *Danger: Men Drinking.* A small black dog was perched on the end stool, watching them.

"Howdy!" the woman said cheerfully. "Come on in and take a look around!"

"Wow," Gwen exclaimed. Her expression changed from uncertainty to wonder. She stepped in and wandered cautiously down one of the aisles.

"It's unbelievable," said Todd, equally happy, and Oscar looked at him. What was wrong with them? This was the store of crazy people. This was the store of someone who was not right in the head. Then he saw something else behind the counter: a display of Green Bay Packers paraphernalia—Topps cards, schedules, four or five felt banners, pictures of players from Paul Horning to Charles Woodson, a *Sports Illustrated* cover from their Super Bowl win in 1997. In the center of it all was a huge life-sized cutout of Brett Favre, who looked about twenty-five. The whole display was ten or fifteen feet wide and extended from the floor all the way to the ceiling.

Todd walked over to the counter, smiling. "This is the last place I'd expect to find a Packers fan," he said. "Are you from Wisconsin?"

"No sir," the woman said. "I just love 'em. I've always loved 'em."

She was like an oversized bird, all wings and splayed

feet, dressed in overalls, with a plaited pink and white shirt underneath. Oscar thought he detected a Midwestern twang, but maybe this was just the sound of rural white people everywhere.

"I grew up in Oconomowoc," Todd said. "About two hours from Lambeau Field."

"Are you an Aaron Rodgers fan or a Brett Favre fan?" the woman asked. "We have a lot of debates around here." She glanced at the men on the stools, one of whom nodded at Todd and raised his glass.

"I'm both," Todd answered. "I loved Brett, but it's kind of hard to argue with Rodgers winning a Super Bowl. Plus he's a California boy."

The woman nodded, as if he'd passed some kind of test. "That's Henry and Carl," she said. "We call Henry the mayor of Franklin. Of course, Franklin only has ten people, and two of them are dead, so it's not saying much."

Both men chuckled and sipped from their beers.

"And Carl's the grandpa of the town, but don't call him old. And I'm Annie."

"*Sweet* Annie," one of the men corrected.

"And that there," she continued, pointing at the dog, "is Vince Lombardi."

Todd grinned. "It's nice to meet you all."

Oscar slipped down another aisle to escape forced social interaction; he suspected that the men at the counter would take one look at him and try to drag him out to the fields. But even from thirty feet away, he could hear the conversation. He learned that the store had opened in 1918 as a train depot, and had been converted into a dry goods store in the 1930s. Sweet Annie's family had always run it, and she lived in the small house in back. They operated on a cash-only basis, with the occasional barter arrangement for locals. Sweet Annie had never visited San Francisco or Los Angeles; the biggest city she'd ever been to was Fresno. "What do they have in those places that they don't have here?" she asked. "Smog, crime, and traffic."

And Todd said, "You're absolutely right."

"And we even have crime here, or at least we did once. See those?"

She pointed to the high windows above the counter, where there were three jagged holes in the glass, spaced several inches apart.

"Are those . . . ?" Todd started.

"Yep. *Bullet* holes. We had some excitement around here about a year ago. Did you happen to see those trailers across the street?"

"Yes."

"Well, turned out some no-good youngster was cooking up some of that meta amphetamine. When the sheriff and his men came to arrest him—we don't have police here in Franklin, on account of it's so small—they got into a shoot-out. A deputy was shot and killed right out on the street there. And we got those three bullets in the window as a souvenir. I was hiding in the back—the cops told me to clear out—but the guys working in the fields next door had bullets whiz right past their heads."

"Wow," Todd said.

"It's a real shame, if you ask me."

"A *real* shame," Henry echoed.

"All those drugs and things coming up this way where it's always been so quiet. We haven't had something happen like that my whole life," Annie said. "But it just goes to show you, there's good and evil everywhere. And you can't get away from trouble if it wants to find you."

"That's for sure," Todd said.

Now Gwen appeared at the end of the counter, looking hesitant. "Sorry to interrupt, but can I ask a question?"

Sweet Annie turned to her. "Sure, honey. Hey, where are you all going anyway?"

"We're going backpacking," Gwen said. "Up in the mountains."

"Backpacking! Adventurers, huh? Which trail are you taking? Booth Valley?"

"No, actually, we're going up to Cloud Lakes."

"Cloud Lakes? That's supposed to be beautiful, although I've never done it myself. Like I said, everything I need's right here in Franklin."

"We're really excited," Todd said.

"Well, it's the bears that scare me," Sweet Annie continued. "One of them made it all the way to Franklin one time. Walked in and helped himself to the worms right there in the refrigerator. You're braver than I am, that's for sure."

Gwen asked, "Do you have any washcloths?"

Sweet Annie shrugged. "I think so, honey. We have just about everything. You just have to look a little while to find it."

And seemingly, they *did* have everything else. Oscar found a display of mugs from national parks—the Grand Canyon, Yellowstone, Glacier, the Everglades. He saw a box of daguerreotypes of unidentified people. Then a rack of back issues of *Field & Stream* and *American Marksman*, mixed in with *Ladies' Home Journal* and *Highlights*. There were cleaning supplies in dusty packages that had never been opened. There was a toy rocking horse, a wood stove, a phonograph. He could not remember when he had ever seen such clutter. And yet Todd and Gwen looked totally content—Todd still talking with the proprietor and the men at the counter, Gwen picking up various handcrafted things, smiling, placing them back on the shelves. He didn't understand this—what exactly did she find so charming? Why wasn't she freaked out by these goofy rednecks?

Then Tracy swept past him, holding a flashlight and two bundles of firewood. "Let's go." She stood impatiently at the cash register until Sweet Annie noticed her and ambled over to ring her up.

Gwen paid for a washcloth and a little embroidered pillow that read, *Every day is a beautiful day.* Todd bought a postcard—the same picture as the one on the door—and fished in his wallet until he came up with a small folded rectangle of colored paper. It was the Packers schedule from last season. He handed it to Sweet Annie. "To add to your collection," he said.

When they were back on the highway, Oscar shook his head. "Well, *that's* not a place I need to go back to."

"I thought it was sweet," said Gwen. "It reminded me of the country stores my great-aunt used to tell me about in the South."

"Really? That woman seemed a little off to me. And those two guys weren't exactly rolling out the welcome mat."

"Oh, they were fine," Todd said. "They're just locals. They're probably not used to seeing city people."

Oscar was about to ask what exactly Todd meant by "city people" when Tracy looked over her shoulder and into the back.

"And did you catch that story about the police shootout?" she asked. "Geez, it makes you wonder."

"It does," Gwen agreed. "And *those* folks were friendly. But I sure wouldn't want to break down out here in the middle of the night. There are a lot of white supremacist and militia groups in the Central Valley, you know."

"Really?" Todd said. But judging from his tone, Oscar thought, what he meant was, *Oh, come on!*

"Seriously. The Visalia area is a Klan stronghold, and other groups are active out here too. Two of them were convicted a couple of years ago for murdering a black kid."

"The Klan," Todd repeated, not disguising his skepticism.

"Really," Gwen said. "You can Google it."

Oscar's earlier irritation at Gwen was gone, and now he felt aligned with her, protective. He didn't appreciate Todd's questioning of her. And he resolved that however unprepared she might be for this trip, he would take it upon himself to watch out for her.

"Well one good thing," Todd said. "Those methed-out creeps that lady was talking about don't have the chops to backpack in the mountains."

"That's for sure," Tracy remarked. "Hey, how do you know all this, Gwen?"

"One of my coworkers brought a bunch of kids up to Sequoia last summer. He found all this stuff on the Internet and was a little freaked out."

"Well, whatever creepy folks there are down there, we're away from them now," said Tracy. "Check it out. We're going uphill."

And they were. The flat straight strip of country highway was now curving and winding upward, a lush valley opening to the right of them. They went up and up, beyond the chaparral and oak-lined hills and into the pines, and as the trees changed, the air did too, and they rolled their windows down to breathe it in. It smelled like forest and rich wet earth; it smelled fresh; it smelled like mountain. Oscar's unease and irritation both faded, and he was excited again. He stared out the window and took in the view— the deep green valley with the river winding through it, the snowcapped peaks behind. This is what I came for, he thought. This is why I'm here.

CHAPTER SIX
TODD

When they finally pulled up to Redwood Station, Todd couldn't contain himself; the car had barely come to a stop before he was out of it. The ranger station was a miniscule one-story cabin, painted a red-chocolate brown. He loved how well these buildings blended in with their surroundings. The structure looked especially small at the foot of all the grand cedars and pines; no sun broke through the canopy of branches. Tacked up on the walls were trail maps, pictures of bear canisters, warnings about proper food storage, and examples of items—food wrappers, sunscreen, deodorant, toilet paper—that had to be packed out of the woods. About half a dozen people were lined up at the counter, waiting to get their permits. Another three or four backpackers were splayed out across benches that had been cut from logs, with heavy packs, water bottles, and bags of trail mix scattered around them. Judging from their sunburns and dirt-streaked clothes, they had just come in from the backcountry.

Tracy took the reservation letter they'd exchange for their permit and got in line. Gwen and Oscar ran off to use the restrooms. Todd walked out of the parking lot and toward a grove of sequoias he'd spotted from the road. He was glad to have a few minutes alone. All morning he'd been wondering if he should have stayed behind. Why hadn't the Pattersons told him they were cancelling? If he'd known ahead of time, he might have made his own excuses. But he didn't find out until he'd arrived at Tracy's, and by then it was too late. Now, several hours into the trip, he wasn't sure how this was going to work. He felt weird being the only white person in the group, but that was just the start of his discomfort. Tracy's usual intensity, which was great for the gym, had kicked into overdrive—and spending a structured hour with someone a couple times a week was very different than being with her all the time. He liked Gwen, and she was easy to look at too—she had dark lovely skin, strong cheekbones, warm brown eyes, and wavy hair that was tied back in a ponytail. She watched everything cautiously, as if looking out from behind a curtain, but when she smiled, it lit up her entire face.

Oscar, on the other hand, had an edge—as if he suspected Todd of something just because he was white. He'd been so cagey at that wonderful store in Franklin, slinking around the aisles like he was getting ready to steal something. With his slicked-back hair and big tattoos, he would have caught Todd's attention too. And that ridiculousness about the men in Franklin, and come to think of it, even Gwen's remarks in the car. The Ku Klux Klan? Really? In 2012? He had a hard time understanding this kind of oversensitivity, but it wasn't worth getting into it. So he'd kept his mouth shut—well, mostly.

As they took the winding road up the gradual slope of the Western Sierra, he'd finally begun to relax. Then they drove down into a canyon, as if through a gateway into an entirely different world. Near the bottom, he'd spotted a great blue heron flying over the river, neck extending and retracting, chest jutting out as far as its head. Its long graceful legs were trailing behind, tapered and liquid dark, like the ink-dipped tip of a fountain pen. His heart had swelled as he watched it swoop down toward the water.

And now, here he was with these magnificent trees. Several dozen giant sequoias with beautiful red-brown bark, each as big around as a building, as a whale. Their skin looked soft and contoured and he wanted to touch them, but to do so would have felt like sacrilege. They gave off a deep silence, as if they absorbed all sound, and their very presence made the noise and clutter of Todd's life—of *all* human dealings—seem trivial, superficial, and temporary. Walking among them, Todd felt like he had entered a cathedral—the grandiose beauty, the quiet, the suggestion of time beyond knowing. He loved the Sierra in all of its seasons—the snow in winter that made the trees seem even redder in contrast; the dogwood blossoms in spring, their broad white petals suggestive of movement, like his daughter's pinwheel toy. The stillness of the forest made something still in him too. He remembered his first trip to the Sierras when he was twelve, with his mother and stepfather. It was seeing the sequoias for the first time— more even than seeing the ocean—that made him feel he'd arrived in California.

He pulled his cell phone out of his pocket—no reception. What a joy it was to be beyond the reach of that tyrannical thing, of incessant e-mails, of connectivity. He understood that his recent thoughts about changing careers were part of some midlife crisis, and he felt like a bit of a cliché. But at least he'd avoided making a fool of himself by buying a fast car or messing with younger women. He knew that women still noticed him—like Rachel, his junior associate, who often stayed late, and whom he'd turned down when she suggested a drink after work because he didn't quite trust himself. He'd burned off his restlessness and frustration by throwing himself into exercise. And by dreaming of coming up to the mountains.

In most ways Todd still felt the same as he had in his twenties, but he realized that wasn't how others saw him. At the firm's picnic last summer, he'd played in the inter-office softball game, Downtown versus Century City. He'd been an All-Pac Ten second baseman in college, and he made sure that everyone knew it. But when he dove for a sharp grounder and landed on his belly, the third baseman and pitcher came running over to make sure he was all right. And when, in the final inning, he ran full tilt from second base, rounded third, and barreled into the catcher at home, players from both teams sprinted over and lay him down on his back to make sure that he was still in one piece.

"I'm *fine*," he'd insisted. "Just bruised up a little."

Then Todd looked up at the circle of faces hovering over him and realized that all of the other players were under thirty. They did not consider him to be one of them. They thought of him as old. It was a moment, all right, and it didn't help that he'd reinjured his shoulder in the collision at the plate, which is what started him on physical therapy. After that, he worked to get himself back in shape.

He walked halfway through the grove and then looked at his watch. Fifteen minutes had passed since they parked. Reluctantly, he returned to the car, but the others weren't there. Glancing toward the ranger station, he saw Oscar and Gwen reading the bear and food storage regulations— and then Tracy, who was now second in line.

There were two rangers working—a blond woman with the air of an old-school basketball coach, and a tall, rangy man in his sixties, mustached and sun-weathered, who was exactly what Todd envisioned when he thought of a forest ranger. Todd joined Tracy in line just as the male ranger yelled, "Next!" And the two of them approached the counter together.

"Hello there," the ranger said, in a deep, mellow voice. His name tag read, *Greg Baxter*. "How can I help you today?"

"We have a reservation for the Cloud Lakes trail," Tracy said. She placed her confirmation letter on the counter. "We'd like to rent some bear canisters."

"Cloud Lakes," the ranger repeated. "I'm sorry, but a forest fire was spotted up at Merritt Dome this morning, and they've had to close the trail."

Tracy stared at him. "You're kidding."

"I wish I were," Ranger Baxter said. "We saw smoke up there last night, and then our helicopter did a flyover early this morning. The fire's right in the area where you're supposed to hike. See, they're talking about it now."

An urgent voice crackled over the walkie-talkie clipped to his belt: "*. . . the fire has crossed the Cloud Lakes trail. Repeat, the fire has crossed the trail. It is approximately 300 acres now and growing. Do you copy?*"

The woman ranger, whose name tag said, *Laurie McKay*, detached her walkie-talkie from her belt and spoke into it. "This is Redwood Station. Yes, we copy."

"*The fire is currently being held by the Ainley River, but it'll probably jump the river in these winds.*"

"We're holding all backpackers here," said Ranger McKay.

"*All hikers in the backcountry will have to evacuate,*" came the voice over the radio. "*Melissa Lakes Station and Dylan Station, do you copy?*"

A few seconds, and then a different voice: "*This is Dylan Station. We copy.*"

Then: "*Melissa Lakes. We copy. We'll evacuate out of the Merritt Dome area and send hikers back toward the trailhead.*"

"This is Redwood Station. We copy," said the ranger. She and Baxter looked at each other. "Bummer," he remarked.

By now, the other people in line had all crowded around the counter. There was a family—a father and mother with their tall, fresh-faced teenage son. There were two rugged-looking guys in their twenties and a single man in his thirties. The family seemed especially upset—they'd flown out from Massachusetts for the hike—and now Ranger McKay turned her full attention to them, trying to calm them down.

Todd couldn't believe it. A fire, on the very trail they were supposed to hike? What rotten luck. "Well, what are we supposed to do?"

"We've been planning this trip for months," Tracy added.

Ranger Baxter shrugged, and sighed. "I know, I'm sorry. The Cloud Lakes are spectacular. But there are some other great trips you could take—a couple of other loops and a few in-and-outs."

Neither Todd nor Tracy answered for a minute. Todd was still envisioning the pictures he'd seen, the beautiful valley, the flower-filled meadow, the photo of the Cloud Lakes at dawn. It was hard to believe he wouldn't be going there. Behind him, the two young guys turned and left; the family was still talking heatedly with Ranger McKay.

"Well, what would you suggest?" Tracy asked. "We've

come all the way out here, you know? It would be a shame to just turn around and go home."

Baxter spread a topographical map out on the counter and pointed to an area that was colored with green and wavy brown lines. "Well, there's the Boulder Creek route. Most people can do it in six days and five nights."

"Too long."

"Then there's the Brenda Lakes trail." He pointed to an area where the lines were much closer together. "But that one's pretty strenuous. Four thousand feet elevation gain the first day, probably twelve thousand feet elevation gain and loss total."

By now, Oscar and Gwen had joined them. They both looked crestfallen. Tracy glanced at them, then back at Baxter, and said, "That might be a bit too much."

"Well, where have you been sending other people?" Gwen asked. She sounded disappointed but maybe a little relieved.

"Honestly, most people have just gone home. They've had their hearts set on Cloud Lakes. But that's a shame, if you ask me. There are plenty of other beautiful places to go." He paused, fiddled with a knob on the walkie-talkie. "Those who *have* decided to stay have done one of the trails I suggested. They'll probably be pretty crowded this weekend."

"All the more reason not to do them," Tracy said. "Isn't there anyplace else?"

The ranger stood up and pulled on his scraggly beard, looking thoughtful. "There might be *one* more place you could try . . ." he said, half to himself. Then, shaking his head, "No, it's probably not a good idea."

"What?" Tracy asked, leaning over the counter.

"Well . . ." He looked at them, lifting one eyebrow and then the other. "There's a real off-the-beaten-path kind of trail just outside of the park. It's the right length trip for you—about thirty miles. It's gorgeous, and you'll get the same variety of landscape as the Cloud Lakes trail—river and meadow, some alpine lakes, then a couple of high passes. And what I believe is the prettiest canyon in the whole Sierra . . . The thing is, no one's hiked the trail in years. It's not even marked on this map."

"How do you know about it?" Todd asked.

The ranger spread the map out with his hands again. They were big, gnarled hands, twisted and aged by years of living in the mountains. "I've been up here a long time— over forty years. I've been to places that aren't marked on the Forest Service map or any other. This trail, I hiked it with a buddy once almost thirty years ago. It was one of my favorite trips ever."

"Well, if it's so awesome," Todd asked, "why doesn't anyone do it?"

The ranger smiled, and his expression was complicated. "It's real remote, and the road to get to it is a killer. The Forest Service doesn't maintain it anymore."

It sounded like there was more to the story, but Tracy was clearly intrigued. "Well, what do you think, guys?" she asked, turning to the others.

"I don't know . . ." Gwen said. Then to the ranger: "Are you sure it's okay?"

"Oh, absolutely! I mean, there *is* a trail; it's just not been maintained. The most you're likely to find, though, is some overgrown brush and fallen trees. But it's beautiful, I promise. Well worth the trouble to get there."

They all looked at each other. Oscar sighed. "Well, it

would be a shame to go home after we've come all the way up here."

"We could at least go check it out," Todd said.

Tracy turned to Gwen. "How about you?"

"I don't know. But if the rest of you think it's okay . . ."

Tracy beamed. "Great! Let's do it." Now she turned back to the ranger. "So—where would we be going?"

Ranger Baxter took out another map, which showed the park and the surrounding wilderness area. All four of them crowded the counter to look. "Here," he said, taking a green highlighter and marking an X in one corner, "is where we are, at Redwood Station. This," he hovered over a line with his pen but didn't touch down, "takes you to the end of the road where the Cloud Lakes trail begins. Here," and now he set the point of the pen down and traced a solid line and then a broken one somewhere north and west of the main trailhead, toward the edge of the map, "is where you'd be going. There's a primitive camp-site about eight miles down at the end of this dirt road, probably a forty-minute drive from the main road. About halfway down there's a turnoff to the left—but don't take that, just keep heading straight down. Once you get to the end, there might even be an old fire ring. Trailhead should be right there too."

Now he stepped away from the counter and ambled over to a small desk, where he opened a drawer and looked through some files before pulling out a single sheet of pa-per. He came back over and placed the paper on the counter. It was a color copy of a hand-drawn map. There were shaded little triangles for mountains, blue arteries for rivers, stick trees, and pebble-like boulders. There were small nota-tions in blocklike print—*Good campsite, Many switchbacks, Lots of fish!*—and simple drawings of a deer, a hawk, a bear. At the top of the map were the words *Lost Canyon.*

"Now this is the best I've got as far as a map," the ranger said. "It's what I used when I did the loop myself. It was drawn by an old-time ranger."

The map looked whimsical, cartoonish, which actually gave Todd some comfort. If this earlier traveler created such a charming representation of this route, how hard could it actually be?

"This is all you've got?" Oscar asked.

"It's all you need," said the ranger. "That, along with a topo map of that area. If one of you guys knows how to read one, you'll be fine."

"I do," Todd said.

"Me too," Tracy added.

"Great! Then let's get you set up with your permit and bear canisters." Baxter smiled. "I'm happy for you guys. There's so much out here that most people never get to see. But you seem up for doing something different."

"We are," Tracy said.

"Honestly, as unofficial as this map looks, it's probably pretty accurate. Some of those old-timers knew every inch of these mountains. Who knows?" The ranger laughed. "A few of them may even still be out there."

"I've heard about some of them, actually," Tracy said. "Guys my grandfather knew, who came in from the eastern side."

"Well, be careful out there," the ranger said. "These mountains are tougher than people think. We have to send out rescue teams every year. So watch yourselves, all right?"

They promised to watch themselves, and the ranger

handed over their pass. Then he gave them four bear canisters—cylindrical, drum-shaped containers of black plastic that would hold all their food and toiletries. They returned to the car, and Tracy swung out onto the road, back in the direction they'd come from. They were all quiet for a few moments, watching the same landscape they'd just passed through nearly an hour before.

Oscar broke the silence. "Did you say your grandfather knew people who lived in the mountains?"

"Yeah, he did," Tracy answered. "People who snuck out of Manzanar."

"The internment camp? Really?"

"Yeah. Mostly they just left for a day or two to go fishing. They'd crawl out under the barbed-wire fence at night and hike up to the rivers at the foot of the mountains, then sneak back in the next night. My grandfather went with them a couple of times. The more adventurous ones would travel farther up, to the lakes, and stay out for three or four nights. Finally the guards wised up, though, and people would get beaten if they were caught. So a bunch of my grandfather's friends just up and left one night and never came back. Mostly men but a couple of women too. For all I know, they're still out there."

"That kind of sounds like the Maroons, the escaped slaves in Jamaica," said Gwen. "They built their own new society in the mountains."

"Exactly. People fleeing bad situations, and starting over, fending for themselves in the wild." Tracy paused for a moment. "My grandfather was always jealous that they didn't take him with them. But he had a family—my mom was five years old and my uncle was just a baby—so maybe that's why they left him behind. After the war, though, he'd go hiking up here; I think he always hoped he would find them."

"Did they ever come down?" Oscar asked.

Tracy shook her head. "I don't know. Not that my grandfather heard . . . I like to think they're still up here, you know? I'd love to do what they did. Chuck everything and live in the mountains."

There Tracy went again, off on a tangent. But it was okay, Todd thought—they were back on course. They continued on the road that ran beside the river, winding back up out of the canyon. The sky was noticeably hazy now to the east from the smoke of the fire, and Todd was glad they were driving away from it.

After half an hour they turned right on the small spur road the ranger had pointed out. They passed a sign that informed them that they were leaving the park. Twenty miles farther on they found a jeep road. It wasn't marked, but there was a big rock formation directly across from it, with a half-circle of big Jeffrey Pines framing the entrance. The turnoff itself was barely visible, overgrown with weeds between the faint tire grooves, and they drove past it and looked at it three or four times before deciding it was in fact the right place. Once they turned, there was a quick, steep climb, and then a bend behind some trees, and just like that they were out of sight from the road. They were truly in the backcountry now, apart from civilization. The road bumped left, right, winding through trees and then reaching a clearing that yielded a glimpse of the peaks to the east. It was the single worst road Todd had ever been on. The potholes seemed to have potholes, and big rocks jutted out, like living creatures poised to rise up and tear through the bottom of the car. Tracy drove a bit too fast for his comfort, negotiating the truck around the rocks and in and out of the potholes, jostling and jolting her passengers.

"No wonder no one comes back here," Gwen said.

They'd all rolled up their windows to block out the dust, and held on to parts of the interior—dashboard, headrest, handle—to keep from bouncing all over the car.

"Yeah, wow," Tracy said. "This isn't fun." And yet everything about her relaxed posture, the ease of her hands on the wheel, suggested that it *was* fun, that she was enjoying this bad road, this test of her nerve and skill. You better know what you're doing, Todd thought. You better not be getting us into something we can't handle.

After twenty minutes they reached a turnoff to the left.

"That must be the road the ranger mentioned," Todd remarked.

"Right," Tracy said. "It looks even worse than this one."

Just past the junction a small log had fallen over the road, and the two men got out to move it aside.

"I hope we make it," said Oscar when they were back in their seats. "And I hope the car's okay. It would suck to be stuck out here, especially if other people don't come back here much."

"We'll make it," Tracy assured him, and then they were quiet, feeling every bump and jolt as they headed steeply downhill again, trying not to get carsick, maybe hoping their collective fears would keep the car safe until they made it to the end of the road.

Which they did, finally—one last dip and bend and they were there. A break in the trees, a small flat area between the walls of a narrow canyon. There was a clearing and, to their delight, an obvious fire pit. When Tracy cut the ignition, they all just sat for a moment.

"That was something," Todd said.

"How long did it take us?" Gwen asked, sounding queasy. Todd was on the verge of getting sick himself.

Oscar looked at his watch. "About thirty-five minutes from the turnoff."

"And how far did we actually go?"

Tracy looked at the odometer. "A little over eight miles, just like the ranger said."

"Well, at least we know we're in the right place."

Then Todd became conscious of another sound, running water—steady and continual, alive. "Do you guys hear that?"

"A river," Gwen said.

"Sounds like a small one, more like a creek," he said. "But still. What a perfect spot to camp."

Todd jumped out of the car and walked through the trees, and after forty feet or so, there it was—a creek running gently through the floor of the canyon, flowing around rocks and under fallen logs. It caught little bits of sun and reflected it back, sharp and bright like shiny jewels. The water was a beautiful blue-green color; it appeared as pure as if it flowed from the center of the earth. He looked up and saw a row of pine trees, their branches all on one side, extending toward him as if holding out their arms in welcome. He felt joy rising in his chest, and his heart and breathing slowed, as if his body was matching the rhythm of the creek. Now he missed his kids terribly and wished they were here—scrambling down to the water's edge to pick up a shiny rock, or standing on the bank with fishing poles. They needed to do *this*, he thought, instead of play dates and video games. He'd bring them back up later on this summer.

He returned to find the others unloading the car—they'd taken out the cooler, the firewood, a couple bags of food, the camp chairs that Tracy had brought. Tracy suggested that they pitch their tents upwind from the campfire, and so she drove with their gear over the rough rocky ground and the others followed on foot. About thirty feet beyond the fire pit they came upon the bottom of a huge fallen tree, its root system unearthed and perpendicular to the ground, its intertwined roots flat but intricate, like a Jackson Pollack painting. Behind the tree, sheltered from wind, was the perfect spot. Todd unloaded his pack and set it on the ground. Then, the happy business of making camp—pitching their two tents about ten feet apart, blowing up their sleeping pads and placing them and their sleeping bags inside, leaving their packs in the tent vestibules.

By the time they were finished, it was almost five. The sun had moved beyond the canyon wall, leaving them in shade, and between that and the elevation—reported by Oscar as 6,728 feet—it was suddenly cool. Todd dug his fleece jacket out of his pack and put it on. But before he walked back to the fire pit, he looked at their campsite. It was a pleasing sight. Two tents, his green Mountain Hardwear and Tracy's orange Big Agnes, against a backdrop of the Pollack tree, the tall shading pines. The canyon was maybe a quarter-mile wide; the steep granite walls must have risen a thousand feet. Behind him, the rippling creek. They were tucked away in a little fold of the Sierras, and he liked how this setup looked, and also how it felt. They were out in the wild, unreachable, and no one except the ranger even knew where they were. He tried to imagine the guys from the country club in this setting, and couldn't.

By the time he reached the fire pit, Tracy and Oscar

had already made a pyramid of logs and stuffed twigs and newspaper into the cracks between them. Tracy struck a match and touched the paper in several places; it blackened and curled, smoke risking quickly, and then the paper and the kindling lit with flame. There was a rusted grate just over the flame, strong enough to hold a pot full of water and pasta. For a moment Todd thought the fire pit was a little too intact, too functional, for a place that hadn't been used in many years. But he let the thought pass. Tracy tended to the pasta, and then to the sauce, while everyone else retrieved their plates and utensils and set up their camp chairs. When the food was ready, Tracy used a sweatshirt to protect her hand and carefully lifted the pot. After dumping the water thirty feet from the fire, she set both pots on a large flat rock and served everyone their meals.

"Last dinner not out of a bag for three days," Tracy noted.

Gwen groaned. "Don't remind me."

"Last beer too," added Oscar, taking a swig from the bottle he'd pulled out of the cooler.

It seemed to Todd that this was the best meal he'd had in months. Tracy's pasta and sauce tasted wonderful, but even better was the setting. They were surrounded by forest, beside a pristine creek, on a small patch of land hugged by canyon walls, which were dark and looming now, like sleeping giants. Through the canopy of trees they could see the first-quarter moon, so bright it was as if what they saw at home was a poor imitation. He felt happier than he had in a long time.

"Cheers," he said, raising his bottle. "Here's to our first night in the mountains."

"Here's to Tracy for making dinner and driving," Oscar said. "And for organizing the trip."

Tracy leaned over and hit him on the knee, and he struck back at her, laughing. "Well, here's to all of *you* for stepping out of your normal lives. Out of the gym too—and into the real world."

"Here's to getting home safely," Gwen said.

Todd could hear her nervousness. Would she be able to do this trip? "For sure," he said, reassuringly. "We'll get home safe."

They ate hungrily and washed their meals down with more beer—all except Gwen, who drank Sprite. Then Todd broke out his own surprise—fixings for s'mores—and they roasted marshmallows on switches, slid them between graham crackers that were loaded with squares of chocolate, and ate. With some beer in him, away from the city, Oscar wasn't so bad, Todd decided. Oscar told stories of his real estate exploits—the times he'd shown houses and walked in on people having sex; the bitterly divorcing couple who'd only speak to each other through him; the mysterious person who frequented open houses and shit in all the toilets. He had them rolling, and even Gwen finally started to relax.

Around seven thirty, Tracy said they should clean up for the night, and so they took some water from the creek and washed their dishes, dispersing the water away from the fire and tents. They stuffed all their food into their bear canisters and covered the empty cooler with jackets in the back of the truck. Tracy reminded them to put their toiletries in the bear canisters too, and Gwen, wide-eyed, asked why.

"Because bears are drawn to anything with scent," Tracy answered. "Even toothpaste, even deodorant."

Todd remembered a show he'd watched with the kids on the Discovery Channel, two black bears ripping a car apart as easily as a beer can to reach a discarded Snickers wrapper. "It should be fine," he assured her. "If no one's been out here for a while, the bears have no reason to visit."

"I'll be all right," Gwen said gamely. "Besides, if a bear comes down from the mountains, he'll get to *your* tent first."

Todd laughed, happily surprised. "I see how it is. So much for teamwork, huh?"

"I'm just saying."

"He's right, we shouldn't see them," Tracy said. "But I have bear spray, just in case."

"Bear spray?" Gwen repeated.

"Yeah, it's super-intense pepper spray, ursine strength." She reached into the bag beside her and pulled out what looked like a miniature fire extinguisher—red, cylindrical, eight or ten inches long. "I brought it just for you. I don't usually carry it on trips in the Sierras—it's more for grizzly country. But I figured it would make you feel safer."

"Thanks," Gwen said, "it does."

Soon they were sitting in their chairs again, staring at the fire. They heard a small but growing chorus of frogs, singing to each other and the night. They decided on a wake-up time—six—and a departure time of eight. They pulled out the topo map and tried to link it to the hand-drawn map, but the features in the landscape didn't easily match. Then they followed the trail to Lost Canyon on the hand-drawn map and estimated how far they'd go the next day. If they broke the route into four somewhat even parts, they'd reach Lost Canyon on day three.

Todd felt the reality of the trip setting in. Tomorrow they were going into the unknown wild with nothing but a hand-drawn map. He was nervous—when he vacationed with his family, he plotted out routes and rest stops and stopping points with to-the-hour precision. This trip was different—less predictable, less certain. But maybe their change in plans was a blessing. He'd wanted to see how he would do if left to his own devices. And now here they were. As he crawled into his sleeping bag in the cramped intimate space of a two-man tent shared with someone he'd just met that day, he felt a surge of anticipation and excitement. Tomorrow, he'd be walking farther away from his life—or maybe farther into it.

CHAPTER SEVEN
GWEN

Gwen woke to total stillness, a quiet so deep and pure she wasn't sure that she was really awake. There were no passing cars, no distant sirens, no voices floating in from the street. As she listened with her eyes closed, she realized that the absence of human sound didn't mean it was silent. Birds were singing—three, no, four different kinds—trees were rustling in the wind, and she could hear the steady murmur of the creek. She opened her eyes and saw that Tracy was already gone. She wiggled out of her sleeping bag, zipped open the door of the tent, and peered out. A clear day—up between the canyon walls the sky was icy blue. But the canyon itself was still in shade, and when Gwen stepped out, she rubbed her arms and bounced on her toes at the cold. There was no sign of movement from the other tent, no sign of Tracy, either. She looked at her watch—5:47—and was glad that she had thirteen minutes before Oscar's alarm woke the guys up and their morning tasks began. She walked into the woods to squat and pee—her original shyness about this act somewhat cured by long hikes in LA. Then she made her way past the tents and up the creek, where she found a boulder at the edge of the water and sat.

For the first time since they'd left the city, she felt truly relaxed. All day yesterday, she'd been uneasy about the trip. She'd enjoyed the cash store, its cluttered charm and odd people, but had been troubled by how dismissive Oscar and Tracy were, and then later, by Todd's naïveté. And she'd felt on guard at the ranger station, where she and Oscar had gotten curious looks from some of the other people. This is our wilderness too, she'd wanted to say— but as usual, she kept her mouth shut. And then the change in route had unsettled her, not to mention their drive down the bumpy and deserted road to get to an unmapped trail.

But dinner had helped. Tracy's competence with the fire, the fact that the fire pit had actually been there, had reassured her. And she was feeling more at ease with the guys, as Oscar's edge dulled a little and Todd loosened up. But she'd also been aware of the world beyond their circle of light, the deep growing darkness of the woods. And as the evening went on she'd grown anxious again—not only about their trip, but about being so far removed from everything she knew, with no easy way to get back. She remembered how she'd felt when her great-aunt died and she was about to enter foster care—the fear and uncertainty, the sense that no one knew or cared where she was. As the darkness had settled around them, the trees transformed into silent sentinels that looked ready to wake up and move. And when everyone shoved their food and toiletries into the black cylindrical canisters, when they debated about how far away from their tents was far enough to place them, when Tracy put the bear spray right next to her in the tent, fear had filled Gwen's chest and prickled her skin; she was sure that a bear would appear at any second, at first indistinguishable and then suddenly there, as if formed of the darkness itself.

But there'd been no bear, not even a hint of one. Just

the hard, cold ground, with a few rocks digging into her, ground that she realized too late was slightly sloped, so that she always seemed to be rolling left, and when she finally did manage to get to sleep, she dreamed of falling over a cliff. It had taken hours, though, to sleep. She had lain awake with her eyes open, listening to the frogs, jumping at every sound in the woods, while Tracy—positioned head to toe—slept heavily beside her. She'd needed to pee but was afraid to leave the tent, the relative comfort of her sleeping bag. And so she'd stayed in one spot, alert and cold, until sleep finally overcame her. The last time she'd looked at her watch, it was almost one thirty.

Now it was morning, though, now it was light, and the fears of the dark had subsided. She was proud to have made it through the first night—and glad to be awake, and alone. The creek was chattering and lively, making its way past mossy rocks and under fallen branches, rushing in the spots where the banks grew narrow, flowing gently when the shoreline receded. The trees looked harmless in daytime, and in the light she saw the bark, the beautiful parallel downward patterns that moved and flowed like water. Gwen heard the high-noted chirping of one bird, the lower calls of another, the insistent tap-tap-tapping of a woodpecker, which she spotted high up in a tree, its red head a blur against the black of its body. The tree was full of pine cones which dangled like earrings. Across the creek she saw two squirrels winding down around a trunk, tails swishing, both of them stopping just above the ground and nattering at each other. She looked up and saw that the top third of the canyon wall was touched by light, so bright it appeared to sparkle. Huge swaths of granite were broken up by small plateaus that housed hearty, improbable trees.

What a beautiful place, Gwen thought. She had never been anywhere like this. She couldn't believe how different it was from the chaparral and dusty trails near LA.

But even as she appreciated the beauty of the spot, she felt sad about Robert. She just missed him, was all. There was so much he had never gotten to do, and it felt unfair that she was in this lovely place that he would never see.

Suddenly she thought of a story that Devon had told her, about a hiker who'd been killed by a falling boulder. It had taken him a long time to die. The boulder, a bathtub-sized chunk of granite, had caught the man square in the chest and pinned him to the ground. The hiker had two friends with him, but they couldn't get the rock to budge. One of them stayed with him while the other went off for help. The trapped man's legs were free, his face unobscured, so his friend talked to him and wiped the sweat off his brow while he slowly bled to death from inside. By the time the rescue workers arrived three hours later, the man was unconscious. It took them the rest of the day to dig him out.

It occurred to Gwen that this was what grief was like. It was like being crushed under the weight of something that she couldn't get out from under, or remove. And she wasn't sure, even as she went on with her life, that it wasn't slowly killing her.

Now she heard voices behind her—Todd and Oscar had emerged from their tent. Oscar was fiddling with his gear, and Todd was stretching, bending over to touch his toes and then leaning sideways. Gwen sighed and walked back to the tents. For a moment she was self-conscious about not having on any makeup, but her concealer was buried somewhere in her backpack.

"Morning," Oscar called as she approached. He was

wearing sweatpants and a jacket and his hair was a disheveled mess, which made him look younger, endearing.

"Morning," she said. "How'd you guys sleep?"

"Okay. Except I woke up once when I heard footsteps outside, thought it might be a bear. But it was just Todd, out to take a piss."

"You do look kind of bearlike," Gwen noted.

"Good morning to you too," Todd answered. Then, to Oscar: "Wish I'd known you were awake. I could have messed with the tent and *really* had some fun."

"Very funny," Oscar said. Then, to Gwen, "How'd *you* sleep?"

"Not so great. I kept thinking I was hearing things. But I feel good now. It's a beautiful morning."

"It is," Oscar agreed. "But it'll be even more beautiful when we have some coffee."

"I think Tracy's working on that now," Todd said.

Gwen looked toward the fire pit and saw that Tracy, who'd reappeared, had a fire going and was placing a pot of water on the grill. "I'll go help her," she said.

Tracy was already in her hiking pants and fleece jacket, with her hair pulled into its usual ponytail. She looked happy and awake, not a hint of sleepiness or stiffness, as if she'd spent the night in a luxury hotel.

"Good morning, sleepyhead!" she called out. "You hungry?"

"I am, actually. Hey, where'd you go?"

"Just up the trail a ways. To see how it looked. I woke up around five and it was already light, and I knew I wouldn't get back to sleep. The trail looks good—clearer than I expected."

"*That's* good."

"Yes, it is. You want some coffee?"

"More than anything else in the world."

Tracy had brought over one of the bear canisters, and now they took packets of instant coffee and made themselves two cups. Eventually the guys came over and they all had bowls of instant oatmeal, which Tracy had brought for the whole group, sitting in their chairs from the previous night and laughing at their nighttime discomforts.

"How is it that you sleep so well outside?" Todd asked Tracy, after it was clear that all the others had slept badly.

"Clear conscience," Tracy replied.

"How do you manage *that*?"

"It's easy. Pure living. Plus, I don't have kids."

Both Todd and Oscar groaned, and Gwen imagined they felt the pull of their families. She was feeling guilt too, about not being able to call her sister on her birthday. And she wondered about the group she missed yesterday, about how Sandra Gutierrez was doing. But in truth, she was glad to be away. She suspected that Todd and Oscar felt the same, because they were, despite their momentary outburst of guilt, both giddy and energized. She was relieved that they seemed to be getting along and weren't trying to out-guy each other.

After they ate, they all washed their dishes and repacked their food. Then Gwen changed out of her sweats and into her hiking clothes. She captured her hair in an elastic band and reluctantly put on a hat; she was not one of those girls who felt cute in a baseball cap.

Then, a flurry of organization. They folded their tents up and Tracy and Todd stuffed them in their packs. They sorted out clothes they didn't need and threw them into the back of the car, Gwen trying to shake the feeling that she was forgetting something crucial. They filled their bottles from the stream and treated the water with a screwdriver-sized ultraviolet contraption. They adjusted and tightened their hiking poles—all except Oscar, who hadn't brought any. By seven forty-five, everything was either in the car or their packs, and the campsite looked as clear as it had when they'd pulled in the day before.

"All right, we need a picture," said Tracy, and so they lined up near the fire pit. They were now in their respective hiking outfits—Gwen in olive pants and an eggplant-colored long-sleeved shirt, Tracy in clay pants and a light brown button-down, Todd in a gray-blue long-sleeved shirt and tan hiking shorts, Oscar in black nylon shorts Gwen remembered from the gym, and a rust-colored pullover fleece. Tracy placed her camera on a tree stump, then ran over to join the group; she hoisted her pack on just as the timer counted down and the camera clicked. She retrieved it, looked at the picture, and held it out for everyone to see. "Off we go," she said. "Explorers in the wild."

Oscar looked over her shoulder and grinned. "What a bunch of dorks."

"There's just no way to look cool, is there?" Gwen agreed, laughing. "With these big old packs and poles."

"I think we look pretty studly," Todd said. "If you don't mind me saying so, ladies."

"I agree," Tracy said flatly. "Carrying forty-pound packs for thirty miles, up to 11,500 feet, isn't my definition of dorky."

"Okay, okay, sorry!" Oscar said, shaking his head. "All right, we're adventurers. We're pioneers in the wild."

Gwen knew what Oscar meant. Sure, a thirty-mile loop in the backcountry was a big undertaking. But they were in the Sierras, in a designated Wilderness Area—not too far from civilization. All of them had steady, responsible jobs; two of them had families. They could pretend to be whatever, whomever they pleased. But in the end they were four adults in their thirties and forties, a lawyer and a youth counselor, a trainer and a realtor. They were not extraordinary people.

They walked over to the trailhead—an unobtrusive passage through a thick cluster of trees—and then they were hiking, and Gwen could hardly believe they were on their way. The trail led through forest, then curved closer to the canyon wall. She was aware in a different way of her body itself—the effort of placing one foot in front of the other; the extension of her arm to plant a pole. And she was conscious of the pack on her back, which was like carrying a small child, except it didn't adjust itself like a child would and simply added weight, so if she leaned left the pack tipped with her, threatening to pull her over; if she stood up straight it pulled her backward; if she bent over the pack pressed her toward the ground. After ten minutes she learned how to use the poles to help distribute the weight, another ten and she developed a kind of rhythm. She was third in line—Tracy led and Oscar followed, Todd brought up the rear. She watched how the others picked their steps and used their poles, and tried to ignore the pressure on her shoulders and hips.

They walked silently on soft trail, through cover of forest. They left the first canyon and entered a larger one. Here the granite walls were more varied—huge rounded domes with clear marks where bits of rock had crumbled off; and cliff walls where the rock had fallen away in squares, leaving shapes like the blunt-featured figures on

Easter Island. After thirty minutes, Todd called out, "Hold on for a minute, I've got to tie my shoe."

Oscar sat down heavily on a fallen log and swung his pack off his shoulder. From the look on his face, he was as glad to stop as Gwen was. She found a thigh-high boulder and lowered herself slowly, resting the pack on the rock to remove the burden from her shoulders. The hip straps dug into her stomach and she breathed in relief as she undid the buckle and slipped her arms out of the shoulder straps. She reached behind awkwardly to grab her bottle and then gave up and turned around, pulling the bottle out of the side pocket.

"I forgot how damned hard it is to walk with a pack," Oscar said, taking off his fleece. His pack, an old-fashioned external frame, looked like a loaded sled set on its heels.

"It's pretty tough," Gwen agreed, and she glanced over at Tracy, who was still on her feet, looking up the trail, bear spray clipped to her belt. She stood there easily, bouncing on her toes, as if she carried nothing at all.

"We've gone one mile," Tracy announced. "Only twenty-nine to go."

Gwen took this in without comment, but her heart sank. They'd gone one mile? With all that effort? What had she been thinking? This was infinitely harder than any hike she'd ever done in LA. How was she going to make it thirty miles with a heavy backpack? Right now, she wasn't even sure if she could make it another mile.

"Why are we doing this again?" Oscar asked.

"Aw, come on," Todd said, hoisting his pack back on. "This is great."

"Yeah, let's go," Tracy said. "Only three more hours until lunch."

Oscar looked at Gwen and opened his eyes wide. "You heard her. Only three more hours till lunch."

Gwen twisted her arms at uncomfortable angles to get them into her shoulder straps, then reclipped the buckles at her waist and chest. She didn't know how she would stand up again. She tried once but the pack was too heavy; she managed to raise herself about three inches and then sat back down.

"Lean forward onto the poles and bend your legs," Tracy instructed, and she tried once, twice, before she finally got her feet set under her and pushed with her legs, shooting up so fast that the weight of the pack carried her forward and almost tipped her over.

"This is going to get easier, right?" she asked.

"Not really," Tracy answered. "You just get used to it."

This didn't reassure Gwen, but as they continued on, she found that Tracy—as usual—was right. The pack was heavy, unwieldy—but she was getting used to it. She stopped thinking about the whole trip and focused instead on placing one foot in front of the other, using the poles to help her as she stepped up onto rocks and as the trail began to slope uphill. They had spread out now, fifteen or twenty feet between them, and Gwen was glad for the space and privacy. The woods around them were green and lush; the trees were clothed with bright green-yellow moss and the ground was covered with ferns. It looked to Gwen like a scene from a children's book, some fictional benevolent forest. Several tree roots sprang up from and reentered the ground, like eels whose smooth, dark backs breached the surface of water. The landscape gave way to more open terrain, and eventually the creek revealed itself to be the fork of a larger river. They followed this new river past huge granite outcroppings like the toy building blocks of the children of giants. They continued under sheer granite walls, meeting up with the river again, where a jumble of fallen boulders caused the water to twist and spray; they walked close enough to feel the mist on their skin.

Suddenly Gwen heard a whooshing sound and locked eyes with a fish, level with her in midair, ten feet away. It was caught in the talons of a huge rust-winged hawk, whose right foot was clamped around the fish below its head, the left above its tail, the bird's wings beating the air as it moved quickly skyward. The fish's mouth was working and it must have been in shock, removed so suddenly from its watery home that it didn't even struggle. Then they were gone and the great bird turned upriver, its large, solid body now dwarfing its prey, the wings moving with efficiency and power. As it flew, water streamed off the fish in a diffuse, falling spray. Rays of light hit the droplets as they fell, and the whole effect was like a million fireflies, or shimmery fireworks floating softly toward the river.

"Holy shit," Todd said.

"That was something," Tracy said, grinning.

"That poor fish didn't know what hit him," Oscar said. "Did you see him? He was looking right at us!"

"That's life in the wilderness for you," Tracy remarked. "One minute, you're just swimming along, minding your own business. The next . . ."

Gwen took a few steps closer to the river. She didn't want a life lesson right now. She didn't want the moment to have meaning imposed; it was perfect and complete as it was. In the distance, she could still make out the tiny figure of the bird, the now-thinning trail of spray.

"Let's keep going," Tracy said, and so they did.

The trail stayed close to the river now, sometimes just beside it, sometimes winding away past a rock formation or through a stand of woods, never out of hearing distance. After another three miles the trail crossed the river. It was serene here, and there were enough rocks to use as stepping stones. When they reached the other side, they decided to break for lunch. They left their packs beside the trail and scrambled back down to the river's edge with their lunches. Gwen sat on the sand, and Tracy a little above her on a fallen log. Todd clambered up on a big rock at the edge of the water, and Oscar, after removing his boots and socks, waded out into the river, where he hoisted himself up onto a rock and sat facing upstream. The usual gray boulders were intermixed here with smooth, shiny black rock, whose wavelike curves and circular indentations had been carved by the rushing water. They looked like sculptures, more beautiful than anything conceived by man.

They ate hungrily—cheese sandwiches for Tracy and Gwen, peanut butter and jelly for Oscar and Todd. They shared a couple of Snickers bars for dessert. Then the two men relaxed on their boulders, arms over their faces. Gwen gazed out at the water, which was so clear she could make out brown and gray rocks submerged far out in the river, as if she were looking at them through glass. Finally, nearly hypnotized by the sight of water sliding over rock, she lay back on the ground and closed her eyes. The feel of the sun on her face, drying her sweat, was heavenly; the smell of the pines and the water made her feel cleansed; the steady sound of the river was soothing and she drifted off to sleep.

It felt like ten seconds before someone jiggled her. "Come on, sleepyhead," she heard, and when she opened her eyes, Tracy was standing over her. "We need to get moving."

Gwen sat up slowly and saw that the guys were already back up at the trail.

"We refilled the water bottles and treated them—yours too," Tracy said.

"Thank you. How long have I been asleep?"

"About half an hour."

When they resumed their hike, Gwen was still half-asleep. The pack seemed heavier now, her hips and shoulders felt bruised, and hot spots were developing on her feet. And she was hungry again too—the sandwich had not been enough. Embarrassed, and feeling like she wasn't pulling her weight, she asked to stop so she could put some Moleskin on her heels. Everyone waited quietly but she could sense their impatience. She got her shoes back on, ate a bit of beef jerky, and was quickly up again.

They continued for ten, fifteen minutes without much conversation. Then the trail veered sharply away from the river and uphill to the right, and they all stopped to assess their course.

Tracy pointed up the river's path with her trekking pole. "Looks like the river comes from out of that slot canyon. No way for us to follow it."

Upriver, forty-foot vertical walls of granite rose on either side of the narrow canyon. Whole sections had broken off in flat irregular shapes like sheets of glass, leaving light-colored scars on the rock beneath. Wherever the river was coming from, it wasn't anyplace they could safely travel.

"What does it say on your homemade map?" Todd asked.

Tracy swung her pack off her shoulder easily and set it down with one hand. She unzipped the lid and pulled out the map. "Seems right. You can see that the trail heads away from the river."

"So . . . it looks like we have some switchbacks coming up," Todd said, looking over her shoulder. "And then there's an open space here, maybe a meadow?"

"This is a lake," Tracy said, pointing. "Right here at the end of it."

"So we're on the right track?" Gwen asked.

"Seem to be," said Todd. "But brace yourself. We're about to go uphill."

Oscar was sitting on a rock, fiddling with his GPS unit, and now his shoulders slumped. "As opposed to what we've been doing for the last four hours?"

"*Steeper* uphill," said Tracy.

Gwen just sat where she was, too tired to speak. She could picture her mother shaking her head, hear Chris's derisive laughter. But what could she do? She couldn't turn around and walk out. So she reshouldered her pack, more smoothly this time, and resolved to keep on going.

The terrain was steep, but it wasn't as bad as Gwen feared. The trail was a ramp of earth and leaves, no rock steps. Still, she was glad for the workouts in Tracy's class, the countless squats and knee drives; without them, her legs—and lungs—would never have been able to handle this load. And it helped that as they switchbacked up the slope, they began to see the wooded valley they'd started from. It was beautiful, and seeing how far they'd come gave Gwen the energy she needed. They heard water again, a stream that was working its way down from another part of the mountain. There was more granite here, massive swirling gentle slopes that flowed downhill in concert with the water. One huge dome was crisscrossed with number-

less cracks, like a pot that had been broken into thousands
of pieces and carefully glued back together.

Within twenty minutes they'd reached the top of the
switchbacks and now they crossed another stream, balancing on a log that had fallen across it.

"Look!" Todd called out excitedly, and Gwen saw the
dark, slick backs of fish, the flashes of pink on their bellies
as they darted and swam. There were so many she might
have reached out and grabbed them with her hands.

"Are they rainbow trout?" Oscar asked.

"No, those are eastern brookies," Todd said. "Damn, I
wish I'd brought my fishing pole."

They stood admiring the fish for a moment—Gwen
had never seen so many in a natural setting, so colorful
and alive. They walked on and wound their way through
the forest, passing a stand of white-barked trees that Todd
identified as aspens, their flat round leaves shimmering
and rustling in the breeze like a thousand gentle wind
chimes. Then suddenly they were out, in a landscape so
different they might have stepped through a wardrobe
into Narnia.

They were standing at the edge of a meadow, a mile
wide and at least two miles long. The lush green reeds
were as high as their waists, and sprinkled through them,
at each creek and rivulet, was an explosion of wildflowers—
purple and red and yellow and orange, bright blue and
scarlet and gold. The river here was wide and meandering,
running calmly along the edge of the meadow; several deer
were standing a quarter-mile away, drinking peacefully at
its banks. The meadow was ringed with taller peaks that
still held pockets of snow. Although Gwen could make out
the gentle sound of the water, everything else was still; the

silence here was even deeper than the silence that morning at camp; it was so full it was a sound in itself.

"Wow," said Tracy. "Wow." And if even *she* was impressed, Gwen thought, then this really was something special.

"Have we died?" Todd asked. "Because I think this might be heaven."

"This is unreal," Oscar said. "I didn't even know that a place like this existed."

"Well, dead or alive, we're here," Tracy said. "If our map is accurate, there's a lake just a bit farther on."

Here the cover of trees was gone and they were in the open sun; they put on sunglasses and sunscreen and lip balm. The meadow and mountains, the running river, only got more beautiful as they hiked. They were silent except for the occasional word from Todd or Tracy to identify a wildflower: lupine, monkey-flower, Indian paintbrush, mule's ears, penstemon, mariposa lily. The grandness of it all left Gwen humbled and moved; it was almost too much to take in. After an hour the meadow narrowed and the two ranges came together; the peak straight ahead was the landscape's gathering point. On each side a stream rippled down a steep mountain wall. And there, surrounded on three sides by mountain, they found the small, pristine lake. The surface glistened in the afternoon sun. The banks in front of them, and to the right, were rocky but approachable; to the left the meadow continued, reaching up to and beyond the lake's end.

"I think this is home for the night," said Tracy.

"This is perfect," Todd replied.

"Let's put our stuff down and I'll look around for a place to set up camp."

Gwen was glad to have a reason to sit; she took off her pack and collapsed. Down the meadow, a deer lingered by the river's edge, still watching them. Its nose was black and wet, its huge ears swiveling in response to sound. Why didn't it leave? she wondered. The lake was so still that the reflection of the mountain on its surface looked like an entirely separate mountain. In her exhaustion she half-wondered if she could swim out and step onto it.

Then Tracy was back. "There's a good spot up there," she said, pointing behind them and to the right. "Flat, protected by some trees, nice view of the lake. Exactly like it shows on the map."

"Good. I'm ready to be settled," Todd said.

Oscar stood up, groaning. "Tell me about it."

The spot Tracy had found was perfect—clear, and nestled in trees, overlooking the lake. Gwen helped the best she could, unfolding the tent poles until they locked into place, clipping the plastic hooks onto the poles. But mostly she felt like she was getting in the way, so she stepped aside as Tracy attached the rain fly, collected rocks to the fill the gaps in what looked like an old fire pit, and gathered, with Todd's help, an assortment of branches and sticks for a fire. Tracy was in a short-sleeved shirt now, black, and Gwen saw how the muscles in her arms shifted with her movements. Her calf and thigh muscles were so solid Gwen could see them through her pants. Even at forty, Tracy looked like she could still mix it up with the twenty-five-year-olds in the pro women's basketball game Gwen had gone to recently with the kids. Tracy's motions were steady and efficient, strong, and again Gwen thought of wolves. What a well-built creature, she thought, looking at Tracy's body. Would she ever feel that confident in her own?

Once camp was set up, Oscar and Todd crawled into their tent for a nap. Tracy changed into some flip-flops and even she lay down now, head resting on her pack, cap over her face. But Gwen, after closing her eyes, sat up straight again. Despite her exhaustion, she was too charged up to rest.

She walked down from their campsite and stepped across a small creek, over to the other side of the lake. The lone deer still watched her from the river's edge. There were a few mosquitoes swirling around her now, but she batted them away. Off trail, the wet earth of the meadow was like tar on her shoes; she stepped quickly so as not to sink in. And what was she trying to get to? She didn't know. Maybe further into the heart of beauty itself. Finally, more than a hundred feet up the side of the lake, the ground was a little firmer. Here bushes grew in heavy green clumps.

There was a patch of easy shoreline ahead, and Gwen decided to go down to the lake to soak her sore feet. She stepped past some shoulder-high brush, about fifteen feet from the water's edge. There was a blur of movement—a tiny form, bolting awkwardly away. It was a fawn—smaller than she'd imagined a deer could ever be, barely the size of a spaniel. It moved uncertainly on legs so fresh and untried that these might have been its first steps on earth.

"It's okay," she said reassuringly, but the baby was gone, stumbling to the next set of bushes. No wonder the deer had stuck around, she thought. She was afraid we were a danger to her baby.

Gwen was about to continue on when she saw a flash of blond fur—another fawn, curled up in a tight ball with its little bony legs angling outward. Was it dead? No, just lying still, head pulled into its body, ears lying flat against its head. When Gwen saw its dark liquid eyes looking up at her fearfully, she understood it was trying to hide. She stepped up to take a closer look at the little creature, its constellation of white spots, knowing she shouldn't but unable to help herself. The fawn burrowed its head deeper into itself. "Oh, honey," she said, "I won't hurt you."

Then she backed away enough to give the baby some space, and it sprang up and wobbled off to join its sibling.

"Don't worry, mama deer," she called out to the adult. "Your babies are fine."

She went down to the water, took her shoes off, and stuck her worn feet into the lake, enjoying the shock of the snow-melt cold. She'd hoped to rinse off in the water, but the numbness in her feet convinced her otherwise. Instead, she submerged one leg up beyond her once-injured knee, to discourage inflammation. After her leg and feet got used to the cold, she looked up at the sky. A few afternoon clouds had floated in over the peaks; they almost seemed alive. They moved through, into, and on top of each other, in shades of white and gray. A chain of clouds like five ghosts linked their feathery arms and rose up to take a bow. Then she heard a noise and looked down at a circle expanding in the lake; a fish leapt up to catch a bug, and then another, their bodies clearing the surface and twisting before landing back in their watery homes. Finally, chilled but happy, Gwen put her shoes on and made her way back to camp. Her joy must have been obvious, because as soon as she arrived, Tracy asked, "What just happened? You look like you fell in love."

"I kind of did," Gwen admitted. "I just saw a couple of fawns down there. This high." She lowered her palm to her knee. "Totally covered with spots. Legs so fragile they could hardly walk."

"Very nice," said Tracy. "They're probably just a couple of weeks old."

"One ran off, and the other was curled up right in front of me. I almost tripped over it. I think that was the mom we saw on the other side of the meadow."

"Two of them," Oscar said. He was sitting at the fire ring, rearranging food in his bear canister. "I didn't know deer had twins."

"They usually do," came Todd's voice from the tent. "Probably to increase the chances that at least one will make it. And they lie still because when they're babies, they don't have any scent."

"How do you know that?" Gwen asked.

"I used to hunt them when I was a kid in Wisconsin."

This hit Gwen like a punch in the stomach.

"That's cool," Tracy said. "Do you still hunt?"

"No," Todd replied, sounding wistful. "I haven't gone in years. I'd still be up for it, but I think my kids would disown me. Not to mention my wife."

"I hunted a bit in Idaho," Tracy said. "I haven't in years either, but I do make it to the firing range sometimes."

"Me too," said Todd. "To work off stress. My family doesn't know that, though." He laughed.

Gwen tried not to hold Todd's comment against him, or Tracy's either. And it was easy enough to forget their conversation, since there was still so much to do. She unscrewed the locks on her bear canister and retrieved a packaged dinner, fixed up a cheese sandwich for lunch the next day. She took a Ziploc bag and some biodegradable soap, as Tracy had taught her, and went down to the river, where she washed her socks, her underthings, her hiking shirt. She hung her wet clothes on nearby branches, trying not to be self-conscious about them. She went off behind a rock and sponge bathed with a couple of body wipes and a washcloth, forgoing lotion out of worry of bears. There were a few raised bumps on her arms and shoulders from mosquito bites—they had bitten right through her shirt. She put on her warm base layer, top and bottom, and then her hiking pants. She layered on her pink fleece and then her purple down jacket, and pulled on a thin wool cap. She tried not to think about what the cap would do to her hair, or how she must look without makeup.

By the time she got back to their camp, the others had changed clothes too. Tracy was boiling water over the fire. One by one, Tracy poured the water into their food packages, and the hard unrecognizable material transformed into food. They were starving. Gwen's beef Stroganoff tasted like a school cafeteria meal, better than she'd expected. The others, once the water did its work, had varieties of pasta and rice.

"This is the most satisfying meal I've ever had," Oscar said, and he didn't sound like he was kidding. They sat on boulders, swatting away the occasional bug, and ate like they hadn't had a meal in days.

"This will make it better," Todd said. He pulled out a flask and took a draw, then held it toward Oscar.

"What is it?" Oscar asked.

"Bourbon."

He let Todd pour him a drink, took a sip, and screwed up his face. Todd poured Tracy a shot and then offered some to Gwen, who waved the flask away.

"Are you sure? It'll help you sleep," Todd said.

Gwen laughed, or tried to. "If it was wine, I'd take you up on it. But I don't think I'm going to need much help."

"Yeah, what a day, huh?" Oscar said.

"Fun, though, right?" said Tracy.

"Definitely," Todd said. "Thank you, Tracy. Thanks to all of you, actually. I didn't know how much I needed this."

"Me too. I love being out here," Tracy said. She looked at the peaks behind the lake. "I can't wait to see what's up there."

"More mountains, right?" said Oscar.

"Right. Then the next pass, and the next one."

"What is it exactly that you want to see?" Gwen asked.

"I don't know," said Tracy. "Beyond."

When they were done, they packed their food, trash, and toiletries into their bear canisters, and hid them in various rocky depressions well away from camp. Then they sat and watched the sun go down, saw the peaks that framed the lake set afire with golden light. Everything looked brighter and more defined in this glow. Gwen could see the golds and reds in the rock, the pink and orange of the clouds. The sky changed constantly, and she thought she'd never get tired of looking. It was light until almost nine.

"Well, I'm beat," Oscar said. "I'm hitting the sack."

"Me too," Todd said. "In fact, I'm asleep already."

"I'm going to look at our maps and figure out our plan for tomorrow," Tracy said.

"You go right ahead," said Oscar. And then the three of them crawled into their respective tents, moving around with their headlamps on, the circles of light hitting the tents from inside.

Gwen stayed up and stared at the sky. The night came on quickly now. The stars began to reveal themselves, and as the fire died down to embers and the headlamps went out, their camp was submerged in darkness. Except it wasn't totally dark, for there was still a slice of moon, and now the sky was alive with stars and cut straight across by a cottony ribbon of white, which she realized with astonishment was the Milky Way. She had never seen the Milky Way before; she hadn't known it was actually real. Here in the mountains, she was filled with a peace that she got from nothing else—not work, not friends, not prayer. She was amazed at where she was, among these towering peaks, in a place that hadn't been shaped by human hands. Although she felt small, there was a comfort in this feeling, something grounding in the vastness of the world. Being outdoors gave her a feeling of equilibrium and grace—a sense of closeness to God—that she was supposed to feel at church, and usually didn't.

Suddenly a point of light shot diagonally across the sky—a shooting star. And then a few minute later, another. Her heart leapt. How long ago had these stars actually existed? How long had it taken for their light to reach her? Tonight, farther into the wilderness, she was a little less afraid. Making it through the first day had made her more confident that she could meet tomorrow's challenges, and the next day's, and complete the thirty miles. She was satisfied—and tired. After one long last drink of water, she opened the door on her side of the tent, crawled into her sleeping bag, and fell asleep.

CHAPTER EIGHT
OSCAR

When Oscar's alarm went off he did not wake gently; the state of sleep shifted into the state of pain. He lay on his back, eyes closed, and couldn't believe how much he hurt—his shoulders, his neck, his upper and middle back, his pecs and abdominal muscles, quadriceps and hamstrings, even the muscles of his ass.

Once, as a teenager, he'd fallen off a motorcycle and when he woke up the next morning, he'd felt like this. He let out a groan and realized he wasn't alone in the tent. But there was no movement beside him—Todd was still asleep, his feet wrapped in a narrow mummy bag directly at Oscar's head. And now Oscar remembered the snoring. It had started as a low rumble and then built into a sound like an eighteen-wheeler idling right beside him. Todd had snored the first night too, back at the trailhead. But nothing like this—this had been a sound louder than Oscar thought a human could make. He'd tightened the top of his sleeping bag around his head, stuck his fingers in his ears. Nothing had helped. The snoring continued, despite his not-so-gentle nudges to try and get Todd to stop. No wonder all the bears had stayed away.

He must have fallen asleep, though, because now he was waking up. Slowly, carefully, he unzipped his bag and slid backward out of it, opened the flap on his side of the tent, and rolled out. It was about ten past six now, clear, and cold. He understood that they were in a beautiful place—the lake was still in shadow, the meadow covered with a layer of dew—or was that frost? He heard the sound of the river and the morning calls of birds, but he was aware of all this only vaguely. Mostly what he felt was his own misery. A vise seemed to be closing in on both sides of his head. And he felt like a piece of plywood was lodged in his back, holding him rigid, making it impossible for him to turn his head or even lift his arms. He thought of his earlier bravado and was annoyed at his own stupidity. He no longer had any illusions about kicking the mountain's ass. His ass was officially kicked.

"I feel like fucking hell," he said aloud. But softly. He knew Tracy would have no sympathy. It was her job to push people past what they thought they could do, and suddenly he felt annoyed at her for not being more understanding about their limits and fears; for pairing him with a Westside white guy who was also an epic snorer; for bringing them out here where they hadn't seen another soul, not one damned person, on a route that for all he knew might lead to nowhere. And Gwen. A nice person, for sure, and not bad company. But she was no more suited to being out here than his mother was. Oscar knew she had struggled yesterday, had watched her stagger under the weight of her pack—and yet she'd kept her spirits up and he was grudgingly impressed. But did she have to be so damned *excited* about everything? Yes, it was pretty out here; that was not a news flash. But he didn't get her reaction to the hawk and the fish. So what if the hawk caught its lunch? That's what hawks *did*. If they all thought hawks were such a novelty they should come to Glassell Park, where the big-ass pushy birds were always circling overhead, swooping down into the canyon to catch squirrels or rats.

And Todd. Okay, well, Todd wasn't as bad as he'd first expected. He seemed to know what he was doing, and Oscar had to admit, after falling behind yesterday, that Todd was in better shape than him. And he was turning out to be a pretty decent guy. But his cluelessness was typical and infuriating. How could he be so dismissive of things that were glaringly obvious? He probably didn't even notice the weird looks that their party had gotten at the ranger station.

Suddenly he felt a sharp pang of missing Claudia. He regretted not calling her before heading to the trailhead, not appreciating her enough in general. They'd met four months ago during Lily's regular checkup, and he probably wouldn't have noticed the nurse taking his daughter's temperature if Lily hadn't blurted out, "You're so pretty!" Claudia had blushed and said, "So are you," and then Oscar blushed too, especially when he saw that his daughter was right.

"Well, maybe Nurse Hernandez," he said, eyeing her name tag, "could go out with us sometime for an ice cream." And Claudia smiled and they all blushed some more, and they met at Griffith Park that weekend, where they rode the merry-go-round and took a train ride and had double scoops of ice cream.

Things had gone slowly—because Oscar was always working, he said, but really he wasn't ready to settle down. Besides, he wasn't sure what to make of this woman, who was so low-key, and so good with Lily. He hadn't let himself realize how much he enjoyed her presence. What he wouldn't give to be lying next to her in a soft, cushy bed, her warm hands dissolving the pain and tension in his body. Why the hell was he out here, anyway? Right now, he missed everything about his normal, everyday life. Right now, even pushy clients and an ever-ringing cell phone weren't seeming all that bad. He had to get over this crankiness; he was stuck with these people for another three days. According to his GPS unit, they were now at 8,445 feet, and they'd traveled a little more than eight miles. Only eight miles! How the hell was he going to make it the rest of the way? Now he stood and bent sideways, touched his toes, pinwheeled his arms, trying to soften the plate of plywood in his back. He scratched the mosquito bites on his legs and arms, at his waist where his shirt rode up—his bug spray had been totally useless. He scratched his face too; his two-day beard was getting itchy. He examined the burst blisters on the backs of his heels and dug some Moleskin out of his pack to cushion them.

Ten feet away, the zipper on the other tent opened, and Tracy emerged, already dressed in her clay pants and red down jacket, looking like she'd stepped out of a North Face catalog. Why was she not beaten up by sleeping on the ground? She was always so ready, whether here or at the gym at five thirty a.m., when most reasonable people were still asleep. Oscar felt another wave of resentment and tried to squelch it.

"Morning," she said. "How'd you sleep?"

"Not so great, actually. As I'm sure you heard, somebody snores."

"Really!" she laughed. "Well, that's too bad. It was all quiet over here."

Now the slippery sound of nylon being pushed aside and Gwen and Todd crawled out of their tents, Todd looking like a hungover frat boy. His hair was a stirred pile of windblown blond, held in place by a faded Stanford baseball cap, and he needed a shave. Gwen's hair was in a ponytail, with several clumps hanging loose. Both looked tired—but also peaceful and happy.

"Morning!" Tracy said.

Gwen stretched, yawned, rubbed her eyes, and then caught sight of the others. "Morning," she said, laughing. "What a motley crew."

"Speak for yourself," said Tracy. She was moving around the edge of the campsite, gathering more sticks for the fire.

"Wow, I did not sleep well," Gwen said. "It was colder last night, wasn't it? And I kept waking up because I thought I heard a bear. How is it that you're not exhausted and sore? It's really annoying." But she didn't sound annoyed. She sounded happy.

They went off to retrieve their bear canisters, which were all undisturbed, then ducked behind boulders to pee. By the time they'd brushed their teeth and splashed their faces with river water, Tracy had made oatmeal and coffee. They filled themselves with warm food and drink, still shivering in their down jackets, and Oscar slowly started to feel human again. As the sun peeked over the range to the east, it lit the crests on either side of the valley and bathed their lake in light. Tracy pointed out their route for the day—up the canyon wall beyond the left side of the lake and toward a notch between the peaks.

"Then what?" Todd asked. "What's after the pass?"

"We head back down into forest, from what I can tell. We'll have to cross a river and then go back up to another ridge."

After they finished eating, they broke camp, Oscar

helping Todd with the tent. He was amazed, as he had been yesterday, that all their tents, pots, clothes, and food compressed into the packs they carried on their backs. By eight thirty they were making their way back down toward the lake, then through the meadow where Gwen had seen the fawns, mud sucking their shoes and splattering their legs. Soon they were traversing up the slope, picking their way carefully through the rock. There appeared to be a bit of trail edging up the side, so they followed it, walking half a mile toward the vertex of the bowl, then doubling back, taking switchbacks up the crumbling slope.

"Watch yourself!" Tracy shouted. "There's a big drop here from a rock slide."

The worn-away spot was only five or six feet wide, and they all stepped through safely, and Oscar remembered a story that Eduardo had told him, about two mules who'd been on a resupply trip when they fell five hundred feet to their deaths. He wished he had thought to bring hiking poles; he'd underestimated how tough this trip would be.

The trail smoothed out but the climbing was relent-less—like taking stairs all the way up a skyscraper. With the weight of his pack and the pain from his blisters, every single step was a struggle. They walked past boulders whose outside layers had flaked off in thin, delicate pieces, like the crusts of pastry shells. They walked over wedges of flat, tombstone-like rock that might have been picked up and shoved diagonally back into the ground. The sun had come over the ridge and changed the temperature from cold to too hot. But the air was still bracingly fresh, tinged with a minty, spicy smell that seemed to come from the bushy plants that covered the slope. And the views were getting better and better. Each time they doubled back, they could see more of the valley, the dark blue lake where they'd camped. The mountain facing them across the lake had a thin streak of white cutting through it, like a scar from the slash of a giant dagger. As they climbed they could see more of the land to the north, the wooded valleys and distant snow-capped mountains. Despite Oscar's soreness the pack felt better today. It was hard work stepping through and over the rocks, but the movement had loosened his muscles. He'd gotten into a rhythm and he was—finally—enjoying the landscape. They reached the pass within two hours.

They stopped for a moment, giddy with accomplishment. Then, at Tracy's urging, they left their packs and scrambled a hundred yards up to the top of the nearest peak. They were now at just over ten thousand feet. The views from the summit opened up to the west, countless ridges and hills, all the way to the distant horizon. Todd and Gwen took turns shooting photos of the group, and Oscar felt himself relaxing. Maybe he *would* make it the rest of this trip. Maybe his back would keep loosening and his head would clear, and he could really enjoy all he was seeing.

They carefully worked their way back to the pass, then continued down the other side. It was steeper here, loose boulders and unstable dirt, so the others all used their hiking poles to brace themselves. The downhill was much harder on Oscar's feet and knees; he felt like the Tin Man, creaking and in need of oil. About halfway down they crossed a flat sheet of water sliding over rust-colored rock—they were on top of a waterfall. They dipped their hats in the water and Oscar draped a bandanna over his head, to shield his neck and face from the sun. They filled their bottles again, looking over the edge where the water fell to some unseen place below. It was a lovely spot, but they soon walked on.

As they approached a cluster of trees, he saw something on the ground, a white and orange object that stood out against the sand-colored earth.

"What's that?" he asked, pointing.

Tracy, who was leading, went to look at it. "Wow," she said.

Gwen, who was right behind her, went over too. She jumped back as if she'd been burned. "Jesus."

Oscar followed and looked over Gwen's shoulder. It was an owl's head, perfectly severed, as pristine as if the bird were still alive. Its feathers were white with a ring of orange rust; they looked downy and waved in the breeze. Its narrow beak was shiny and its eyes were wide open, staring up at them. It was hard to believe the rest of the body was gone. There was no blood—the head had been removed with surgical precision.

"Wow," Oscar said, echoing Tracy. "That is fucking weird."

"Must have been an eagle or a hawk," Todd said. "It probably dropped him."

"It still looks alive, doesn't it?" Oscar said.

"Yeah, it's amazing," Tracy said. "It's beautiful."

"It does look alive," Todd said. "Must have just happened."

"It's creepy," Gwen said. "I don't want to look at it anymore."

She seemed genuinely freaked out and Oscar didn't blame her. Sure, the head was beautiful in a macabre kind of way, but it was hard not to take it as an omen. He became even more certain that it signaled bad luck when, within a few minutes of resuming their hike, they heard the sound of water—not the gentle trickling of the river in the meadow but a louder sound, active, insistent. Oscar's stomach tightened. This was real water—how big and fast would it be? And how the hell would they get across it?

Todd must have been thinking the same thing because now he remarked, "You hear that? Doesn't sound like a creek."

"What'll we do if it's too big to cross?" Gwen asked.

"It won't be," Tracy assured them.

They were all quiet for the next few minutes, watching their footing, and with their voices still, the river grew louder. They hiked down through one last steep section and then suddenly there it was: a solid mass of moving, churning water, twenty feet wide, big and full and serious.

They stood four abreast at the edge of the woods, about ten feet up from the bank.

"Well," Todd said after a few moments of quiet, "that's a heck of a river."

It was like a living thing, the river, steady and strong, arguing with itself and with them. The water flowed past them quickly without flourish or drama; it stepped down several terraces, rounded a corner, and disappeared from view. But the sheer mass of it—the steady inevitable progression— made Oscar wonder about the strength of the current. It looked powerful and indifferent. And cold.

"How deep do you think it is?" Gwen asked.

"No way to tell, really," Tracy said. "Not until we start to cross it."

"You actually want to try and cross this thing?" Oscar

blurted out. "No way, Tracy. This is serious. This is too fucking much for me."

Tracy stared out at the river for so long that Oscar wasn't sure she'd heard him. Then she said thoughtfully, "There's *got* to be a way. Let me just go upriver for a bit to see if there's an easier spot."

"I'll go down," Todd said, and Oscar looked at him, surprised.

"Really?"

Todd shrugged. "It's worth checking out. It would suck if there was an easier place just around the corner and we didn't even bother to look."

Were these people crazy? Were they out of their fucking minds? Oscar thought of the tourists who died every year in Yosemite, the ones who stepped over railings and past clear warning signs. But while he hated to admit it, Todd's calmness eased his own nerves just a little. And he discovered to his own surprise that he trusted this guy's judgment more than he trusted Tracy's.

"Well, I'll wait here," Gwen said, bending to unshoulder her pack.

"Me too," Oscar said, unfastening his waist straps and letting his own pack fall.

Todd made his way downstream to the left, feet crunching on fallen branches, and Tracy walked off to the right. Soon Todd was around a bend and out of sight; Tracy's figure grew smaller but stayed visible as she walked along the riverbank. Oscar sat down and rooted around in the top of his pack and pulled out a Snickers bar. A lizard ran out on the boulder beside them, feinted in their direction, and then scooted away. In the silence the sound of the river was louder—patient and steady, speaking to the trees and the ridges above them, a conversation as old as time.

"Want some?" he asked, holding the candy bar out to Gwen.

"No thanks. That poor owl made me lose my appetite."

"Yeah, this is more than we bargained for, huh? Not exactly a leisurely stroll."

"Oh, I've been having a great time," Gwen said quickly, glancing at him. "But *this*," she said, gesturing toward the river. "I don't know, it just makes me nervous."

"Do you get the sense," Oscar said carefully, "that we're in a bit over our heads?"

"Maybe." Gwen sounded noncommittal, and Oscar realized that whatever doubts she might have, they were still about herself and her own abilities—not about the wisdom of taking this unused route, not about the judgment of Tracy.

Todd returned in a few minutes, looking discouraged. "No luck," he said. "It actually gets worse down there—after that bend, there's some rapids."

Tracy came walking up jauntily and after she heard his news, she said, "Well, there's a spot up there that might work. A little wider, the water's slower, no big rocks below—and a fallen log across the whole river."

"Is it big enough to walk across?" Todd asked.

"No. It's too skinny. But we could probably hold on to it and wade."

This didn't sound promising to Oscar, but Todd, replied, "Well, okay! Let's go check it out!"

They all reshouldered their packs and made their way a quarter-mile upriver. When they got to the spot that Tracy had found, Oscar's heart sank again. Sure it was wider here—maybe twenty-five feet—but the "log" was more like a sapling. The rocks beneath the water looked slippery and dangerous. This was no place to take a fall.

"That's not much of a log," Todd remarked, echoing his thoughts.

"I know," Tracy said. "But it's all we've got."

The fallen tree lay about two feet off the surface of the water, a few jagged points sticking out where branches had broken off. Oscar's eyes followed the length of it to the stump on the other side, where the trunk was still attached by some strands of wood. The color of the exposed flesh there was shocking in its lightness; the tree might have fallen just that month, that very week.

"I'm not sure it'll hold," Todd said now. "It's not attached by very much."

"It'll hold," Tracy said.

"Well, maybe one of us should test it first."

"I'll go," Tracy volunteered. She set her pack down and loaded her phone and bear spray into the lid. She collapsed her poles and shoved them into her pack handles-first, the points sticking out of the top. Then she sat on a rock and removed her shoes. "It's too dangerous to wear your flip-flops," she said. "You could really fuck up your feet. So take your socks off and put your shoes back on. Unclip the clips of your sternum and hip belt. If you lose your footing and start to get pulled backward, let the pack go or it'll drag you down with it."

Oscar listened to these instructions with a detached wonder. Were they really learning how not to drown? Yes, they were. Before he knew it, Tracy had put her shoes and pack back on and had scrambled down the bank.

"Uh, what if we *do* lose our footing?" Gwen asked.

"Try to keep your head upstream and your feet down-

stream so they can brace you against any hard obstacles,"
Tracy said. "And pray like hell."

She took hold of the tree and stepped sideways into the
water, which quickly came up to her calves and then her
knees. Her poles swayed behind her like antennas. About a
third of the way across, the water reached her thighs, and
she slowed down and gripped the log more tightly. Oscar
could see the force of the current pulling her back, extending her arms until he thought she'd lose her grip. But she
didn't. Even as the water reached almost to her waist, even
as her knuckles grew white from the effort of holding on,
she stayed on her feet, she kept moving. Oscar looked at
her face and saw that she was grinning.

Then she was across and she pulled herself up onto the
bank, letting out a whoop of triumph. "Piece of cake!" she
yelled out. "Who's next?"

Todd looked soberly at Oscar and Gwen. "Let's go
across together. I'll go first, and Oscar, you go last. Gwen,
you stay in the middle."

"I don't know if I can do this," Gwen said.

"Sure you can," Todd replied reassuringly "And we'll
be on either side of you."

"Are you sure the log can support all of us?" asked
Oscar.

"I'm *not* sure," Todd said. "But I'd rather take my
chances than have Gwen try to cross on her own. But let's
hold on to each other, all right? And keep your center of
gravity low."

Todd and Gwen collapsed their poles and stuck them
into their packs. Todd maneuvered through the branches
and plunged in first. He grabbed the log with his left hand
and held on to Gwen with his right as she gingerly stepped

in after him. Then it was Oscar's turn, and he gasped as he lowered his foot in the river. The water was fucking cold— like just-melted ice. "Jesus," he said.

"Just ignore it if you can," Todd instructed. Slowly, slowly, they crab-walked sideways into the river, each man with one hand on Gwen's shoulder strap and one hand on the log. The rocks underfoot were slick and unstable. Oscar stepped onto one and it gave way beneath him; he grabbed the log with both hands in a panic. But he regained his balance and took hold of Gwen's strap again. As the water crept up past their knees and then their thighs, Gwen made a noise between a groan and a yelp.

"It's okay," Todd shouted, "you're doing great!"

But it wasn't just the cold that bothered them now; it was the force of the water, the current pushing against them, as if the river had intention and purpose. Each time Oscar lifted a foot the current pulled it away; it took all of his strength and focus just to set it down again. The sound of the water was all around them, louder now, more insistent, as if the river was displeased with their presence. The bark was rough and sharp against his hand, but the tree held firm. Slowly, slowly, they made their way across. When they reached the other side, Tracy helped Todd out, then Gwen and Oscar. When he was clear of the water, Oscar scrambled up the bank and sat down. He had never been so glad to feel the ground beneath him.

Gwen collapsed beside him. "Thank you, God."

"See, I told you we could make it," Tracy said. "Piece of cake."

No one answered—they all just sat and tried to catch their breath. Oscar's pack was wet about halfway down; he didn't want to think about how soaked his stuff must be.

"Hey, we need to dry off," he said, beginning to shiver. "Think we can find some sun?"

They looked around. The canyon was already in shade, and the sun had moved past the upper wall.

"No luck till we get out of the woods and up on a ridge," Tracy said. "But it would be good to change clothes, if you have anything dry."

They dug through their packs with varying success. Gwen changed back into her clothes from yesterday. Todd put on his shorts from the day before but his shirts were all soaked; he wore his fleece on bare skin and draped a half-wet shirt over his pack to dry. Tracy undid the bottom half of her convertible pants and removed the wet legs, not seeming to mind the wet tail of her shirt. She was cheerful, visibly charged up that they'd made it across the river, and Oscar realized that it wasn't that Tracy didn't *feel* the privations of being in the wilderness; it was that she actually embraced them.

Oscar didn't share this enthusiasm—especially once he'd examined his clothes and couldn't find a single dry item. He had one pair of cargo shorts that was only half wet, but all of his tops were soaked. He changed into the cargo shorts and kept the same shirt on—at least the shoulders were dry.

"We should dry off pretty quick once we're moving," Tracy said.

"Does anyone need to rest for a bit?" Todd asked.

"Not here," Gwen said. "I don't ever want to see this river again."

They collected their wet clothes and stuffed them into their packs. They reengaged their poles. Then they lifted their packs onto their shoulders, heavier now with all the wet clothes, and trudged back downstream, where the trail, or what they hoped was the trail, continued. They wound their way through a flat area of wood and started to climb again. Although they couldn't see very far through the trees, Oscar thought from the way the sky opened up that the top of the ridge wasn't far away. He was right. After half an hour of switchbacks, they'd reached the gap— and a clearing where the sun finally hit them. Far off in the distance, to the east, they saw a larger set of mountains— endless, imposing, majestic, their flanks draped with snow.

"Wow," Oscar said. "You want to take a break?"

"Yes!" Todd said. "Let's stop and dry off." He stripped off his fleece and put his shirt back on.

"And eat," Gwen added. "What a view!"

"All right," agreed Tracy, but she sounded distracted. Oscar was about to get annoyed again—couldn't she see they all needed to rest? But then he saw where she was looking and he understood why. Straight ahead of them, descending gently and parallel to the ridge, the trail continued on. But to the right there was another trail, which angled sharply down into a different canyon.

"We seem to be at a junction," Todd remarked.

"There's more than one trail out here?" Gwen asked. "Isn't that kind of weird?"

"Not really," Tracy said. "There's probably some offshoots. Maybe one of these is actually a game trail. Or maybe it leads to a campsite."

Oscar didn't like to think about the second possibility— after two days of worrying that they were the only people out here, now he hoped that this was true. "Well, you have the map, right? Maybe that will tell us."

"Maybe," Tracy said. "Let's take a look. And eat."

They all sat heavily and removed their wet shoes and set them out to dry. Oscar was relieved for the break. He squeezed dollops of peanut butter onto a bagel and bit off huge chunks, and then wolfed down an apple. He hadn't realized how hungry he was.

The others were silent, eating their own lunches. Tracy finished off her sandwich and pulled the maps and compass out of her pack. She lay the topo map out on the ground and ran her fingers over it, as if trying to feel the right way to go.

Todd leaned over her to look at it and made a disgusted sound. "That thing is useless. Lost Canyon isn't even *on* there."

"I know, but there's some landscape features we can work with," said Tracy. "This must be the river we just crossed. And maybe this is the ridge we're on now."

"I don't know. And an inch on that is, what? Five miles?"

"Yeah, you're right. There's no real detail. Let me look at the other map." She unfolded the photocopy of the hand-drawn map, the top left corner of which was now wet. She held it carefully with one hand, looked at it, and frowned.

"What?" Todd asked.

"What?" Oscar echoed, and now he got up and made his way behind her.

"It just gets a little blurry here," she said. The line marking the trail had bled from the river water; the writing was now unreadable. Still, there clearly was the lake where they'd spent the night, a set of bumps that must have been the pass from this morning, and wavy lines that might have been the river. The trail continued up to the ridge where they'd stopped, and then veered right toward

Lost Canyon. There was no sign—at least not as far as they could tell—of a trail straight ahead.

"It must be the trail going that way," said Tracy, pointing right.

"I don't know," Todd said. "It looks like we should be heading *here*." He tapped the paper to a point on the ridge.

"But the loop has us always bearing right," Tracy countered. "What do you think, Oscar?"

Oscar wasn't sure. All he knew was that they had already traveled five miles over rough terrain and he was feeling damned tired. He couldn't believe that they were trusting this hand-drawn, faded, and now waterlogged map that had been made by God-knows-who, who might have been stoned or nature-drunk or just plain mischievous when he put these images on paper. Oscar took the GPS unit off his waistband and tried to pull up a map. But he hadn't bought the detailed topo software, so all he could see was that they were somewhere in the mountains, with Fresno to the west. And that they now stood at just under 8,300 feet. There was no detail whatsoever. "I don't know."

Todd was fiddling with Tracy's compass, shifting and adjusting the black wheel on a rectangle of plastic. "That's almost due east," Todd said, pointing at the distant range. "And this," he gestured toward the more defined trail, "goes south."

"So does this other one," Tracy argued. "It just heads southwest a little."

"It could be either one," said Oscar. "Gwen? What do you think?"

Gwen was staring off, exhausted, not really engaged. "What?"

"Which way do you think we should go?"

"I don't know," she said. "It's up to you guys."

"Well, I think we go down," Tracy said. "Why don't we give it a shot? If it doesn't seem right, we can always backtrack and take the other trail."

They could, but the thought of having to climb back up the slope with their heavy packs did not sound appealing to Oscar. He was pissed they were in this predicament, but what could they do? "Okay," he agreed.

And Todd said, "All right, we'll try it. But let's reassess in a mile or so. Okay?"

They packed up their trash and put their socks and shoes back on. Gwen looked disheveled—a few strands of her hair were escaping from her hat, and her face was covered with sweat. Todd's neck and cheeks had burned through his stubble and he looked dried out; his legs were streaked with mud from the river. Even Tracy seemed worse for the wear. Her black hiking shirt was dusty and there was a big bruise blooming on her shin, which disappeared when she zipped her pant legs back on. Oscar knew he looked no better. But he realized he *liked* how they looked. They'd spent two nights in the backcountry, hiked almost fourteen miles, crossed a river, and topped out at a significant pass. They were battle-tested now. They were for real.

Tracy started down to the right, cutting steeply into the tight new canyon. Bushes and branches grew everywhere, scratching Oscar's legs, and he was about to wonder aloud if this was a game trail when they were suddenly past the obstacles and the path opened up. It was narrow, but it was definitely a human trail—there was a deliberateness to the way the ground was cleared, and a few rocks and logs had been positioned to create steps. This wasn't the smoothest, easiest trail, but it seemed to be the right one.

They'd hiked about twenty minutes when Tracy yelled, "Ow! Shit!" She turned back toward them, covering her shoulder. When she moved her hand, there was a dime-sized circle of blood—and a small piece of curved metal protruding from her flesh.

"Are you okay?" Gwen asked. "What *is* that?"

Todd looked closer. "It's a fish hook."

"How weird," Gwen said. "Let me get my first aid stuff." And quick as that, she slung her pack off and produced a small red bag, out of which she pulled tweezers, some kind of wipe, Neosporin.

Todd rolled Tracy's sleeve up and held her arm in his hand. "It hooked you good, but I think we should be able to pull it right out. Can you take it?"

"Sure," Tracy said. Her face was resolute.

Todd took out his Leatherman, opened the scissors, and cut off the short, curved end of the hook. Then he switched the tool to pliers and carefully pulled out the long part of the hook, working in a curving motion to follow the path it had taken through the flesh. Tracy's face looked like she had smelled something awful—but there was no cry of pain, not even a sharp intake of breath. Then it came free, a sharp, bloody piece of metal, and the blood trickled out of the two small wounds. Gwen pressed some cotton against them, and they all stood and looked at each other.

"Are you okay?" Oscar asked, feeling useless.

"Yeah. It'll be fine. But what the fuck? What's a fish hook doing way out here?"

"There's probably a creek down here," Todd said. "Maybe someone just lost some equipment."

"In a tree?"

Todd shrugged. "Who knows? Didn't the ranger say there are guys who live out in these woods?"

Once the bleeding had slowed, Gwen dabbed some Neosporin onto the wound, applied a fresh ball of cotton, and pressed two strips of tape into place.

"Thanks," Tracy said. "You're an expert."

"I'm with kids a lot," Gwen replied. "You wouldn't believe some of the stuff they get into."

As they continued down into the canyon the trail grew indistinct, until finally they reached a point where there was no trail at all, just a solid tangle of bushes and trees. The ground was covered with fallen pine needles and the forest was so thick here they couldn't see more than twenty feet ahead. They stopped in a small clearing and looked at each other. One especially large tree was trailing its limbs like an exasperated woman, arms flung down and palms turned up in surrender.

"Uh, we seem to have hit a dead end," Todd observed.

"Yeah," Tracy said. "Weird."

They all stood silently for a moment. In the quiet they heard the trickle of an unseen creek.

"Well," Tracy said, "maybe you or I could go explore and see if the trail starts up again."

Todd shook his head. "I don't know that it'd do any good. I think we should just go back."

"Oh, come on," Tracy said. "It can't hurt to look around a bit, can it?"

They faced off now, quietly, but in clear disagreement. "What do you guys want to do?" Todd asked the others.

Gwen shrugged. "I don't know. I'm following *you*."

Then Tracy asked, "Oscar?"

"I'm not sure, either. The only thing I know for sure is that I have to take a piss."

He unclipped his hip and chest straps and dropped his pack; it hit the ground with a leafy thump. He trudged off into the woods, not looking back. This was bullshit, he thought. This was ridiculous. Here they were, lost on some stupid-ass trek that was making them tired and confused, when they could have been on one of the established trails, they could have been with other people, they could have enjoyed the camaraderie and key valuable information that comes from traveling a popular trail. But no, they had to come out *here*, in the middle of fucking nowhere, where there were decapitated owl heads and random murderous fish hooks, and wander down a stupid path that was probably a black bear superhighway.

He kept walking until he was out of sight, energized by his anger, unzipped, and let loose against a tree. The release of his piss felt incredible; he enjoyed the sound of it hitting the bark. That was better. He stood there holding himself, with his eyes closed in tired relief. He was relaxed now in a calm, mindless way. The others all seemed far away and he didn't care what they were doing. He wasn't in any hurry to get back.

A piece of cold metal touched the back of his head. His heart skipped a beat and he blurted out, "What the—?" But he knew what it was even before the firm shove and the male voice that said, "Don't move."

He shuddered—as if the gun had shot him through with ice. "Uh, okay, okay," he managed, raising his arms. He saw the pattern of a bug's slime lining the bark; he saw a squirrel scurry into his vision and then away. "I don't

have any money, okay? I don't have anything. I'm just passing through."

There was no answer, just the gun against the back of
his head, and the quick, harsh breathing of whoever was
holding it. Now he thought of something, and repeated
what he'd said in Spanish: "No tengo dinero. Sólo estoy
pasando."

"No me importa el dinero," the voice replied, wavering. "¿Qué estás haciendo aquí? ¿Quién eres?"

"Mira, yo no quise molestarte. Cualquier cosa que es-
tés haciendo, a mi no me importa." And he *didn't* care what
the man was doing there. He didn't even want to know. He
just wanted the gun to be removed from his head. But if it
was, that would scare him too, because the man might be
stepping back to shoot. He wondered if this tree with its
bug-stained bark was the last thing he'd ever see. An image
of Lily flashed before his mind—laughing, her fat cheeks
dimpled.

"¿Quién está contigo? ¿Estás con la policía?"

"¿La policía?" Oscar said. "No, sólo estoy aquí de
excursión."

"¿Entonces quiénes son los demás?"

Oscar had thought that maybe he could pretend he
was alone, that he could somehow spare the others. But it
was too late; this man, whoever he was, already knew they
were a group. He might have watched them approach from
wherever he'd been hiding. He might have even followed
them down. Oscar had to convince him they didn't mean
him any harm.

"Sólo otros excursionistas," he said. "No la policía."

"No te creo," said the man. "Nunca viene ningun ex-
cursionista para aqui." He jammed the gun into the back

of Oscar's head again. "Regresate con ellos. Los quiero a todos juntos."

Oscar was still shaking and even though he'd just relieved himself, he felt like his bladder was loosening. He was aware that his zipper was open, his penis still out, soft and vulnerable. He reached down to close his shorts and this brought another jab to the head.

"Sólo estoy cerrando mis pantalones," he said.

"Okay, hazlo rápido."

Once he'd zipped up the man said, "¡Ándale!" and Oscar started to walk with his hands up, as commanded, back to where the others were. I should make a break for it, he thought. But if he did he knew the man would shoot. Maybe with all of them together the odds would be better; maybe they could overpower this guy.

Oscar tripped over a rock and almost fell. When he recovered the man said, "¡Ándale!" and he kept walking. But in that moment when he was twisting to regain his balance, Oscar caught sight of his captor. He was just a kid. Maybe sixteen, maybe eighteen, with shiny black hair that needed a cut, sand-colored skin, bright eyes that were lit with excitement. Only about 5'6", 5'7", and skinny—not a big kid, not at all. It was strange to see him on the other side of a gun, dressed in camouflage. The kid didn't seem hard or cold or particularly tough. Mostly he looked scared. But this was probably the most dangerous state of all. Any false move and he could shoot.

Oscar walked until he saw flashes of Todd's blue-gray shirt, Tracy's gray and red pack. Under his breath he said, "I'm sorry."

"That must have been an epic piss!" Todd called out when they heard him coming.

But then Oscar stepped into the clearing with his captor behind him, the gun to his head, the kid now holding him by the shoulder. Oscar didn't say anything. What was there to say? But he saw the others' faces as they took in the scene. It was all so surreal, and if he hadn't been gripped with fear he would have found their reactions comical. Todd's face was slack; he looked completely confused. Gwen stayed frozen on the log where she'd been sitting. Tracy's face was the strangest—animated, angry, as if annoyed that this kid had disrupted their plans. And maybe just a tiny bit excited.

"What the hell do you want?" she asked aggressively. Was she trying to get them shot?

"He doesn't speak English," said Oscar brusquely.

"¿Qué dijo?" the kid asked him.

"Ella sólo quiere que sepas que no queremos causarte problemas," Oscar lied.

"Vete pa'lla," the kid said. "Ve y parate con ellos."

And so Oscar stepped away from him, half-glad to escape the pressing mouth of the gun, half-scared that he'd now be facing it. He went and stood at Gwen's side and now all four of them were together. The kid swept the gun back and forth in front of them, wild-eyed, his hands and arms shaking.

Chapter Nine
Todd

When Oscar first stepped out of the woods, Todd thought he was seeing things. That couldn't be another person behind him. That couldn't be a gun at his head. But it was, and it was, and now they were all facing it. The gun waved before them in a big messy arc, and Todd could tell by how the kid held the weapon that he hadn't used it much, if ever. This only made him more dangerous—like those once-a-year hunters on opening weekend who fired at anything that moved. Todd thought of Brooke and Joey but pushed the thought away; he needed to focus. Now the kid yelled something in Spanish, which Todd didn't understand, but the urgency did not need translation.

"He says to get closer together," Oscar said, and they all stepped toward each other.

"What does he want, money?" Todd asked. The kid did look pretty disheveled, his camouflage clothing caked in dirt, large sweat stains under his armpits. "I don't have much but he can have what I've got."

"I don't think so," Oscar said. "I don't know what he wants."

Now the kid reached behind him and produced a walkie-talkie, which he brought to his mouth and shouted into, voice urgent and high.

"He's trying to connect with someone," Oscar said.

"No shit."

"I mean someone close by."

The kid kept pressing the button on the side of the device, yelling into it, but he only got the buzz of failed reception.

"Vámanos," he said finally, and gestured to his left with the gun.

"He wants us to go that way," Oscar said.

"Where?" Todd asked.

"He hasn't said."

"Well, what if we don't?" Tracy asked. She lifted her arms aggressively.

As if to answer, the kid pointed the gun at her head.

"All right," she said, so calmly that for a brief wild moment Todd wondered if she'd known about this, been part of it somehow, had set it up as another test of their mettle.

Gwen reached for her pack but the kid shook his head no, and so she straightened up again, face slack with fear. Wherever they were going, they'd have to leave their stuff behind. This wasn't good. They were in their hiking clothes, which were still a bit damp. It was after four and the sun had already dropped behind the ridge. Everything was in shadow and the air was cool. What would they do as the temperature fell?

Todd, walking first, started straight into the woods where the kid was pointing, but a few translated commands adjusted him to the right, until they came to a small creek and a solid rock wall jutting out into the water. The boy gestured for him to step onto a boulder a couple of feet out in the creek, and when he did, he saw that a trail continued beyond the rock face. Grabbing the wall for balance, he swung out and stepped back onto the shore. He walked, tripping over some black PVC piping which ran across the trail. Three dead fish lay half-submerged in the shallow creek, lifeless tails swaying in the water. What looked like a car battery lay directly in the creek. After a quarter-mile, they saw a thick field of knee-high plants, lush and green and fernlike, growing in a clearing amidst a dozen sawed-off trees.

"No wonder," Tracy said.

"Yeah, huh?" said Oscar.

"What?" Todd asked.

"It's weed," Gwen said, disbelieving.

"A whole *lot* of weed," said Oscar.

"No wonder," Tracy said again. "We've stumbled into a fucking pot farm."

Now the boy yelled again and walked up beside them. Oscar answered something swiftly in Spanish. And then to the others: "He wants us to shut up and keep moving."

Todd held up, waiting for the others to pass; as Tracy and Oscar stepped by, they looked at him questioningly. But he knew what he was doing. He wanted to be in back, closest to the gun. It looked like a Glock—he'd shot these himself at the shooting range. If the kid tripped or got distracted, if there was a lapse in his attention, Todd wanted to be within arm's reach so he could turn and grab it. He didn't want the women to be closest to the gun, not even Tracy. She might spin around and try to pull the gun from his hands, endangering them all. And Oscar, he wasn't sure about him, not after seeing how much he'd struggled these last two days; not after he'd let himself get caught off-guard, ambushed while he pissed in the woods. He knew this wasn't fair, but he couldn't help but feel it.

They walked slowly up to, and then around, the field of marijuana, which gave off a skunklike odor. Todd stared absently at Tracy's back, wondering if each sight he took in would be his last. Soon they reached a makeshift camp—a brown tarp roof anchored to the top of a boulder and covered with branches, the corners stretched and attached by rope to trees. Underneath was a sleeping bag and a pile of clothes, as well as a backpack, canned foods, some plastic storage bins. Beside the shelter, in the open, there was a camp stove set up on a large sawed-off tree trunk, a chainsaw, and several bottles of propane. There was a folding table with machinery Todd didn't recognize. Trash was everywhere—empty cans of refried beans and corn, crushed beer cans, plastic wrappers; crumpled, greasy tin foil and tamale wrappers; empty bottles of hot sauce and whiskey. It was strewn about in a semicircle forty feet wide, as if a tornado had hit. There were empty plastic containers of pesticide, as well as half a dozen fertilizer containers, painted green and brown. There was tray after tray of rat poison.

Todd got it now. The kid was living out here, tending to this field. He might have been here a week, he might have been here a month, but either way, they'd surprised him, he hadn't expected anyone, and now he was as freaked out as they were. What a fucking disgusting mess, Todd thought. He was sure that the kid was illegal. This is what we get for not protecting our borders. A gunman in the forest, interrupting our trip, and enough pot to supply the state for a year.

The kid made them stand together in front of his shelter while he tried again to rouse someone on his walkie-talkie. But all he got was more static. He hit the instrument against a tree, trying to jolt or punish it back into functionality. Todd thought about rushing him, but the gun was still in his other hand. This wasn't the moment, not yet.

"Who do you think he is?" Gwen asked softly.

"I think he's just tending the garden," Oscar replied. "But I worry about who he's working for. Probably one of the cartels."

Todd couldn't quite take this in. He'd smoked pot a few times in college, and he knew it came from somewhere. But a Mexican drug cartel, out here in a national forest?

"This has got to be worth hundreds of thousands of dollars," Tracy said.

"Maybe millions," said Oscar.

"I can't believe we stumbled onto this."

"I can," Oscar retorted, voice rising. "We should have stayed in the park. We should have stuck with one of the trails that people actually hike."

"Hey, hey, stop it," Todd said. "This doesn't do us any good."

And now the kid stepped close again, drawn by their elevated voices. His breathing was fast and shallow and his cheeks were flushed. He held the gun up with more authority, but Todd still wasn't convinced he could use it. You're just a boy, he thought. Come closer, just two steps closer, and look away for a second, and I will have that gun out of your hand before you know it.

The kid unleashed a string of sentences and Oscar replied, trying to talk in calmer tones. Todd's annoyance at Oscar vanished now; he was glad that one of them could talk with this guy. The kid took a few steps backward, eyes and gun still on them, toward his shelter.

"He's telling us to go with him," Oscar explained.

And so they walked over to within ten feet of the shelter and stood while the youth rifled through a couple of bags and then opened one of the bins. A look of relief came over his face and he pulled out something black—a phone, bigger and bulkier than a standard cell. A satellite phone, Todd realized.

The kid stood up and pressed the phone to his ear. He watched them, eyes darting back and forth, as if they had cornered him and not the other way around. Then he brought the phone down and punched in a number, put it back up to his ear. After two or three attempts, he spat out a curse. He lowered his head for just a second, taking his eyes off them, but not quite long enough for Todd to take advantage. Then he looked back up.

"Vámonos," he said again, waving them away.

"He wants us to move," Oscar said. "I think so he can get reception."

And so they started walking again, Todd still in back, Tracy, then Oscar, then Gwen, who was leading the way. They continued upstream past the end of the garden, where something smelled so horribly foul that Todd had to hold his breath. Then the canyon wall receded, changing from a vertical face to a tree-lined slope.

"Maybe one of us pretends we need to pee," Tracy said to Todd in a voice that was a little too loud. "I mean, you or me. And when he turns to keep watch, the other can jump him."

"Let's wait and see where he takes us," Todd replied, whispering. "There might be a second when he's distracted with the phone."

"Whatever we do, we need to divert his attention." Tracy's body was tense, taut, ready to explode—like a cocked gun—and Todd raised his hand to calm her.

"¡Cállate!" the kid yelled, and Todd felt the muzzle of the gun against his shoulder. He shut up. But he knew that Tracy was right. They had to wait until he was distracted, or distract him themselves. Then they had to wrest the gun away. And they needed to do this before his cronies arrived and all hope of escape would be lost.

"¡A la izquierda!" the kid yelled out now, and Oscar turned around and looked at him.

"¿Aqui?"

"¡Sí, pa'lla!" the kid yelled, and so Oscar turned left, heading through a small break in the trees and up a wooded slope.

"Where is he taking us?" Gwen asked, voice shaking.

"How the hell do I know?" Oscar said, but they all scrambled up the slope, reaching out to grab trees to keep their balance. The footing was tricky. The slope was a tangle of strewn-about branches, fallen logs, loose rocks, and dense trunks. The hill had eroded so much that some of the roots were exposed. One tree's roots looked like an old man's crossed naked legs; another tree had wrapped its dry gray branches around a small green sapling, as if trying to suck the life from it. Todd glanced behind him a couple of times to see if the kid was struggling. But he was doing okay; he slipped and slid like the rest of them, but never lowered his gun. Sharp fallen branches and broken-off twigs stabbed Todd in the legs with every step. He couldn't avoid them, couldn't stop to tend to one bad scratch even as the blood trickled down his leg.

After about ten minutes they reached a bare rock shelf with a fifty-foot wall of granite behind it; for the first time since they'd left the junction on the ridge, they could see clear through to the sky.

When all of them had gathered, the youth made them stand on one side of the ledge while he stood at the other end and pulled out his satellite phone. He punched in the number with his left hand, gun still in his right, and this time he got through. They could hear the phone ringing on the other end, even from ten feet away. After three rings a loud male voice answered.

"¿Hola, José?"

The boy's face went slack with relief. His eyes brightened and almost welled with tears. "¿Miguel? ¡Gracias a Dios que te alcancé!"

"¿Qué pasa, José? ¿Hay algún problema?"

"Un problema, sí, Miguel. Tengo aqui a unas personas. Se acercaron mucho a las plantas."

"¿Es la policía?"

"No, no la policía. No creo. Nomas gente, excursioneros. Pero nos encontraron, Miguel. ¡No sé qué hacer!"

"Mierda. Mierda. ¿Cuantos?"

"Cuatro."

"¡Cuatro!" A pause. "Tienes que dispararles. No podemos dejar que la gente sepa en donde queda el jardín."

The boy's eyes filled with tears now. "No sé si puedo, Miguel. Dos son mujeres."

"What is he saying?" Todd whispered tersely to Oscar, who looked pale as a ghost.

"He's saying . . . the other guy is telling him to kill us."

Todd knew he had to rush the kid now, whether or not there was a clear opportunity. He heard the voice on the other end, louder now, insistent. "Hágalo."

The kid's head jerked back suddenly, and Todd thought he was reacting to the voice on the phone. But then he saw there was a perfect dark hole in the boy's forehead, just above his right eyebrow. The boy dropped the phone and stared at them open-mouthed. But he didn't really see them, his brain was already shattered. His body was still moving, though, flailing to hold on to life.

"What the—?" Tracy said, and then they heard the report, echoing back from the other side of the canyon.

The boy's legs had buckled and he slumped sideways and fell, his left arm pinned beneath him, right arm flung in front of him, legs extended—right leg forward—as if they were trying to lead him to safety.

"José? José?" came the voice through the phone—which had landed on the rock just in front of them.

Tracy stepped forward to pick it up but Todd held her back. She was all action and reaction, impulse and nerve. Jesus, didn't she ever think?

"Don't," he said. "We don't know where the shot came from." He thought it had come from above them and possibly from the left. Was it a ranger, maybe? The police? Whoever it was, Todd felt a wave of relief. Their captor had been shot; he was lying dead in front of them. Maybe now their endless awful day could finally be over. Oscar was right—they never should have taken this trail. But no matter. They were safe now, or at least on their way to safety. They could end this goddamned trip and go home.

Gwen was breathing hard, almost hyperventilating, and when Todd looked at her, he saw that she was crying. Oscar just stared at the dead kid, fingering the GPS unit still attached to his belt as if it could somehow help them. Tracy, despite Todd's warning, had stepped out farther on the ledge and was scanning the ridgeline above them, and now she pointed somewhere to their left. "I think it came from up there."

"Someone's a damned good shot," Todd said.

And then they heard a new voice shout, "Stay right there! I'm coming down!"

Todd allowed himself to lean against the granite wall and close his eyes for a moment. Now, the images of his children appeared, and he was flooded with joy and relief. They were saved. In front of him the voice still crackled from the satellite phone.

"¡José! ¿Qué está pasando, José? ¿Estás bien?"

"This creeps me the fuck out," Tracy said. "Let's at least get the phone."

"Let's not," Todd countered. "It'll have fingerprints. Maybe that'll help the police identify the kid and catch the rest of these bastards."

Gwen sat down beside him, and he could feel that she was shaking. "Hey," he said, putting his arm around her. "Hey, it's okay now. We're going to get out of here."

"I can't believe this," she said, voice shaking too. "I can't believe this is happening."

"I know. But it's over now. We're going to go home." Looking out, Todd noted absently that they could make out the small canyon into which they'd accidentally wandered, the thick expanse of forest. Most of it was in shadow now, but the tops of the trees on the opposite ridge were lit bright orange, as if dipped in fire. How crazy that this pristine and gorgeous place could be the scene of what happened today. How sad that John Muir's paradise had become home to a giant pot farm.

They heard branches breaking, someone coming down the slope on the far side of the wall, and they all stood up to greet whoever had rescued them.

It was a man, young, sliding with a rifle strapped over

his shoulder, moving surprisingly fast. A flash of white fur accompanied him, zigzagging down the slope. In another moment the man stepped down the last few feet and stood squarely on the shelf, pulling the rifle and a backpack off his shoulder. A rangy, coyote-sized dog jumped down after him. It was mostly white, spotted, half its face covered with black, as if it were wearing an eye patch. It kept its distance, skirting the edge of the cliff.

The man was in his twenties, white, about 5'9", with close-cut light brown hair. He wore a dirty white T-shirt, worn blue jeans, brown work boots, and wire-rimmed glasses. Todd heard Gwen's sharp intake of breath, and sensed Tracy standing up straight, ready to fight. He was confused by their alarm. This guy had shown up to save their asses—from Mexican drug runners, no less. Now he walked over to the dead boy on the ground, picked up the fallen gun, and shoved it into his own waistband. He turned toward the four of them and flashed a broad grin.

"Howdy do," he said.

Chapter Ten
Gwen

When the man turned and offered his weird, off-pitch greeting, Todd said, "Jesus, are we glad to see *you!*"

Gwen was silent and he seemed oblivious to this, as well as to Tracy's hanging back, to Oscar's hostility.

The newcomer looked at Todd as if talking to a slightly retarded child. "Yeah, you got yourself into quite a jam."

"It was crazy," Todd said, and now a flood of words came out. "We were just minding our own business, and suddenly that little shit comes out of nowhere and corners Oscar with a gun." He gestured at Oscar. "And then he took us back to a pot field, of all things, and he was trying to reach someone on his phone, but I guess there was no reception, so he brought us here."

"I know," the man said. "I was watching you from up on the ridge. But I couldn't get a clear shot at him until he stepped to the edge." He wiped his brow with the back of his hand and readjusted his glasses. His arm, like the rest of him, was wiry and thin. His movements were quick and jerky, as if all of his nerves ran close to the surface. Several tattoos were half-obscured by his shirt sleeves. "No reception, huh? You gotta know which phones actually work out here."

Just then the phone crackled again and the voice called out, "José? José?"

The man walked over, picked it up, and yelled into it, "José can't come to the phone right now!" Then he turned and flung the phone off the ledge; it traveled fifty feet before hitting a tree.

The dog, seeing the flying object, rushed over to the edge and barked. Except what came out of its mouth wasn't a bark at all, but a choked-off, stifled wheezing sound that died in its throat.

"Stop it!" the man yelled, kicking her in the chest. "Be quiet, you stupid furball, you mangy stray, you useless bitch!" The dog cried out and slinked away, back over to where she'd been. She lay down and put her head on her paws, still whimpering.

Gwen's stomach turned, and even Todd seemed taken aback. Still, he said, "Well, buddy, that's one way to end a phone call."

The man looked off at the ridge in the distance, as if he were just another hiker enjoying the view. "It won't be long before his greaseball cronies show up and find him. And the beauty of it is, they'll think *you* did it."

Something shifted, there was a sudden intensity, like the feeling Gwen sometimes got in South LA when a strange car turned the corner, moving slowly, windows inching down.

Todd asked, "Hey, who are you, anyway?"

The man turned back toward them, a grimace on his face. Small red blotches appeared on his pale cheeks. His eyes were the color of ice. "I'm a concerned citizen, and a farmer. My brother Gary and I have some *interests* up here, and we don't appreciate anyone interfering with them. Especially not Mexican nationals."

"You're a farmer?" Todd asked, and Gwen wanted to kill him. Could he really be that stupid?

"Yeah. My family's had a ranch in the Central Valley for three generations. My other brother still runs it. But cattle are a drag. So Gary and I branched off, since I need income for my other activities. We've been growing our most lucrative crop up here."

Now even Todd seemed to understand what he meant; he sat down, deflated.

"Look, man," Oscar said, "we weren't looking for any trouble."

"Well, you sure did find it, though, didn't you?" The man scratched his head suddenly, as if something had bitten him. Then he stopped. "I gotta thank you, though. We knew the Mexicans had some gardens up in the mountains but we didn't know where. We didn't think anyone came back here anymore on account of the bear dump. So when I saw you all turn off at that old abandoned road, I figured you must have known something, or that you might even have a grow back here yourselves."

"The bear dump?" Todd asked.

"Yeah, the place where they used to get rid of problem bears." The man lifted his rifle slightly, as if preparing in case he saw one. "Back in the day, the tourists in the park used to feed the bears like pigeons, and so the bears got used to helping themselves. They'd go up to people and lift the backpacks right off their shoulders. One of them attacked a little kid once. When it got bad, the Park Service would shoot them—and then they'd bring them out here. That road you took, there's another turnoff about halfway down that leads to a cliff. The rangers would dump the bears over the edge."

Behind her fear, Gwen felt a wave of revulsion. She remembered the other dirt road they'd passed. She remembered the ranger's hesitation when he first brought up the trail. Could this story be true? Silently, she started to pray.

"Some hikers discovered the dump maybe thirty years ago," the guy continued. "And then all hell broke loose. There were a couple hundred bear corpses hanging out of trees, smashed on rocks. Some of them had been skinned for their fur." He spat out a stream of brown spit, chewing tobacco. "My dad saw it, said the skinned ones looked like huge naked men covered with muscle. I wish I had seen them." He sounded momentarily wistful. "Anyway. After that they shut down the road."

"That's explains why no one comes back here," said Todd. "And why the road's not even on the topo map."

"Exactly. Which makes it pretty convenient for other purposes, I guess. Fucking Mexican bastards. So when I saw your car turn off the road at that old abandoned exit, I figured I'd just tag along behind you."

He looked out at the view again, ran his hand down the barrel of his rifle. "It's pretty country up here. Glad to see it. And you've made the trip easier on me, thanks. That fire pit at the trailhead was real nice. Didn't use it since I didn't want you to see the smoke, but it was a beautiful spot to camp. The lakeside spot was pretty too. But that river crossing was a bitch."

Now he looked right at Gwen, and her blood ran cold.

"You probably needed some help, didn't you? You don't look like you can carry much of a load. But that's how it is in general, isn't it? You people not carrying your load."

Oscar took a step forward and said angrily, "Hey, shut up, man."

The man casually brought the rifle up to his shoulder. "Not so fast, brown boy."

Oscar stopped in his tracks. "Fucking asshole."

"Be careful now. I've already shot one Mexican today. I shoot another, and I'll probably get a prize. Hell, if I shot you and the black one here, my friends would probably throw me a parade!" He chuckled, then swept his rifle back and forth across the group of them, and Gwen instinctively drew back.

"Whoa," said Todd, jerking her toward him. She looked behind her—there was a drop of at least a hundred feet. Six more inches and she would have stepped right off the cliff.

She closed her eyes—her heart beat wildly—and took several deep breaths. Fear built on top of fear. Todd had just kept her from falling to her death, but was that any worse than what she faced now? She had come here to get *away* from the threat of violence and danger. But as scared as she'd been of José, he was just a kid, as freaked out as they were. This guy was different. This was a scary murderous man who seemed delighted to have them in his sights. She noticed his tattoos again—the number 14 on one arm, and what looked like the bottom of a swastika against a red and black flag on the other. The man lowered the rifle but still held it diagonally across his chest. Please, God, she prayed, please help us get out of here.

"Actually, my name's not Asshole," he said, sounding jaunty again. "And it's not Buddy either. You can call me A.J. And this here's Timber. I just got her a couple weeks ago, at a rodeo. Someone had taken her and given her back already, and now I know why. She steals everything that's not tied down and she's pretty useless as a sheep or cattle dog. And she barked too damn much, so we had to get that taken care of."

The dog sat alert, the tips of both ears falling forward. Little black spots were scattered across her white coat; she looked like cookies-and-cream ice cream. Despite A.J.'s dismissals, she gazed up at him, awaiting a kind word, a gentle touch.

"Look, man," Tracy said now, stepping forward. She'd been quiet, and Gwen had seen her trying to read the situation, the calculation almost visible in her eyes. "Oscar's right. We're not trying to cause any trouble. We don't care what you're doing up here. Hell, we didn't care what *he* was doing." She gestured at the dead youth between them. "We're on vacation, on a backpacking trip. We just want to get our stuff and go home."

A.J. turned toward Tracy as if seeing her for the first time. He looked interested, even amused, and Gwen prayed that she wouldn't do anything stupid, lunge at him or curse him and get them all killed. He faced her squarely and shook his head. "Sorry, it's a bit more involved than that. Hey, are you a Mex too?"

Tracy glared at him. "I'm half Japanese and half Irish." Gwen was glad she didn't add the usual finishing touch: *And 100 percent trouble.*

"Half Jap!" A.J. grinned, seeming genuinely pleased. "Well, this is my lucky day! Where are you all from anyway, the United Nations?"

"No, genius," Oscar said. "We're from LA."

"*That* hellhole. Well, that explains it. Too bad you didn't stay there." He lifted the rifle now and brushed some dirt from the barrel. "Because as I was saying, the situation here's kind of involved. See, we need to get rid of that garden, let the Mexicans know they're not welcome. And now I've told you about *our* garden too. Do you know where it is?"

They all looked at him, confused. "N-no," said Todd.

"Well, I'm not going to tell you!" He laughed loudly.

Gwen looked at his eyes, which were almost colorless, but with a spark of something, anger or insanity, that ran through his body too, providing a jerky, stilted energy. It was like he'd been plugged into an electrical outlet. She had seen this kind of look two or three times over the years, in the eyes of the occasional people she'd met who were truly psychopaths.

"I'll tell you this, though. Gary came up the morning after you left and he's on the trail a half-day behind me. He's probably at the lake by now and he'll be here in the morning. Then we'll figure out what to do with you. Well, most of you anyway . . . You! Stanford!" he said, gesturing at Todd with his rifle.

"Me?" Todd responded, lifting his head, absently touching his cap.

"Yeah, you. What's your story? What are you doing with these people?"

Todd drew himself up straight, looked at him warily. "They're my friends."

"I guess you're some kind of colored-people lover, huh?"

"I guess I am."

They glared at each other and Gwen thought for a moment that A.J. might shoot. But then he laughed, a burst of sound that was more like a curse. "I thought so," he said. "Fucking traitor." He shook his head in disbelief, then spat on the ground. "All right, then. All of you. Let's get down to that garden. I want you to show me where those fuckers were camped." They all stared at him until he lifted the gun again. "Come on, now. Let's get moving down this slope."

And so they reversed their course of earlier. Oscar stepped off the ledge and headed down first, followed by Gwen, Tracy, and Todd. Tracy was looking all around, as if trying to find a path of escape.

"Don't you try to run off now," A.J. warned, but it wasn't possible, because just getting down the hillside with its unstable steep dirt and loose rocks, its slippery pine needles, took all of their concentration—and because this man, unlike José, seemed perfectly comfortable moving around in the wilderness with a gun in his hand.

Gwen glanced back a couple of times and saw him stepping confidently down the slope, sideways and balanced, as if he'd been making his way down wooded slopes his whole life. The dog ran ahead of them, her spotted white body flashing between the trees, her long, fringed tail acting like a balancing force. As they entered tree cover again, Gwen felt claustrophobic, worse because the light was now failing. There were trees, trees everywhere, some that had fallen into each other, dead branches and living ones reaching out and entangling her, making her feel like she would never get loose. Within a few minutes they'd reached the spot with the horrible smell. The dog ran off to the right and sniffed at something crumpled and brown.

"Timber, leave it!" A.J. commanded, but she lowered her shoulder and then flipped onto her back, rolling with joy and abandon.

"Damnit, you nasty-ass dog!" A.J. yelled. He stepped over, never taking his eyes off Gwen and the others, kicked the animal hard in the side, and yanked her up by the collar. Her shoulders and back were covered with a sticky brown substance; on the ground the source of it was unrecognizable.

"Fucking dead deer. Probably died from the rat poison." A.J. shoved the dog along with his foot, not saying another word until they reached the edge of the grow. When he saw it, he let out a low whistle. "Nice crop," he said, admiringly. "Bastards."

He plucked a single leaf off a plant and held it to his nose, then shook his head. "If these were a little further along, we'd think about taking them." He threw the leaf down. "We need to put these fuckers out of business."

He directed them down the trail until they reached the campsite, and when he saw this, the color came up in his cheeks; it was as if he'd found that someone had not only broken into his house but had taken up residence there. He gripped his rifle so hard that his knuckles grew white. "Motherfuckers," he said. Then he turned to the others and pointed his rifle. "Stay there."

He went to José's duffel bags and pulled out the contents—clothes, shoes, an extra blanket, and a one-eyed teddy bear. God, José was just a child, Gwen thought again. A scared kid who didn't want to be here. A.J. opened up the bins and searched through them, pulling out boxes of crackers and cans of soup. The dog, who now smelled awful, rushed over to stick her nose in an open bin; A.J. threw a plastic food container that hit her squarely on the back and sent her slinking off again. Then he went over to the stove, which Gwen thought now might not even be for cooking, but for something related to the plants. A.J. looked at all of this, then turned the table heavily on its side. He picked up a shovel and started to beat the stove with it, striking it over and over again. He did this one-armed, swung the shovel like an ax, still holding the rifle in his other hand. He seemed to be doing this more to express his anger than to destroy the equipment, since he couldn't do much damage one-handed. The sound of metal on metal made Gwen wince.

"I can't believe the balls of these people! Right under our fucking noses. Right in our national forest!"

Had Gwen not been in the situation she was in, she would have found this amusing, a drug grower and Confederate sympathizer and God knew what else, sounding like a ranger for the National Park Service.

Now he took the shovel and started smashing up the rest of the camp—bins, the tarp and tent, the cooking equipment. He swore with each impact, cursing the Mexicans, the dead boy on the ledge above them, pausing only to pocket a bar of soap he found in one of the bins and to pick up his glasses, which had fallen off during a particularly violent swing.

In the midst of this Gwen heard Tracy say, "We've got to do something. He's going to kill us."

"I don't know," Todd replied. "Maybe we can reason with him."

Gwen had had enough of this. "Todd," she said, using the tone she'd use with an unreasonable teenager, "Tracy's right. He's going to kill us. And he can't let us go after what we've seen and heard."

"We've got to move quick," Oscar added. "His brother's coming."

"Hey!" A.J. yelled. "You be quiet over there. No talking, no plotting, no crying for Mommy. Just shut up and do what I say." He dropped the shovel and came back over to them. "Come to think of it, we need to get rid of your stuff too. Let's start with your maps and compass. And your GPS."

Tracy glared at him, but when he lifted the gun, she produced the maps and compass. He gestured for her to drop the plastic compass and then smashed it with his foot. He did the same with Oscar's GPS. Then he pulled a lighter out of his pocket and lit the corner of the topo map, which blackened and curled and then vanished into nothingness. He repeated this process with the map of the Lost Canyon trail; the part that didn't burn was a soggy mush. He then made them empty their pockets, which produced a knife out of Oscar's front pocket and a Leatherman out of Todd's.

A.J. approached them and patted them all down. Gwen endured the rough feel of his hand on her body, touching her at the hips and stomach, giving her ass a squeeze for good measure. "You're a pretty one, for a darky," he said. "And not too skinny either." She felt dirty and invaded and terrified, and curled into herself when he was done.

Something blared loudly, an alarm or a phone, and it took Gwen a moment to realize that it couldn't have been José's. A.J. reached into his backpack and pulled out a satellite phone. "Iridium," he said. "Best choice for the backcountry." He took a few steps away from them but kept his rifle against his hip. "Gary!" he said cheerfully. "We were just talking about you!"

He listened to the reply.

"Yes, all four of them. The Mexican kid's gone off to a better place. But we're still here, and we're about to go pick some plants." He listened again and said, "All right. I'll keep everyone entertained until then."

He hung up and clipped the phone to his belt. "That was Gary, my brother. He says hi, and he looks forward to joining the party. But work before play, right? So let's go tear up some plants before it gets too dark."

Was he serious? Tear up plants on a day when they'd hiked seven or eight miles with heavy packs, crossed a fast-moving river, run into one scary guy with a gun only to end up in the hands of another? Gwen was tired, bone tired, and she was hungry. And on top of that her bladder was full.

"I have to pee," she said aloud.

"So . . . pee!" said A.J.

"I'll just go off over there." She gestured toward the woods.

"You're not going anywhere. You're staying right here in my sight."

She couldn't believe this. Oscar was standing next to her, and she saw the expression of horror on his face.

"I won't run, I promise. I'd just feel better if I could go over there."

"Well, I wouldn't," A.J. said, lifting his rifle a few inches. "And it's really all about me, you understand? It's all about the man with the gun. So why don't you just stay here, where I can see you."

And so she stayed close, and the others all looked away, and they might have closed in around her except that A.J. stepped up nearly level with them so he could see better. Even though she turned away so she was facing him sideways, she still felt terribly exposed, felt his eyes as she undid her pants and shoved them down and squatted, the cool air a shock against her skin. She was shamed by her nakedness, shamed by the sound of the piss hitting the ground. She felt something taken from her, his greedy appraisal, and she thought she might be sick. She didn't want to look down and acknowledge her embarrassment, so instead she stared up between the trees. The sky was a darkening blue, open and free; she wished she could be drawn up into it.

When she was done, she stood quickly and pulled her pants up. Oscar touched her on the shoulder protectively.

"That was very entertaining," A.J. said. "Thank you. A heck of a view. Maybe you and me, we can spend some time together later."

"Don't even try it, you bastard," Oscar said.

"Watch it," A.J. warned.

"You talk shit about her, and now *this*?"

"I'm an equal-opportunity guy when it comes to females," A.J. said. "Besides, the darker the berry—"

"Fuck you."

"Shut up," A.J. said, shoving the rifle into Oscar's belly. Then: "Anyone else need to pee? . . . All right, one more thing I've got to take care of and then we'll go." He looped a rope around the dog's collar and led her to the edge of the creek. With the rifle still in one hand, he used the other to pick her up by the collar and flip her on her back in the water. She yelped and cried and struggled but he yelled, "Shut up!" and held her down with his boot, gun still pointed at them. Now he pulled out the bar of soap from the camp and turned her on her side, soaping up her fur where she'd rolled in the carcass. He stepped down so hard he might have crushed her ribs, but the dog lay passive and quiet, eyes wide open in fear and distress. When he was finished, he lifted his foot and removed the rope and the dog leapt up to the shore, shaking the water off, staying away from A.J. Her tail was so far between her legs that the tip of it touched her chest.

A.J. directed them up the trail. For a few moments

there was no sound except their shoes breaking twigs and the panting of the dog, who slithered between them. Then A.J.'s voice rang out loudly.

"*We're off to see the Wizard*," he sang, "*the Wonderful Wizard of Oz!*"

Gwen felt the hair rise on the back of her neck.

"What's wrong with you guys? You don't like music? What a bunch of party poopers."

When they got to the edge of the garden, A.J. tied the dog to a tree and led them between the rows. "Okay. What you're going to do is tear the plants out. Grab them as close to the ground as you can, so the roots come out with them . . . All right, go on, get working now. And no smoking on the job, ha ha!"

They all looked at him, at the plants, at each other.

"Good thing it's still so early in the season. A month later, and they'd be taller than you. Now go on!"

Finally Todd, with an expression that Gwen couldn't read, took a few steps forward, bent over, and pulled up a plant. She was furious at him, unaccountably. Did he think cooperating would help? And she felt guilty for her anger— he was in the same mess that they were. And then she felt annoyed again, annoyed at the guilt, annoyed at her con- fusion of feeling.

"Good man," said A.J. "Now, the rest of you, do what he's doing."

Oscar sighed and stepped forward, and when Gwen saw this, she gave up and did the same. Tracy glared at A.J., not moving, until he leveled the rifle to her chest.

"Go on, Jap," he said.

So she stepped forward too, and soon all four of them were tearing up plants, spaced a few feet away from each other. A.J. leaned against a tree trunk and pointed his rifle toward them.

"This used to be *our* country." He turned on a big flashlight so they could see in the growing dark. "Fifteen, twenty years ago, when I was a kid, it was all white people up here, or mostly white, and the Mexicans knew their place. But then things started to change. They invaded this business like they've done everything else. They've come into here, Sequoia, Humboldt, Mendocino. And that's only California. Some homegrown traitors have even gone into business with them!" With the rifle still under one arm, he pulled a cigarette out of his pocket and lit it. "But not us," he said, blowing out a mouthful of smoke. "We had to take a stand. We want our country back. We want to restore my people to their proper place as the head of everything—and send the rest of you fuckers back where you came from."

He took a drag from his cigarette and glanced at the dog, who looked at him uncertainly, then lowered her head. "The cartel killed a buddy of mine last December when he stumbled onto one of their gardens. Now we've killed one of theirs." He whistled. "This is a shitload of money here, boy. Whew! They're going to be *pissed!* But you know, if the fucking US government would only legalize drugs, it would drive all these bastards out of business. We could grow our crops openly and not have to sneak around."

Gwen heard his rants but only half-listened. Her whole body hurt. The muscles in her legs were tight; her toes felt raw. And her back was pierced through with pain every time she bent over. She felt a growing panic as the night came on, as the forest closed in around them.

They worked for what seemed like a very long time,
A.J. allowing them periodic breaks to eat the almonds and
peanuts he'd taken from the camp, to have a gulp or two of
water. Gwen's back hurt even worse now, and her hands
were raw from handling the plants. A.J. kept the light on
them, and the moon was bright, so they were able to see
despite the darkness. Time seemed both to expand and
hold still, and Gwen had no idea what hour it was. She felt
A.J. turn his eyes on her periodically; once he winked at
her and leered. She shuddered and avoided looking at him.

She thought vaguely of the strangeness of what she was
doing, how the fields in these mountains connected with
the violence in Mexico, the murderous rivalries between
gangs in LA. She knew people who smoked, of course, but
had never tried herself. She had seen what drugs did to too
many kids in South LA—robbed them of their senses, and
futures.

Finally, Tracy stood up straight and said, "I have to
take a piss."

"Well, go on. But stay right here in my sight."

Tracy took a few steps through the garden and A.J. followed, stopping about ten feet from her and not far from
Oscar. The dog lifted her head and looked up. Todd was to
the left of them, and Gwen not far behind. She saw Tracy
stop a couple of feet from a tree. Then Tracy pointed suddenly and yelled, "Shit! Watch out!" and they all looked up
to see what was there. A.J. looked too, and Tracy slipped
behind the tree.

"Hey!" A.J. yelled, too late. He made for the tree but
Todd cut to his left and A.J. dropped the light and swung
toward him. Then Tracy flashed out between the trees and
A.J. raised the gun to shoot, but Oscar came up behind

him and struck him with a branch, bringing the full force of the wood against his skull. A.J.'s glasses flew off and he dropped the rifle and crumpled to the ground, and Tracy rushed over and kicked the gun away. A.J. lay there groaning and Oscar hit him again—in his midsection, his shoulders, his head. Finally he was still. Todd bent over and took the phone and José's handgun from his waistband, and Tracy gave him another kick. She knelt and pressed two fingers to A.J.'s neck.

"Still breathing."

"But at least he's out," Todd said.

They both looked over at Oscar. "Hey, great job," said Todd, giving him a fist-bump. His newfound respect was evident in his voice.

"You too," Oscar replied. "Both of you."

"How the hell did you know to do that?" Gwen asked. She picked up the flashlight and aimed it between them, creating a circle of light.

"I didn't know," Tracy said. "We just did it."

"When you slipped behind that tree," Todd said, "shit, I didn't know *what* we were going to do."

"That was crazy!" Gwen said this admiringly, not knowing whether Tracy had been brave or stupid. Was there a difference? she wondered.

"I figured you guys would step up," Tracy said. She stood and clapped both Oscar and Todd on the back. "You took care of business!"

Todd examined the satellite phone, and Gwen felt a surge of hope. Maybe it was as simple as calling someone; maybe they'd be able to connect to the outside world.

"I don't know how to work this," Todd said. He fumbled with the buttons and Tracy looked over his arm.

"It's password protected," she said.

No one spoke, but Gwen saw her own despair reflected in the others' faces.

There was movement on the ground and they all jumped. A.J. twitched and Tracy kicked him hard—in the side, in the head. His lifted shirt revealed a few inches of stomach, and his flesh there was shockingly pale. A bit of blood streamed down from his temple. But he stayed out.

"What are we going to do with him?" Oscar asked.

"I don't think there's any choice," Tracy said. "We have to kill him."

"We have to *what*?" Gwen said. Her heart was beating out of her chest. "What are you talking about, Tracy? That's crazy!"

"Is it?" Tracy's features were clear and sharp-looking by the light of the flashlight. She stroked her chin as if the question was merely academic, but she looked like she was enjoying herself. "Think about it. He's already killed a man. And from the way he shot that rifle, it probably wasn't the first. He thinks we all deserve to die—and now we know about his business. There's no reason to believe he would have let us live."

"But still," Todd said, "all we've done is show up in the wrong place at the wrong time. If we kill him, it's a whole different story."

"Exactly," Gwen agreed. "We don't want that on our hands. José's death is on *his* hands. We had nothing to do with it."

"But who's to say that anyone will believe that?" Tracy argued. "The kid is dead, and there's no way to prove who did it. Look," she said, leaning toward them, "right now, the main issue here isn't who gets blamed for the kid's death. The issue is us getting out alive. We need to get the hell out of here before A.J.'s brother shows up. Not to mention the kid's people. And we need to fix it so this piece of shit can't follow us."

"Agreed," Todd said. "But we can do that without killing him."

"I'm not so sure we can."

"This is crazy, Tracy," Todd said, echoing Gwen. "You're fucking batshit crazy. We can't do this. I can't do it. I've got a family to go back to, children, a job. Whatever you're thinking of doing, I can't be any part of it."

"You're already part of it," said Tracy. She gestured at the man on the ground, and then up toward the slope, where somewhere José's body lay. "Everything has already changed."

They let this sit, averting their eyes. Gwen felt a chill go up her spine, an opening into another kind of fear. They'd gotten past the immediate danger, two direct threats to their lives. But the fact was, they were out in the wilderness completely on their own. The phone was useless, and there was no other way to reach out for help. No one—at least no one good—was coming for them.

Now Tracy turned to Oscar, and the shadows from the flashlight made her cheeks look smooth and hollow, her entire face more angled and wolflike. "Oscar, what do you think?"

"I don't know," he said, shaking his head. "My mind says you're right. But my gut . . ."

"Look, there's plenty we can do to incapacitate him," Todd said.

"Like what?"

"We could tie him up and put duct tape over his mouth."

"But then he could die out here," Tracy said, with a tone of interested pleasure. "So what would be the difference? Why not just kill him now and get it over with?"

"Stop," Gwen said. "Just stop." Her head felt like it was about to burst. "I can't believe we're standing here talking about *killing* a person. Debating it like we're talking about which trail to take. Tracy, we can't do that. It's not even an option. We've got to figure out something else."

They were all looking at her quietly. Gwen was sure that Tracy was going to overrule her. But something shifted in Tracy's face now and she looked human again.

"All right, Gwen," she said. "We'll figure something out."

They dragged A.J. over to a tree, the two men holding onto his shoulders, Tracy and Gwen each taking a leg. They emptied his pockets, recovering Oscar's knife and Todd's Leatherman, plus a worn Swiss Army knife and some matches. Tracy covered his mouth with duct tape. They leaned him back against a tree in a sitting position, his chin falling onto his chest. Then they double-tied him—first binding his wrists together behind the tree and then wrapping his upper body with rope. Tracy and Todd both knew complicated knots to secure both sets of bindings.

When they were done, there was no way he could get his arms loose. They stepped back and examined their handiwork. Gwen felt queasy looking at him—he could die like this, and they would have done it; she knew Tracy was right. But there was still a difference, she told herself, between leaving him to luck and actually killing him.

"Where's the dog?" she asked now.

"I don't see her," Oscar said.

"Me neither."

Todd walked over to where Timber had been tied up and lifted a frayed rope end. "I guess she had better places to be."

"Should we worry?" Oscar asked.

"No. We're not going to be able to find her anyway."

Gwen felt mildly disappointed about the dog being gone. But it was probably better not to have to worry about her.

"I still think we should do something else with A.J.," Tracy said. "Make it impossible for him to follow us."

"Yeah, I think so too," said Oscar. "He's not really incapacitated. Hopefully his teeth aren't as good as his dog's."

"I could shoot him in the leg," Tracy offered.

Gwen thought, Are you crazy? You must truly be crazy. Tracy seemed almost cheerful about this turn of events, as if it were part of a grand adventure they'd all laugh about later at the bar. But Todd had a more practical response: "Someone could hear the gunshot, though. Not a good thing if other people are coming."

"You're right," Tracy conceded. "Then what? Break his leg? Cut him?"

"How about we just break his glasses?" Gwen suggested. They all looked at her blankly. "The way he squinted when they fell off, I don't think his vision is too good. He probably couldn't make his way through the woods without them."

"Even if he could," Todd added, "he wouldn't be able to see well enough to shoot us."

"Good idea, Gwen," Oscar said, and so it was decided.

Tracy went over to the spot where they'd first knocked him out and picked up his fallen glasses. She brought them back to where the others stood and crunched the lenses under her shoe.

"That's for my compass," she said, with one twist of her heel. "That's for Oscar's GPS." Then: "Let's go get our stuff," and for a moment Gwen didn't know what she was talking about. And then she remembered their packs, farther back in the clearing where they'd first encountered José, left there what seemed like a lifetime ago. Tracy was right about one thing: everything had changed.

"We should figure out what we really need to take," Todd said. "We should probably travel light."

"Good point," said Tracy. "We'll only take essentials." She walked over and picked up A.J.'s rifle.

Just before they turned to walk back toward their packs, Gwen swung the flashlight back toward A.J. He was still passed out, chin on his chest, a growing lump on his cheek. There was a trickle of blood running down the side of his face and a strip of duct tape over his mouth. He looked peaceful, almost harmless. He was bound securely to the tree, and seeing all this, Gwen felt a complicated mix of emotions. Anger and hatred and fear all bubbled together with a strange wish that he wouldn't die, that they wouldn't be responsible. I hope I never see your face again, she thought. Then she swung the light away and left him in darkness.

Chapter Eleven
Oscar

They hiked without speaking, but their passage seemed terribly loud. The sound of their boots kicking rocks and breaking twigs reverberated through the woods. There was just enough light from the first-quarter moon that they could see where they were going; still, Tracy switched on her headlamp several times, light muffled by her fingers, to make sure they were staying on track. In these moments, all their faces looked haunted and ghostly, deep dark shadows where eyes should have been. And the trees. They looked weirdly alive in the short bursts of light, or maybe undead, malevolent creatures looming in the dark.

They were headed up the same trail they'd come down the previous afternoon, a lifetime ago. Their loads were less than half of what they'd been the day before, but everything else seemed heavier. Originally they'd planned to spend two more days in the mountains, but now, instead of hiking eight miles each day, they'd push to do all sixteen at once. And so there were things they could leave behind— sleeping bags and tents, and some of the food, the heavy bear canisters. Since it was probably as cold right then as it would get, they left most of their extra clothes. They carried water, some food, and Tracy brought her bear spray. They worried that whoever found their things might blame them for José's death, but they worried more about getting out of the mountains alive. They debated about leaving a couple of the big packs behind, but no one wanted to feel like they were taking less than their share, so they all still carried their packs. The only new things they added were guns. Tracy took José's handgun, and Todd carried A.J.'s rifle.

It was three thirty in the morning, and Oscar couldn't believe where he was or what he was doing. He thought of his daughter, asleep in his mother's house; he thought of his mother and Claudia. What would he say if he could talk with them now? He had never imagined himself in a situation like this.

Now he wished that they had killed the skinhead creep, or at least maimed him in some serious way. They had him secured pretty tightly, but who was to say they hadn't made some error that left room for him to wiggle out of the bindings? And what if his brother showed up? Even though Oscar believed what the people at the Franklin Cash Store had said about the bad element in the area, and what Gwen had said about white supremacists, he'd never imagined that he'd meet such guys himself. He never thought he'd see racial hatred so naked and frank— so much more in-your-face than the subtle prejudice he was used to. Oscar's emotions had been jerked around so much that he felt an emotional whiplash. The terror he'd experienced when the gun first touched his head had settled into a fear so steady and deep he forgot what it was like not to feel it. Then the confusion and relief of their first captor being shot, followed by an even deeper fear.

He'd always associated pot gardens with aging hippies, pleasantly stoned older folks who ate pot brownies and strummed '60s-era guitars. And he smoked out himself at parties sometimes—who didn't? But it had somehow not really occurred to him that there were higher stakes, and dangerous people, or that he could ever run into trouble. He'd known, of course, about the Mexican drug cartels, and he sometimes saw slick, intimidating men driving tricked-out BMWs and Mercedes through Glassell Park. There was a direct line between those arrogant guys and members of the Avenues, who actually distributed the drugs on the street. But even with his awareness of the Mexican mafia, of the gangs, Oscar hadn't made the next step in his mind—connecting the everyday worry about the Avenues and the suppliers in fancy cars to the actual place where the pot was grown, the actual people. And wrapped up now in his surprise and fear there was also growing anger: anger at the trouble the dealers caused in his neighborhood; anger that he, by virtue of being Latino, could be seen by anyone as somehow connected to them.

He had worked so hard his whole life to disassociate himself from that element. And now he'd stumbled onto it, in the middle of nowhere. One thing was for sure—if he got out of this, he was never going to smoke again.

The woods and dark seemed endless and their progress was slow. Several times he was startled by a shape in the woods, a still, hulking presence that might have been a bear. Ever since A.J. had described the dead bears, Oscar had seen them in his mind, imagined the horror of running into the furry carcasses, or even worse, the marble-like bodies of the ones that had been skinned. They were long gone, he knew that logically; they'd been dumped off a cliff. But he still thought of them, and feared them, and was relieved each time when the shape he saw revealed itself to be a boulder or a fallen log. Finally they gained the top of the ridge, the place where the trails intersected. They lowered their packs, sat down, and exhaled. It was windier here so they put on their jackets and zipped them up to their chins. Ahead of them, the silhouette of the eastern mountain range. Above them, the quarter-moon, which seemed to shine more brightly than usual. By its light, Oscar could make out the others' faces.

"We can't go back the way we came," said Tracy. "A.J.'s brother is coming."

"José's people too," Gwen added.

"We don't know that," said Todd. "We don't know which way the Mexicans might be coming."

Oscar fought down his annoyance. Were the people coming for A.J. the Americans? The whites? "Should we just take this other trail?" he suggested. "The one we didn't take yesterday?"

And as he said this, it occurred to him how different everything would be if they *had* taken this trail yesterday; how their choice to take the other trail, made in good faith but with limited knowledge, had led to the death of one man and the abandonment of another; to all their confusion and terror.

"We should," Todd said. "We should stick to what we know. And without our maps, all we really know is that this trail goes to Lost Canyon and eventually loops around to our car."

"But the trail is the first place they'll look," Tracy said. "We should leave it and find another way."

"You really comfortable doing that without a map and compass?"

"We know generally where we're going."

"But wait," Gwen said. "If A.J. followed us, that means

he knows where our car is. What if they've done something to it? What if someone else is there?" She sounded slightly hysterical.

They all sat with this possibility for a moment.

Then Todd lifted the rifle. "Well, we do have these guns, if we need them."

"No, she's right," Tracy said. "We don't know what we might find." She was quiet, they were all quiet, and then she lifted a pole and lightly struck the ground. "I'll tell you what. I think we should forget the loop altogether. I think we should go cross-country and out the other side of the mountains." She pointed to the dark silent shapes in front of them. "That way, for sure we keep A.J.'s brother behind us. It shouldn't be more than a day or two's walk, and we'd come out into the Owens Valley."

"Really?" Oscar responded doubtfully. "That looks like a long way."

"We saw those mountains yesterday," Todd said, "and they look pretty big. How can we get over them?"

"There are a bunch of passes. I've been through a couple of them, coming in from the other side. I know the range looks big, but we can get over it, I promise. And once we do, it's just a few miles down."

"I don't know," Todd said, and kicked the dirt. "That's a lot of ground to cover."

"It is," Tracy replied, voice firmer now. "But it's doable. I know it."

"With as little food as we have? And no real sense of where we're going? Not all of us may be up for it, Tracy."

Gwen looked away; she must have realized that she was the weakest link. Oscar was silent, and Todd's uncertainty increased his own fear.

"We can handle it," Tracy said. "And we'll make do with the food. Besides, what choice do we have?"

She was right, and they all knew she was right; they needed to walk out. They had to walk away from A.J. and his brother and whoever might come for José; away from their car at the trailhead; away from who and what they had been.

"We should stay on the trail for a while yet," Todd said, "as long as it still follows this ridge."

Tracy nodded. "Sounds good. Let's do it."

"Hey, you guys, speaking of food, I need to eat something," Gwen said, and Oscar realized that he was hungry too. He hadn't noticed the growling in his stomach, the weakness in his limbs; his hunger had been obscured by exhaustion and fear.

"Why don't you eat an energy bar?" Tracy suggested. "All of us should do that. But we should keep going—we don't want to stay up here on top of this ridge. We'd be too easy of a target."

The night was loosening its grip on the sky. Oscar noticed color and definition now, the blue of Todd's pack, the red of Tracy's jacket. The sun was still well behind the mountains, but the sky was turning gray. As he watched, the first spots of pink touched the bottom of the clouds. It was almost dawn.

"She's right, we should keep moving," Todd said. "When we get some miles behind us and reach a less exposed spot, we can stop for a proper breakfast."

Oscar sensed Gwen's frustration, but she didn't protest. Instead, she bent over to unzip the lid of her pack and pulled out an energy bar. He did the same. Then they lifted on their packs and started to walk. They made their way along the level ridge, hiking fast, aware of how visible they'd become in the growing light. The clouds to the east were now a deep salmon. On their right they could see into the narrow canyon where they'd spent the afternoon and evening—not all the way down to the bottom, but far enough to make out a few of the granite ledges and out-croppings. Somewhere down there was José's body. They'd talked of burying it, or covering it, but decided they didn't have time, and Oscar, despite his anger at the kid, had felt bad about leaving him there. At least he'd be more easily found, he reasoned.

The trail bent right, then straightened out again, de-parting one ridge and following another before angling gently down a slope. Oscar breathed a sigh of relief when they dipped beneath the second ridge—no one could see them unless they were standing directly below. Eventually this trail would lead to Lost Canyon.

They were just starting to settle into a comfortable pace when there was a flurry of movement behind them. Gwen gasped and Oscar jumped and they all looked back, just in time to see a flash of white fur whip around the bend, a feathery waving tail.

"Jesus Christ!" Oscar exclaimed. "That scared the hell out of me!"

The dog jumped up on him—panting, smiling—then ran to greet Gwen, Todd, and Tracy. She play-bowed and gave her strange, muffled bark again, then bolted in a fast circle around them. She sashayed back over to Gwen, of-fering her backside, and when Gwen didn't immediately lean over to pet her, she flipped onto her back, twisting and grunting, tongue lolling out the side of her mouth.

Tracy glanced back down the trail. "Fuck, I wonder if A.J.'s behind her."

But there was no one. This was strange. A.J.'s dog, but no A.J. She'd disappeared by the time they'd finished tying him up. Where had she gone? And what did her presence mean now?

"I don't think he's with her," Todd said. "I think she just followed us."

"Well, that's a little weird, don't you think?" Oscar said.

"Not necessarily." Todd bent over and called the dog to him. She ran over, tail between her legs with just the very tip wiggling. She pressed the side of her face into his leg and swung herself around so that more of her body was touching him. Todd scratched her ears, ran his hand over her head, patted her on the side. She looked up at him adoringly, tongue hanging out in bliss.

"She's not bonded to him. If she were, there's no way she would have let us handle him like we did. Makes sense—he's only had her for a few weeks, right? And he wasn't exactly treating her nicely."

He bent over and the dog jumped up to lick him, so quick and hard that she jabbed him in the face. He pulled up, spitting, laughing. She scooted close to him again, then burst away and ran another loop, moving in quick, jerky motions.

"She's a little crazy, huh?" Tracy commented.

"She's a border collie," Todd said. "It's part of the job description. Plus, I think she's still a pup. She's probably not more than ten or twelve months old."

"Well, what do we do with her?" Oscar asked. Sure, she was cute, but this was no time to be worried about lost dogs. They needed to get moving again, and fast.

"We don't need to do anything. We can see if she follows us."

"I don't think that's a good idea," Tracy said. "What if she runs back and leads A.J. to where we are? Or someone else, for that matter. She might not be attached to A.J.—but who's to say she's not attached to his brother? She could give away our location just by barking."

"Her vocal cords have been cut," Todd said. "That's why she doesn't have a voice."

"Why would anyone do that?" Gwen asked, disgusted.

Todd shrugged. "I guess A.J. didn't like the barking." He sighed. "Look, let's let her come along. If she stays with us, she won't be able to help anyone else."

They were all quiet for a moment, considering this.

"She'll have to eat," Tracy said now, breaking the silence. "And we're short of food already. I don't know, Todd. I'd rather just leave her here. Tie her to a tree."

"That didn't work the first time. And if someone finds her, then they'll *really* know we were here."

The dog was sitting between them now, looking at them earnestly, as if she knew they were discussing her fate. Her ears were standing straight up on her head, tips falling over slightly. Each time someone spoke, one ear swiveled in that person's direction. Gwen bent to pet her but when she raised her arm, the dog fell to her side and cowered.

"It's okay," Gwen reassured her. "I'm not going to hurt you." She knelt and petted the dog, who pressed her head against Gwen's hand and touched her with her paw. "We can't leave her." Gwen looked up at all of them, and then back down at the dog, and for the first time in what seemed like days, she smiled.

Oscar watched this, unsure what to think. There were so many stray dogs running through Glassell Park that he'd hardened his heart against them. A couple of his neighbors were always picking them up and taking them to the animal shelter, but he just tried to avoid them, especially when he had Lily. He'd taught her never to approach a loose dog, and had cursed the irresponsible people who didn't secure their yards, or who abandoned dogs up in the hills. His vote would have been to leave this dog behind.

"Look," Todd said, "she didn't do anything to protect A.J. last night, and she just ran miles in the dark to catch up with us. I think it's pretty clear she wants to be with us. Let's just keep going. I think it's going to be okay."

"Whatever," Oscar said, sick of talking about it. "While we're stopped, though, should we figure out where we're going? We seem to be veering right again. When should we start to cut across?"

They all looked around to get their bearings. They couldn't see the big range anymore, since it was hidden behind the ridge, but from where they stood, it would now be to the left.

"The sun's rising from that way," Gwen noted, pointing back up to the top of the ridge.

"If that's east," Todd said, "then that's where we should go."

They were only about a hundred vertical feet from the top, and the slope did not look steep.

"I think we can just head up this way," Oscar said, "instead of backtracking to where the trail left the top."

"All right, let's go," Tracy said. She stepped off the trail, and the others all followed. They fanned out and climbed up in a parallel line. Even though the slope was gentle, the ground wasn't solid; the small pebbles and dirt gave way beneath their feet, and the others used their poles to steady themselves. With each step forward Oscar lost half a step; the effect was like going up a down escalator. The dog ran up the slope in short energetic bursts; she reached the top quickly and then came back down again, sliding, dislodging rocks and dirt, but excited, encouraging them forward. Once, twice, Oscar slipped and reached out with one hand to stabilize himself. The rocks felt cool to his touch.

It took about ten minutes to reach the top, and when he did, Tracy and Todd were already there. Gwen arrived a couple of minutes after Oscar, and they all bent over, catching their breath, while the dog weaved through them, jumping up to give them whiskery kisses.

"That was harder than it looked," Gwen said.

"*Everything* has been hard out here," Oscar replied. Then he looked up. The big range they'd seen earlier was straight in front of them now. The sun was just coming over it, sharpening its lines against the sky. In the growing light they could see a valley, a big, winding chute they'd have to make their way through, with broad green meadows and still blue lakes, and stretches of woods between them. The jagged peaks to the east cast long shadows across the landscape and sent concentrated rays of light toward the ground. All of this was framed by more peaks on either side of the valley, which Oscar saw, as the sky lightened, were capped with snow. The sight was breathtaking. And even as he knew they had to get through the valley and over the mountains, his heart rose in his chest. This was the High Sierra, rugged and pristine. This was really something.

"Wow," Gwen said.

"Wow is right," Oscar said. "Where *are* we?"

"Somewhere in the wilderness," Tracy said. "Exactly where, I don't know."

"That's a hell of a lot of land to get across," Todd said. "How far did you say it was, Tracy?"

"Well, we just need to get through the valley and over that range. We should be able to do it in a day."

"*You* might be able to," said Gwen. "Tracy, that's really far. And I don't know about you guys, but I'm exhausted."

"All right, maybe a day and a half, maybe two," Tracy allowed. "But that's it, that range is what we have to cross. And the Owens Valley is right on the other side."

"You make it sound easy," Oscar said. "But those peaks are pretty big. And there's snow."

"I'm telling you guys, we can get over them. There are a bunch of passes, and it shouldn't be hard to find a way across."

Todd was holding his poles in one hand, resting the rifle on the ground with the other. Oscar turned to him now, putting aside his annoyance because Todd's evenness, his calm, gave him comfort. "What do you think, Todd?"

He was quiet for a moment before he answered. "I've been trying to pick out a route. One that also provides some cover. I think we head down this way." Todd pointed toward the left. "Hug the canyon wall and get down to those woods. Once we're in them, no one can see us. We can hike through those and then toward that meadow, where there are some boulders to hide behind if we need to. There are a couple of lakes for water, which is good. And once we get down, we'll have a better sense of what route to take over that range. It seems like there's a bit of a saddle there, between those peaks to the left. That actually looks pretty passable, and there's not much snow. Provided we can find a way up to it."

This sounded good to Oscar—thought out and logical. Gwen turned to Tracy and asked, "What do you think?"

"It's as good a plan as any," she answered, shrugging.

"It's the only plan we've got," Oscar said. He hoped that Tracy wouldn't try to argue, and she didn't. They all looked at each other, as if psyching each other up.

"Well, here goes nothing," Todd said. And then he slung the rifle back over his shoulder and put his hands through the straps of his poles.

Oscar watched him go over the edge. Then, with a deep breath and quick silent prayer, he took his first step onto uncharted earth.

Chapter Twelve
Todd

They sidestepped down the slope, carefully at first, but then with bigger strides, using the natural steps formed by the slabs of rock. Above them the sky had turned a silvery blue. The peaks on either side of the valley were lit with brilliant light. Even in his state of exhaustion and worry, Todd couldn't help but notice the beauty.

It took more than an hour to reach the first stand of trees, and once they were safely under its cover, they stopped and put down their packs. After carefully leaning the rifle against a boulder, Todd took off his shoes and shook out some pebbles. His toes looked and felt like they'd been pounded by a meat cleaver. His calf stung where he'd been scratched by a branch. Gwen sat down against a tree, crossed her arms on her knees, and rested her head against them. The dog came over and licked her hand and Gwen petted her without glancing up.

Tracy, still standing, tilted her head back and finished off what was left in her Nalgene bottle. "We're going to need water."

"Yeah, I'm almost out too," Oscar said.

"There's a couple of lakes farther on," Todd said. "We can refill there. Or maybe we'll cross a stream before then."

"Let's stay here for a minute." This was from Gwen, who still hadn't lifted her head.

They all looked at her. "We need to keep moving," Todd said.

"I need to rest, you guys." And now she looked up. The early-morning light revealed how tired she was—deep hollows had formed beneath her eyes, her skin looked gray, and wisps of hair had come loose from her ponytail. "We haven't slept since the night before last, and haven't had a meal since lunchtime yesterday. I'm exhausted, and I need to eat."

Todd leaned toward her. Of all of them, she was the least suited for this trip to begin with, let alone for what they had to do now. And she'd seemed even more shaken than the rest of them by their encounters with José and A.J. But he couldn't let himself think about that now. They had many miles to go, a formidable range to cross. He wasn't entirely sure she'd be able to make it. "Gwen, look, we're all tired. But we can't stop yet. We may have someone behind us, we may have *two* guys behind us. And we need to open up some distance between us and them. If we wait, we'll be an easy target for someone with a high-powered rifle. But if we get going, we'll have a better chance. Once we get farther into the valley, we can stop for a rest."

Gwen did not acknowledge his words; she stared straight ahead as if no one had spoken.

"He's right, Gwen," Tracy said gently. "We need to keep going. Let's do this next stretch and then we can stop to rest. Okay?"

Todd was anxious to get moving—not only out of fear, but also because, although he wouldn't admit it, he knew exactly how Gwen felt. Now that he was sitting and had his shoes off, he couldn't imagine getting up again. His muscles were all tightening up; his left knee had gotten sore. He felt the lure of sleep; it was like the pull of the abyss, deadly, irresistible. He fought this and said, "We can do this, Gwen. We can go a little farther."

Gwen still did not speak. The dog, who'd been sitting beside her, gave her a sly kiss on the leg. "All right," she said finally. "But just give me a minute to deal with my feet." She quickly took off one shoe, revealing a swollen heel and big toe, cut and applied some Moleskin. She re-tied the shoe and stood back up. Todd put his socks and shoes on too.

"Good job, Gwen," Tracy said. She stripped off her jacket and stuffed it into her pack. Then she walked off in the direction they'd been heading, and the others fell in behind her.

They marched on without talking. The ground was nearly level; they were moving through the bottom of the valley. A bright blue Steller's jay shot through a cluster of trees, turning sideways and touching each trunk lightly with its feet, like a skier running a slalom course. They passed a tree with a giant mushroom growing out of its side, like a white, fleshy ear turned downward to hear messages from the ground. Then Todd stopped to point out a clump of coarse black hair, stuck on the side of a tree.

"Look," he said. "A bear used this tree to scratch his back."

Oscar squinted at the hair, and shivered. "Wow, he must have been a big one."

"Is there any other kind?" Gwen said. "Let's keep going."

They kept walking, a bit faster, and then suddenly they were out of the woods. It was lighter now, almost seven a.m. The peaks on either side of them were lit orange and gold in the early-morning sun. They were flanked by huge boulder fields, amazingly white, like giant snowballs that had rolled downhill. Beyond them, at the end of the valley, massive spires and sharp pinnacles with sheets of snow draped between them extended thousands of feet into the sky. Todd's heart lifted, despite everything. He'd never seen such grandeur. He looked again at the corridor between the turrets and pinnacles, which framed the valley all the way to its end. It was like strolling down an avenue lined with cathedrals. It was like walking into the arms of God.

Directly in front of them was a basin they had seen from the top. But what, from that vantage point, had looked like a small break in the trees now revealed itself to be a bigger open space. It was probably a mile across, maybe more—the land was uneven, patches of green and brown interspersed with slabs of granite. In the middle of it all was the lake. A small stream fed into it and then flowed out the other side. This in turn, Todd knew, would eventually lead to other water, one of the countless rivers that rose up in California and flowed all the way to the sea.

"Well, there's our water," he said.

"Yeah, good," Gwen said. "But look at those mountains."

Now Todd looked up ahead of them and saw why Gwen was worried. He'd been so focused on the beauty around him that he hadn't thought about what awaited when they got to the valley's end. From the ridge, the peaks to the east had looked formidable but distant. From here, he could see the full scope of them. The range they had to cross was massive, a jagged spine of sharp barren peaks, easily over 13,000 feet. But he was still overcome by a sense of awe, and a sudden understanding of the land. The western Sierra built gradually, with gentle foothills and lush valleys and hospitable forests. Now they were approaching the starker eastern Sierra, where one plate of the earth had pushed under another and thrust the mountains into the sky.

"How are we supposed to get over those?" Oscar asked, sounding disheartened.

"We can totally do it," Tracy insisted.

Oscar looked uncertain, even angry. "I don't know, Tracy. I think we're in deep shit."

"We can do it," Todd agreed. He was examining the peaks closely. "There's that shoulder I saw before, between the two peaks. It looks lower than the rest of the range." He paused. "There's a pass way to the right too, but that looks farther away. I'm thinking left. That's probably our best bet."

But from the valley floor this seemed very high, and terribly far away. Todd's confidence snagged, began to falter—but he fought this and looked squarely at the others. "Let's go," he said. "We need to keep moving."

He expected some protest from Tracy, but she said, "Sounds good. Let's do it." Then: "But I'm thinking you should ditch your jacket, Gwen."

Gwen turned to her. "Why?" She looked down at her fleece, which was fuschia. "Oh."

"Do you want mine?" Todd asked.

"No thanks. Hopefully my shirt will be enough."

They stepped away from the cover of trees and out into the open, and Todd flinched involuntarily, expecting a shot. Nothing came. They picked their way over the soft springy earth, passing boulders as big as trucks. With each step they could see more of the slope they'd descended that morning; it was bathed in brilliant light. There was no movement, and Todd was relieved.

"It doesn't look like anyone's up there," Gwen said, as if reading his mind.

They all paused and looked back. "You're right," Tracy said. "Well, let's keep moving before someone is."

They walked on, the dog darting in front of them, charging up boulders to survey the land, sprinting ahead of them and then coming back. Her nose took in all of the interesting scents; she scratched the ground gingerly and peed on whatever she found. Finally she ran ahead and kept on running, disappearing over a rise. When they gained it, they saw where she was: at the edge of the first lake they'd seen from above, looking back at them, as if to say, *Here it is!* She tried to announce it but again the weird muffled bark; her mouth moved but they heard no sound. Awful as her muteness was, Todd was glad for it now—a bark here could be heard for miles around.

They scrambled down a clump of boulders and onto the flat land around the shore. As they filled up their bottles, they realized they'd left their water purifier behind.

"We'll need to boil the water," Todd said.

"It'll be fine," Tracy countered. "It looks totally untouched back here. Besides, what do you think the explorers did back in the 1860s? Or the Indians? You think they all had filters or SteriPENs?"

"This isn't 1860. There's a lot more people in these mountains. Plus, there's all the animals."

"Okay, but do you really want to take the time to set up the stove?"

Todd saw the logic in this. No point in worrying about bacteria if they were going to get shot trying to boil it away. "You're right," he said, and drank from his bottle. The water was so refreshing it brought tears to his eyes. He drank an entire thirty-two-ounce bottle, refilled it, and this time sipped more slowly. It was warmer today, and humid. The air was thinner too, and he understood that his slight light-headedness was not only exhaustion, but lack of oxygen. He noticed how pretty the lake was, crystalline blue, with the huge peaks set behind it. If they were still on vacation, if they were here to relax, they would have stopped at a place like this, swam and rested and enjoyed a leisurely meal, stretched out on the rocks in the sun.

But within five minutes they were moving again, around the lake's shore to the left. The sun was high enough now that it was glinting off the water. Something broke the surface and gained the air, splashing down again: a fish. How good it would be to catch it and cook it, he thought. His stomach rumbled with hunger.

On the other side of the lake they climbed up onto another flat area. More peaks were starting to come out of the shadows and reveal themselves, like stage actors stepping into the light. Now they could see the lush green of the land, of the small meadow they were approaching. Springing from the green were wildflowers, purple and yellow and red, in shades so full and pure it was as if the rest of the world's color was muted. He saw a cluster of lupine, not fully in bloom, each tubelike flower bright purple on top but still green at the bottom; they looked like caterpillars emerging from their cocoons. He shook his head at the strangeness of it all. This was a kind of beauty that few people ever saw. And at any moment he could be shot, he could be dead.

"What's that?" Gwen asked suddenly, pointing to the ground with her pole.

Todd looked down at a huge pile of scat, dark brown and loose, as big as a pile of pine cones. Interspersed in it were bits of grass, and red berries, which seemed to have passed through the creature whole. "That," he said, "would be bear scat."

Tracy nodded. "We're not the only ones who needed water."

The muscles in Gwen's jaws tightened, and even Todd felt a twinge of nerves. The bear hair on the tree could have been left at any time. This scat, though, suggested a bear was still close by. He glanced over at Tracy to make sure the bear spray was still clipped to her belt.

"How recent?" Gwen asked.

Tracy bent over and examined it. "It's not super fresh, but it's not old, either. I'd say it's from within the last twelve hours."

"Don't worry," Todd said, sounding more confident than he felt. "He's likely to avoid us. We're scarier to him than he is to us."

"I don't know, man," said Oscar. "You guys keep saying that, but there were those killings just this year, in Yellowstone."

"Those were grizzly bears," Todd said, echoing Tracy's reassurance of earlier. "Not black bears. We don't have grizzlies in California."

"And if they do come around," Tracy added, patting the gun tucked into her belt, "we can always take care of them."

"There's no need for that," Todd said. Why did she have to be like this? He was so angry at Tracy, and at himself, for allowing her to convince them to take an unused trail. For letting himself get carried away by someone else's madness. "Besides, we don't need to be shooting any guns. That'll lead whoever's out here straight to us."

"I'm just saying."

"Let's not even joke about it."

"Well, at least we have bear spray."

The dog, who'd still been running ahead, now came back. She approached the pile of scat and sniffed it curiously. Then she looked up at them, tail and ears lowered.

"See," Gwen said, "even *she* knows to be afraid."

But then the dog took off again, shooting ahead of them. "Let's follow her lead and get going," Todd said.

They continued through the valley, the full sun now in their faces, the air feeling thick and uncomfortable. Every few minutes Todd looked back at the slope behind them, which seemed farther and farther away. No sign of life.

They reached a second stand of woods, near the end of the valley; it felt wonderful to be out of the sun. They walked on until they reached a small clearing. Three huge boulders made up the edges on the near and left sides. Even if someone approached from the way they'd come, he could walk up to the boulders and not know they were there.

"This is a good spot to take a break." Todd stopped near a tree that had grown around a rock; it looked like a tired old woman who'd sat down to rest.

"These are amazing," Gwen said, looking up at the top of the largest boulder. It was as tall as a two-story house. "How the hell did they get here?"

"Glaciers," Todd replied. "They're called erratics. They got carried down on a floe of ice."

"Like a bottle carried by the tide."

"Exactly."

They set down their packs, wandered off to relieve themselves, came back, and collapsed by the boulders. Tracy set up the stove and boiled water. The others had oatmeal but Todd needed something more substantial, so he ate a freeze-dried dinner. He'd started to get shaky from exhaustion and hunger; he'd never realized so clearly the relationship between food and the use of physical energy.

"That was delicious," Oscar said, finishing up.

"I'm glad." Tracy rattled her spoon in her bowl. "Because that's the end of the oatmeal. Except for the one that Todd didn't eat."

"*What*?" Oscar said.

"We're going to be out by tonight, so I only brought one for each of us."

"Well, what else do we have left?" Gwen asked.

"Whatever you have left. You all have at least one freeze-dried dinner, right? And whatever snacks you brought."

A somberness descended on all of them.

"I'm pretty much out of snacks," said Oscar. "I think I have half an energy bar."

"I just ate my last dinner," Todd said.

"You can share mine if you want," Gwen offered. "I have that and some Luna Bars."

"I have some jerky and my dinner. And a couple of bars." Tracy paused. "Look, we'll be fine. We'll be over that range tonight, tomorrow morning at the latest. As long as we've got water, we can make it a day without food."

Oscar didn't look convinced. Gwen either. Todd knew that Tracy was right, but he was still annoyed—they should have talked about this before they left their stuff. But right now, he was too tired to think about their food supply and how much farther they had to go. He had eaten a real meal for the first time in twenty hours, and the heaviness of sleep was upon him.

"Why don't we rest here for a bit," he suggested.

"Great idea," Gwen agreed.

"I think we should keep going," Tracy said. "We have momentum now."

"Tracy," Gwen said deliberately, "I know we're in a hurry. I get it. But I'm so tired I can barely walk straight. We have a big uphill climb coming, and if I don't get some rest, I'm never going to be able to do it." She petted the dog absentmindedly; even the dog seemed to agree. She was spread out on her side, feet twitching, fast asleep.

"She's right," Todd said. "Let's everyone recover a bit. Take a nap, you guys. Oscar, can you set your alarm? We'll leave again in an hour."

"Sure," Oscar said, looking relieved. He fiddled with his watch.

Tracy shrugged, but relented. "All right."

Todd set the rifle down within arm's reach. It was only a .22 caliber, and pretty old at that—but at least it would provide a measure of protection. He lay down where he was, using his pack as a pillow and the lid of his cap to shade his eyes. Now that they weren't moving the air was cool, and the breeze felt good on his face. A few small rocks pressed into his back, but he was too exhausted to care. Almost as soon as his eyes were closed, he fell asleep.

Chapter Thirteen
Gwen

A cold, wet nose against her jawbone, a whiskery muzzle, a warm tongue licking her skin. Gwen yelled, "Hey!" and pushed the dog from her, but when Timber saw that Gwen was awake, she rushed in again, grunting happily. For a moment Gwen forgot why she was there— and then she remembered everything. Their hike, the wrong turn, José, and then A.J.; the confused and hurried nighttime hiking. She looked at her watch: 1:17. Shit! They had stopped at nine thirty, had laid down around ten, and were supposed to rest for an hour. What happened?

"Hey, you guys!" she called out, struggling to get up through her soreness. "Hey! We slept too long! We need to get going!"

Behind her Tracy stirred. Gwen shook Oscar by the shoulder, and then Todd. The dog trailed after her, licking everyone's faces, pawing at arms and shoulders.

Oscar and Todd sat up groggily; Tracy was already on her feet.

"Jesus Christ!" Todd exclaimed. "What happened? How'd we sleep so long?"

Oscar was fiddling with his watch. "I think I set the alarm wrong. I set it for eleven *p.m.*, not a.m."

Todd's face flushed. He got to his feet and took a few pacing steps. "Goddamnit, Oscar."

Gwen was angry too. How *could* he have? How could he have messed up such an obvious thing?

"I'm sorry, you guys," Oscar said. "I fucked up."

"You fucked up, all right," said Todd, whirling around. "We lost two hours. We gave them two more hours to catch up with us, and now . . ." He looked at his watch. "Now we're smack in the middle of the day, when anyone can see us."

Oscar fiddled with the zippers of his pack and didn't reply.

"Look, there's no use making a stink about it," Tracy said calmly. She had her pack on already. "All we can do is just go, all right?"

"I'm really sorry, guys," Oscar said again. Then absently, "I can't find my damned Clif Bar."

"I'm missing mine too," said Tracy. "One of you hungry people steal it while I was sleeping?"

"No," Gwen said. And then she saw two torn-up wrappers just outside their circle, with several visible tooth marks.

As if on cue, Timber came over and licked her. This time Gwen noticed the hint of peanut butter on her breath.

"The friggin' dog went right into my pack and took it," Tracy said.

"Goddamn," Oscar said.

"A.J. did say she was a scavenger," Todd remarked.

"I know, but shit, that was the only one I had."

"It's all right," Gwen said. "You can have some of my stuff."

"Plus, we'll be out of here soon," Tracy added.

Gwen hoped so, because despite her offer to Oscar, she was worried about their lack of food. Already she'd felt light-headed and wobbly-legged—and it looked like the hardest part of their hike was yet to come. But she couldn't worry about that right now.

Within five minutes they were hiking again. They didn't speak; they were sober and scared. And yet Gwen, despite her stiffness and to her surprise, was actually feeling better. She'd needed the sleep, and she felt replenished. The Moleskin made the pain in her feet bearable, and her knee was holding up. Her body had grown accustomed to hiking; it moved more easily through space and discomfort. And while she wished they had more food, she couldn't really begrudge the dog for raiding their supply; she'd been glad when Timber had caught up with them on the trail. She liked having something sweet and alive to keep her company. The dog's energy and joy were helping push her along.

In another ten minutes they'd reached the edge of the woods and they stepped into the open again. They were near the end of the valley, at the foot of the range they'd first seen yesterday, with a steep, exposed climb ahead. And yet Gwen felt good, almost exhilarated, that they had gotten this far. The climb would be a challenge, she knew—and it was hotter today, and the altitude was making it hard to breathe. But it was the final challenge. Once they reached the pass, it was just a long walk down to the Owens Valley. They wouldn't be back in civilization, not quite yet. But they'd be able to see it was there.

"I think we go up along the right," Tracy said, and they all looked to where she was pointing. It did seem to be less steep in that direction, and it was possible to imagine a route.

"Where's the pass, though?" Todd asked. This close to

the range, they could no longer take in the whole of it. The gaps that had seemed so obvious from farther back were now obscured.

"To the left of us, the one you saw before. I think it's beyond that little peak there, right past that darker outcropping." Tracy pointed. "I noticed it while we were at the lake. I was looking for a landmark we could see from here."

Todd nodded. "So we bear right, and then cut back to the left."

"That's what I'm thinking."

"That looks like a lot of loose rock," Oscar said. "Are you sure we can make it up that way without sliding?"

No one answered for a moment, and Gwen realized that Todd and Tracy were so irritated with him that they were ignoring him altogether. But now Tracy turned to him, with a show of patience. "No, I'm not. But I *am* sure that if we go up more directly, we'll run into vertical rock. So I'll take my chances."

They began to hike—Tracy first, Oscar behind her, followed by Gwen, with Todd bringing up the rear. They walked over hard-packed earth, granite, and pockets of mossy growth, sometimes pulling themselves up on slabs of rock that were too big to gain in one step. There were two, three tiny streams of snow melt trickling down. The peaks were offering water from their snowcaps to the lower elevations, feeding the rivers and lakes. In some of the green pockets a few wildflowers grew, hearty clusters of maroon, clumps of purple and blue, the orange and yellow candy-looking plant she'd seen two days before, that Todd had identified as columbine. There were rock shelves with bursts of bright pink flowers growing out of every crag. But she couldn't really enjoy this beauty, could only acknowledge it distantly; she was becoming too aware of the opposite ridge and the valley behind them and the chance that someone was there. When she looked back, though, she saw nothing, just empty sloping land, starting to darken in shadow as the sun moved west.

She had no idea how long they hiked, so skewed was her sense of time. Then the last of the ground cover gave way and they were in a higher, open landscape—rock and scree, just as Oscar had noticed. The slope was dotted with windblown trees, cinnamon-barked and sturdy, swirled into shapes that made them look alive, like trees from a fairy tale. But even these would disappear as they moved farther up. The top of the range was a monolith of brown and gray, stark and barren as the moon. They could make out the jagged tops of the peaks here, and they looked sharp enough to cut.

It was getting harder to hike, harder to cope with the heat, harder to put her feet down without them sliding out from under her. She chose larger rocks that looked more stable but each step was an effort; she felt her calves and thighs begin to quiver. Two, three times she slipped and used her poles to catch herself. Once something scurried between the rocks—a furry brown animal the size of a terrier. Gwen gasped.

"Marmot," Todd explained. "Nothing to worry about."

"We've been going an hour," Tracy called over her shoulder. "And we're making good progress. I think we can reach the pass before dark."

No one answered, and Gwen realized that the others, like her, were struggling just to breathe. They weren't on any trail here; they were picking their way up through steep, uneven rock. They must have been at an elevation of ten or eleven thousand feet by now—Gwen breathed fast and hard but she couldn't get enough air in her lungs. She wondered if the others felt the same. They kept trudging, climbing, sweat streaming down their bodies as they labored upward in the afternoon sun. Blisters had started to form on her hands from the friction of the poles. The reflection of the light off the granite was so intense that she couldn't look at the peaks directly, not even with her sunglasses on.

A cloud moved over and they were suddenly in shadow. The sun emerged again, and then another cloud, followed by a gust of wind.

"That feels good," Gwen said aloud.

"Yes, finally," Todd said. "Some shade."

Then they heard a rumble of thunder.

"Uh-oh," said Oscar, and they all stopped to look. Dark clouds were coming in over the peaks. They were approaching fast. In another few minutes the bottoms of the clouds were visible, perfectly flat and very dark. There was a sudden flash, as if a lightbulb had been lit inside a cloud. No sound for several seconds. And then it came—a deep rumble that started on the other side of the mountains and came toward them like a giant, charging beast. In front of them, the dog lifted her head and gave a mute bark. The hair on her scruff stood up straight.

"We've got to move quick," Tracy said, "before it reaches us."

"We can't outrun it," said Todd. "It's going to be here any minute."

"What do we do?" Gwen asked, trying not to sound panicked. Before the trip, she'd worried about lightning as much as she'd thought about bears. She had convinced herself the fear was irrational.

"Well, we can't stay here," Tracy said. "We could try to go back down to tree cover."

Todd shook his head. "No. We'll never make it down in time."

"We need to get near some boulders then, not be the highest thing."

"Nothing here is really big enough."

"So what should we do?" Gwen asked again, and in the time before anyone answered, there was another burst of light, an actual bolt this time, nearly sideways, still contained by the cloud. As if the lightning were a new life trying to break from its shell, cracking the surface open from within. Then a few seconds later, a crash of thunder.

"We need to get up to that clump of trees!" Todd shouted. He was pointing toward a small stand of windblown pines. It still looked far away. The dog circled back and tried to press herself against him, tail between her legs.

"Are you supposed to be near trees in a lightning storm?" Oscar asked.

"Not a single tree. But a group of them is good."

Gwen glanced over to the opposite range, which was still in the sun, even as the sky to the east grew dark. The clouds were building on each other, layer after layer, like an avalanche tumbling uphill. They now crossed over the top of the range, rain falling in wavering sheets. Gwen couldn't believe how exposed they were, how helpless. They might have been pioneers, it might have been 1850, for all the defense they had against the elements.

"Let's get moving," Tracy urged. Another bolt of lightning, followed by thunder, which opened into itself, each crack fuller and deeper and louder than the last. The dog barked and did a panicked little dance around them.

They had switchbacked left in the direction of the trees, and now they attacked the slope at an angle. The wind picked up, howling as it swept through the canyon. It sounded like a living thing. Gwen tried not to look to her right at the approaching storm, but she couldn't help it. In front of them a lone bird took off from the ground and was swept sideways and away, like a leaf.

A bright flash lit the entire sky, followed by thunder so loud Gwen thought the earth had cracked open. The sound traveled down into the valley, rolled and rumbled between the walls, turned a corner, and continued to rage. The echoes then joined with the original sound and thundered all over again.

"Let's get a move on!" Tracy shouted, and she started to run, slipping with every third or fourth step.

The clouds swirled, black and gray, and now the last of the sun was blotted out. The sky was dark as night. This is not just seeing a thunderstorm, Gwen thought. This is coming face-to-face with one. This is entering the place where storms are made.

"We're almost there!" Tracy yelled over the wind. The stand was maybe a hundred feet away. Then the sky went even darker and the storm was upon them.

Rain, harder and colder than any Gwen had ever known, soaked her to the skin. The wind blew her hair into her face; the straps of her pack whipped and hit her. Gwen cursed herself for leaving her rain gear behind. But then the sky went white again, blinding, followed by a crack of thunder so violent she felt her feet take leave of the ground.

They reached the trees and Todd yelled, "Throw your poles and your pack away from you! Crouch down on the ground! Put your hands behind your neck! And spread out!"

Gwen moved in frightened disbelief. Spread out? Leave the others when she wanted to huddle with them? But everyone else was moving, and so she did too, dropping her poles and her pack, scrambling twenty feet downhill, crouching between several trees and covering her head. The dog burrowed into the space between her legs and arms. Gwen had thought the trees would make her feel safer, but they were scrubby and small, and they whipped and tossed so violently she thought the wind might pull their roots from the ground. No matter what Todd said, she would have felt better under a wide-trunked pine.

"Don't move, you guys!" Todd shouted. "Just stay like that! Hold tight!"

Another crack of thunder, then two quick flashes, followed by a deep, slow rumble, as if the gods had taken hold of the peaks and were shaking them. The ground trembled beneath Gwen's feet and she started to pray, eyes closed, heart in her throat, choked with terror. She could hear Oscar praying too, pleading to see his family. She had never felt so powerless, so small. Up the slope, Tracy was letting loose a curse with every new flash of light. "Mother *fucker*!" she yelled after an especially close strike. "Move *on*, you fucking fuck!"

Gwen was shivering, and she felt the rain pelting her arms and head. The dog cried and trembled beneath her. Then the hair stood up on the back of her neck. There was an audible buzz in the air, electricity crackling around them.

"Strike coming!" Todd yelled, and then a light so bright and vivid that Gwen thought it was the end of the world. She heard screams, male and female, and knew that one of them was her own. The earth rocked and bucked as if from an earthquake. Then a sharp crack unlike the earlier sounds, the sound of wood giving, a crash of impact. Slowly Gwen opened her eyes. She felt herself uncertainly—arms, legs, head. She wasn't hit. She looked at the dog, who peered up at her, mute with terror. She raised her head, against instructions, and found the others looking up too. A hundred feet away, there was a tree with a gash in its middle, the top half broken off, fire burning at the spot where the lightning had hit.

"Holy shit!" Tracy shouted, exhilarated.

"Keep your head down!" yelled Todd.

"Did you fucking see that?"

"Yes! Shut up and stay down!"

But that strike was the worst of it. The next few flashes were close but not directly upon them. Ten minutes later the heart of the storm had passed over them. Twenty minutes after that the rain had stopped. Now it fell on the lake where they'd refilled their water; Gwen saw the drops hit the mottled surface and then fall more gently, creating circles that expanded into each other. They watched the storm's progress as it moved across the valley and over the opposite range—the dark clouds, the diminishing flashes of light. By now the rain had doused the fire in the tree, leaving a fresh black simmering scar and the scent of burned wood.

"You all okay?" Tracy called out as they stood up stiffly, shaking their limbs, taking account of themselves.

"That was fucking close," Oscar said. "Jesus Christ."

"Yeah, seriously," said Todd. "We were lucky."

"I've never experienced anything like that," Oscar laughed. "I almost pissed my pants!"

"I've been in thunderstorms before, but this was something else." The dog ran over to Todd and shoved her head between his legs. He bent over and stroked her back.

"Is everyone okay?" Tracy asked again.

They all nodded. Gwen was still too shaken up to speak.

"That was amazing!" Tracy said, grinning.

Gwen looked at her, too tired to respond. Really, Tracy? she thought. She walked off without speaking, making her way back to where they'd discarded their things. She picked up her pack and poles, and brought them back to where the others stood. Tracy had recovered her pack too, and now she set up her stove behind a tree whose trunk and branches were folded in on themselves like a person in some elaborate yoga pose.

Todd pulled out his flask and unscrewed the top. "This'll help us with the cold. And also with the shakes."

They stayed for twenty minutes behind the shelter of trees, warming their bellies with tea and whiskey, reassuring the dog, standing around the concentrated heat coming from the stove, trying to dry their clothes. The storm was completely over the far ridge now, and the sky above them was clear and blue. The plants and trees in the canyon all looked fresh and new, the rocks were polished clean.

"We better get moving, guys," Gwen said. "If I stay here much longer, I may not be able to get up again."

Tracy packed the stove, and they all looked up toward the top of the range. From where they stood, they could make out a small gap between the peaks, half-covered with a field of snow.

"How long do you think it'll take to get up there?" Gwen asked. She'd learned that she couldn't really judge the time it took to cover any distance. Ground she'd thought would take a long time they'd covered quickly; other spots that seemed close had taken hours to reach.

Todd squinted toward the top. In the poststorm light, Gwen noticed his sandy gray stubble, the scruffy hair beneath his ball cap. He looked like a lion who was just past his prime, weather-worn and tired, but still strong.

"Might be two more hours," he said. "It looks like a couple of miles, if we head left and then traverse. But there's no telling what the going is like."

"Looks shorter to me," Tracy said. "And there may be places we can scramble straight up."

"It'll take what it takes," Gwen said, surprising herself. She was sick of this conjecture. Even though she'd asked the question, she now realized she didn't care about the answer. What did it matter if it was two miles or twenty? They needed to get over the damned pass, was all. They needed to get out of these mountains.

They started up the slope in the same order as before, with the dog again leading the way. Gwen's clothes were wet and clammy, which was bearable in the sun, but each breeze sent a shiver through her and made her worry for the coming of night. She pulled the bottom of her shirt away from her body to help things dry; she tried to ignore the wet squishing in her shoes. But it felt good to be moving again, planting one foot in front of the other, inching toward the pass, toward safety. She felt her legs getting stronger with every step. She felt her lungs expand and take the oxygen they needed from the air.

Soon they were above the tree line, the only plants the

hearty, close-to-the-ground wildflowers that might have been here since the birth of the range. Above them the spires loomed sharp and foreboding, and it scared Gwen to look at them, so she looked instead to the west. They could see the whole valley they'd walked through, shadows starting to engulf the far end.

They walked fifteen minutes, twenty, moving steadily up the slope, their clothes finally beginning to dry. They were hiking about fifteen feet apart now, not speaking, each lost in his or her own thoughts. When I get home, Gwen told herself, I'm going to take a long, hot shower and fall asleep in my bed. She couldn't wait to get back to the ordinary, to the habits of everyday life. She imagined, with an eagerness that startled her, going back to work and seeing the kids.

Suddenly Oscar's shoulder jerked forward and he fell to the ground. He hit with a thud and cried out in pain.

"Oscar! Are you okay?" Gwen yelled, snapping out of her reverie. He must have lost his footing or sprained an ankle.

Then she heard the report. She stared at Tracy blankly as she registered what this meant; instinctively she dropped to the ground just as something whizzed past her head and another gunshot echoed through the canyon.

Someone was upon her and she realized it was Todd; he pushed her down and covered her with his body.

"Keep your head down!" Tracy yelled, and they did, and then the three of them crawled over to Oscar. He was on his left side, facing upslope, hand holding his right shoulder, curled into himself and moaning. Blood flowed from between his clenched fingers.

"Let me look," Tracy said, but he didn't respond so

she pried his hand away. Gently Tracy and Todd turned him onto his back. Gwen saw the ripped sleeve, the fabric soaked with blood. The others held him and peeled back the sleeve, revealing a bloody groove of ripped flesh. The mountain lion on his shoulder had been cut in half.

"He fucking shot me!" Oscar cried. "I can't fucking believe this!"

Gwen couldn't believe it either. She lay speechless as the others tended to him. The dog had run back down the hill and now she settled on her belly, staring, as if even she were aware of the gravity of the situation.

"The bullet only grazed you, Oscar," Todd said. "It took a chunk out of your shoulder, but it didn't stay in."

"Where the fuck *is* he?" Tracy asked, raising her head and trying to look into the canyon.

Todd pulled her down again. "Careful!" Then: "I think down there somewhere," pointing to a spot in the general direction of where they'd started that afternoon. "There, or one of the side slopes. Somewhere in range. Can't be more than a couple thousand feet."

"A.J. must have gotten loose," Tracy said. "He must have had another gun."

"I knew we should have killed him," Oscar said, writhing in pain. "Goddamnit, we should have taken him out when we had the chance."

Gwen felt the accusation there but tried not to let it bother her.

"Save your strength," said Todd, holding him still. "We need to get you out of here."

"We need to get *all* of us to a less exposed spot," Tracy said. "There's some rocks up there—do they look big enough for us to hide behind?"

Gwen and Todd looked to where she was pointing, at a small pile of boulders about forty feet away.

"They'll have to do," Todd said.

It seemed like the longest distance she'd ever travel. They started moving on their bellies through small rocks so sharp it was like crawling through glass, and immediately a shot rang out, and then another, one ricocheting off a rock just below them. Gwen saw the dust flying up from the impact; she heard the others swear. She had managed to gather both her poles and one of Todd's; the other had skittered down the slope. Oscar, with Todd's help, pulled himself along with his one good arm. Todd still had the rifle over his shoulder and he glanced down a few times, as if gauging whether the shooter was within range. Tracy reached for her gun but Todd yelled, "No! Let's get to the rocks."

We are not really doing this, Gwen thought. We are not really crawling on our stomachs on an exposed mountainside, trying to avoid getting shot. But they were, they were, and somehow between praying and careful movement and plain good luck, they made it to the cluster of boulders. Several of them were couch-sized, and as they slid behind them, another shot hit a boulder nearby, a small cloud of dust and tiny rock bits bursting out from the spot of impact. Then the shooting stopped. A.J. or whoever the shooter was must have realized that they were protected, at least for now.

Todd and Tracy got Oscar behind the boulders and laid him flat on the ground. Tracy balled up her jacket and placed it under his head. The boulders were tall enough that they could sit up safely, and so they did. Todd looked grim, and even Tracy had a different expression on her face, as if even her most outlandish hopes for the trip had not included *this*.

Oscar was breathing fast, eyes closed, repeating, "Jesus. Jesus Christ."

He might die out here, Gwen thought. They might *all* die out here—it was looking more and more likely. They were trapped by a gunman on an exposed mountainside, with little food, no water, and no path of escape. She thought of her family, her friends at work—all the people whose lives would continue without her. She thought of what they'd think if she died.

But she couldn't give in to panic—not now, not yet. There were things to be done, there was help to give, and this is what she'd focus on. She twisted around to her pack and unzipped the main compartment. She pulled out her first aid kid, scanned the contents, and quickly got to work.

A rock jutting into his side, and piercing pain in what had been his right shoulder. He gripped the round of it, as if to hold it together. The pain was bigger than the place where the wound was; it consumed his whole body. Something soft was placed under his head. Someone cut away his wet sleeve. Then something tried to pull his hand from his shoulder. It touched him and he screamed.

"Sorry, Oscar." A voice, scared and worried, probably Gwen's. "We've got to stop the bleeding. I'm sorry, there's going to be a bit more pressure."

Something pressed and he felt a searing pain; they might as well have stabbed him with knives. He gasped but managed not to scream again.

"We're almost out of gauze. This is soaked," a voice said.

"Here, use my extra shirt."

"Won't that get the wound dirty?"

"We can press it over the gauze. We've got to get the bleeding to stop."

His breath was quick and shallow, he wasn't getting enough air, but he could not slow it down. His heart skittered and skipped like a nervous bird. I am panicking, he thought consciously. I am falling apart. He opened his eyes and saw the blood all over his front and hands; he closed them again quickly. He was aware of how much farther they had to go, and he knew he couldn't make it. He thought of Lily and his mother, their beautiful faces, which would cloud with sorrow if he didn't come back. But these were distant thoughts, outside and apart from his central awareness, which was: I've been shot, I'm shot and bleeding, this may be the end of it all.

How could this have happened so quickly? One second he was hiking, relieved to have survived the thunderstorm. Then the impact like a spear through his shoulder. It had sent him tumbling forward and only then had the pain come, the awareness of ripped flesh, the shocking forever change in his physical being where the bullet had torn through his body. He'd hit the ground hard, scraping his forearm and cheek. When he saw the blood he knew what had happened. He'd tried to rise again but he couldn't get up; the next shot ricocheted off a boulder right in front of him. Somehow he'd been dragged and shoved behind this large boulder. And the pain kept coming in waves, each one bigger than the last.

"The bleeding seems to be slowing down," someone said, and he felt a change in pressure against the wound, a slight letting up.

"Let's try to get it cleaned up and bandaged," said someone else. He did not know who was talking and he didn't care; they were all outside his pain, all not-him; he was locked in himself and yet away from himself, so that it took him several minutes to realize that the groans and cries that filled his ears were coming from his own mouth.

"What are we going to do?" one of the voices asked. "He's got us totally in his sights. We can't move!"

"We've got to take him out of commission," said someone else.

"How?"

"We've got to ambush him, like he just did to us." This was a male voice, Todd's.

"How the hell are we going to do that?"

"There's only one way to do it," Todd said. "I've got to wait until dark and go down there and find him."

"Are you crazy? He could shoot you."

"As opposed to what he just did?"

"But you don't even know where he is. He could be anywhere."

"He could. But wherever he is now, he can't stay there. There's no cover, and he's as exposed as we are."

"So what are you saying?"

"I'm saying he's probably going back down to that bit of wood, the place where we slept."

"You think so?"

"Yes. There's no other place. It's where we'd go if we could, if our positions were reversed. At least until it was safe to move again."

Silence for a moment.

"Look, let's figure this out later. Right now we've got to get Oscar stabilized."

"There *is* no later. We've got to decide what to do. I need to go back down and take care of that guy, and the rest of you have to get over the pass."

"He's right," said one of the other voices. Tracy? "There's no other way." Then: "I can go down with you."

"No, you need to get the others out. Oscar and Gwen can't make it without you."

A pause.

"I guess you're right."

Silence for several seconds. Then Oscar felt someone

close to him again. "This may hurt, Oscar," said the first voice again. "But we need to remove this compress. And then we're going to bandage it up again."

There was a moment, and then another, when nothing happened, and Oscar lay breathing fast, his body tense. And then something pulled against his raw ripped flesh and a violent pain coursed through him. He screamed again and his heart jumped and fell and then he passed out.

Chapter Fifteen
Todd

He left as soon as it was dark. After checking and double-checking the plan with the others, he pushed off from their hiding place behind the rocks and made his way down the slope. By the time he left he couldn't make out their features, and in a way he was glad, because he didn't really want to be able to see them. Not with the task that he knew he'd be best suited for. Not with what he had to do now.

The going was rough because of all the loose rocks, and he was moving straight down in the dark. This was more dangerous than traversing—it was easier to slip, or to trigger a rock slide that would alert A.J. or his brother that he was coming. But traversing took time, and he didn't have time; he needed to get down to where the shooter was and ambush him at first light. He chose his footing carefully and used his one pole, but even so, he stepped on a loose rock and felt it give way, wrenching his legs apart. Then he was on a patch of loose scree and skidded ten feet downhill. His elbow hit the ground and his jacket tore; the butt of the rifle, which was slung over his shoulder, jammed into his side. But at least the rocks stopped when he did, didn't make noise or tumble farther down the slope. His missteps, little avalanches, stayed his own.

The stars were out and the sky was filled with streaky

clouds, remnants of the afternoon storm. This was good—
the moon two nights ago had been so bright it had lit the
entire canyon. Two nights ago, at the campsite where Gwen
had seen the fawns. It felt like a lifetime ago, and it was.

The moon was still behind the eastern range, and he
wasn't sure when it would top out and spill light into
the canyon. Or if it would at all, with the clouds above
him shifting and combining, splitting apart again. Right
now, as he was making his way down the slope, the others
would be moving up, leaving the rocks and trying to gain
the pass under cover of darkness. They wouldn't be able
to move very fast. Oscar had lost blood, he was weak and
in terrible pain. But he was grim and determined. Todd
looked up to check if there was any sign of movement, even
a flash of white fur. The dog had lifted her head when he left
but had stayed with the others. He couldn't see anything—
the whole slope was encased in moon shadow, the same
shadow that protected him too.

It had been years since he had stalked a target at night,
but as he grew more sure-footed, the old feeling, the familiar adrenaline, returned. Despite hardly eating or sleeping, despite his earlier coldness, he felt good, he felt alive,
stronger and more alert than he had in years. He remembered early mornings in Wisconsin, moving in the dark to
reach the deer blind in the woods before the sun came up;
he remembered a quality of stillness and fullness in the
air, as if the night itself anticipated violence. But then he'd
been hunting for creatures—deer, sometimes birds. Now
he was hunting a man.

From the moment he'd heard the gun's report, he'd felt,
along with fear, a burning anger. Anger that one of their
group had been shot and that the rest of them were tar-

gets. Anger that they were desperately trying to escape because they'd stumbled onto someone else's mischief. Anger
that he'd been reduced to crawling behind a rock, which
would give him the chance—just the chance—to make it
home to his family. And most of all, anger that he'd been
so fooled by A.J. that he hadn't recognized the danger, had
even been glad when A.J. first shot the Mexican kid and
made his way down to the ledge. Gwen and Oscar had
been right, and his unwillingness or inability to see this
guy for what he was had contributed to their predicament.
When A.J. made those ugly cracks about them, Todd saw
that he meant it, and he understood something that he'd
never known before. But by then it was too late. He should
have grabbed José's gun when it was there for the taking.
He should have backed A.J. off as soon as he saw him.
They should never have been in the position to be led back
to the camp and then forced to destroy the garden. Oscar was right—they should have incapacitated A.J. when
they left—broken a bone, blinded him, or killed him. Todd
had been trying to do the right thing, the human thing,
and he'd been swayed by Gwen and her principles. But
decency meant nothing when you came up against a man
who wasn't decent. He had made a huge mistake in dealing
with A.J. He wasn't going to make another.

Below, maybe a half-mile farther down, he could
just make out a stream, the moving water catching light
from the moon. That must be the bottom of the valley, he
thought. That must be the stream that feeds the lake. The
bit of forest where they'd slept that morning was farther to
the right, and he was more certain than ever that the shooter
would have retreated there. He decided to continue his
path straight down, putting him to the left of the woods.

Then he'd circle around and enter from the other side. If the shooter had watched them go up the slope, he'd have seen them traversing more to the left, and that's where he might still look. It occurred to Todd that the shooter might be doing what they were doing, taking advantage of the darkness to move. What would he do if the shooter was making his way up the slope? He didn't know, and the thought of it worried him. He looked toward the woods and then scanned the slope to his right. No movement from below, and none above.

Suddenly he could make out the opposite ridge and the slopes on either side—the moon was peeking over the mountains. Shit. He moved behind a large boulder and looked out from behind it. The entire valley was visible now; it looked haunted and beautiful. He saw the lake where they'd filled their water bottles, the woods, the place they'd started hiking uphill. He looked behind him up the slope, afraid to see the movement of the others. But there was nothing—either they were too far away or they, too, had taken refuge from the light. Or, he thought worriedly, remembering Oscar's grimace, maybe they haven't even left at all.

He waited ten, fifteen minutes and the canyon went dark again; a curtain of clouds was drawn over the moon. He left his hiding place and continued downhill, veering even farther left, away from the woods. The going wasn't any easier—he was still slipping, and he'd tweaked his knee when he'd fallen—but there was a rhythm to it now. He held onto boulders or the occasional tough-rooted plant, jamming the rifle against his shoulder, his back. He was glad he hadn't brought his pack—just a bag of nuts that had escaped the dog's scavenging and a water bottle clipped to his belt with a carabiner. Anything else would have bogged him down. He couldn't see very well, but every once in a while he got a glimpse of the stream's reflection, and that was enough to aim for. His body was moving of its own accord. Adrenaline had taken over.

He tried to imagine his children home in their beds—quiet, and helpless in sleep. What would they say if they could see him now? What would Kelly say? Nothing in their lives together had any relation to this. He had never felt so apart from them, or been so afraid. And he had never felt more full of purpose. If he was able to do what he was supposed to, A.J. or his brother would soon be dead. The others could get over the pass without danger of being shot at again—and then they'd be on their way down the eastern slope and into the Owens Valley. He'd be left to get out of the mountains by himself. But he'd have made it possible for them to escape.

Oscar's gunshot wound had turned his stomach. The blood, the quick bruising, the impossible mess of the flesh, where the muscle and skin were supposed to be smooth, unbroken. It was hard to see the agony, the horrible pain, Oscar crying and moaning and holding onto his shoulder, rocking until Gwen told him to stop, told him to hold still until the blood flow could be staunched, which it was, after some time, with her help. Todd was impressed with Gwen's efficiency, the quickness and matter-of-factness with which she used a shirt to apply pressure, the competence with which she attached a bandage. He knew she was afraid, but she seemed glad to have something to do, a person to attend to, a problem that was within her reach to solve. He thought of Kelly, who was fastidious about their children's most mundane bug bites—she would not have been able to handle this. Tracy had helped too, opening the bandage wrappers, handing over the scissors, but mostly she had stared up at the ridge trying to find the way over, and Todd had felt a welling anger at her, frustration with her stubbornness, the clear knowledge that they would not have encountered such trouble if she hadn't pushed them to take this unused trail. But there was no use dwelling on that; they were where they were. And it was Tracy who would have to lead the others over the pass, while Todd went back to kill their pursuer.

He continued down the slope, going faster when there were larger rocks to use as steps, and slower on the scree, more mindful of being quiet as he got closer to the valley floor. Twice he had to lie flat behind a boulder when the moon reemerged, but as he peered out over it he saw no other movement; either the shooter was being careful too or he had never left his position.

Finally he reached the bottom and returned to springy earth. He stopped and looked around. In front of him, behind him, the looming dark shapes of the mountains, the sky still streaked with clouds overhead. He could no longer see the stream but he could hear it; the running water was more audible than it had been in the daylight, and he wondered if the darkness somehow amplified the sound, or muted all the other senses, the body adjusting to what sensations the world had to offer, making up in hearing what it lost in sight. He heard everything—the water trickling over rocks, the wind through the brush, a lonely creature calling in the dark. And he knew that if he could hear so well, the shooter could too; he needed to be quiet, as stealthy as he could, even here, a half-mile from the woods.

He started walking, experimenting with how to pick

his feet up and put them down again—if he moved too fast, there was a sucking sound when he pulled up a shoe, and a muffled splash when he stepped back down. But if he moved slowly, the softness of the tundra absorbed all sound, and he could walk nearly silently forward. After fifteen minutes, he reached the small stream. He could only see the general movement of water, could not make out where the rocks were, or where he might step—he moved up and down the bank but found no obvious crossing. Did he really need to cross the stream? Yes, he thought. He did. Better that he circle back and approach the shooter from behind. He did not want to run into him head-on. He knelt down, taking the cold water in his cupped palms and drinking thirstily. He refilled his water bottle. He splashed some water on the scratch on his leg, which was feeling hot, infected. Then he stood up again, and found what looked like the easiest way across, and stepped onto a rock a few feet from the bank. But there was no rock or branch to step on next, so he braced himself and stepped straight into the water, the shock of cold taking his breath way. With an effort, he swung his other foot onto the opposite bank and then hopped one-footed in the river with the help of his pole until he was close enough to step out. But the one wet foot made him cold, and reminded him that his clothes weren't yet totally dry from the storm, and he needed to get moving again.

He walked toward the opposite slope, moving more quickly across this solid ground. He felt terribly exposed—if the moon should reemerge now, he'd be caught out, nothing to hide behind, nowhere to go, like a burglar in someone's kitchen with the light switched on. But soon he reached a cluster of rocks and slipped safety behind them.

He sat down, ignoring his wet foot and throbbing knee, and ate a handful of peanuts, feeling the energy course through him, the needed fuel. He checked the rifle to make sure that nothing had broken or jammed; checked that the safety was on. And while there was no way it could have fallen out, he also checked the ammunition.

He tried to imagine what A.J. would do, tried to get inside his head. A.J. had to have known that he hit one of them; he would have seen them dragging Oscar behind the rocks. So he knew that one of them was hurt, maybe dying. If Oscar was dead, they could leave his body, but if he wasn't, they'd never leave him—especially not with someone coming after them. So A.J. knew they would continue up the slope, but when? It would be hard in the dark, with no trail and an injured man, and a slope that was treacherous even in daytime. If they waited until daylight, though, they'd be easy to pick off. So it would make sense for them to leave in the dark, or as close to dawn as possible. It seemed that A.J. should try to make his way up the slope in the dark, so what was stopping him? Maybe he thought he'd be too clear of a target, coming up the slope unprotected. Maybe he was still suffering from the effects of his beating. Or maybe he knew that he could easily overtake them, even if they got an earlier start.

Then another thought occurred to Todd and chilled him to the bone. What if someone was coming from the other direction? Just over the crest of the mountains was the Owens Valley, and a string of small, lonely high-desert towns. A.J. could have called or signaled someone who was now coming from the east. The same way that Tracy and the others were heading out of the range, someone could be heading in to cut off their escape. Maybe that's why A.J. could afford to stay still. Maybe he knew he had them trapped, like a base runner caught between bases, the fielders slowly closing the gap.

But maybe not. The satellite phones seemed spotty out here, and of course there was no cell reception. A.J. was probably alone. Or joined only by his brother coming in from the west. Tracy and the others would be safe going east. This is what he had to tell himself.

He walked along the valley floor, the land rising on either side. Behind him, the big peaks loomed but the range was now shrouded in darkness. If the others were moving, they were totally hidden, and this, he decided, was why the shooter stayed still. Looking east, everything was dark and obscured. West, any movement would be visible.

He reached the edge of the woods and skirted around to the left until he came to a granite boulder with a sprig of plants beside it. This was the point where they had entered the woods yesterday morning, and it was a good place to enter again. He remembered roughly the path they'd taken under the cover of trees, how long it was before they'd reached the house-sized boulders. But when he stepped in from the open sky and into the shelter of the woods, he realized that this would be different. Away from even the small light of the moon and the stars, this world was almost totally dark. He waited for his eyes to adjust but in the black of night, all of the trees looked the same. A minute in, he spun around and wasn't sure which direction he'd come from. Finally he righted himself and held out one arm, reaching to touch trees before he walked into them. Each step he took was painfully slow; he lowered his feet gently so as not to snap a twig.

He walked this way for twenty minutes and covered

very little ground. He was hungry and thirsty, but afraid to open his bag of nuts; any sound was amplified in the dark. Now he stopped and reconsidered his strategy. How close did he want to get to this guy? How close *could* he get, really? He couldn't shoot him in the dark unless he was right on top of him, and there was no way he could get that close without being detected. He needed to be within range, but at a safe distance. And the only way he could do that would be with light.

And A.J. could be anywhere, anywhere in these woods, or if he'd left already, anywhere in the canyon. Todd might have walked right past him already and not even known it.

But he didn't think so. He thought he knew where he was. A.J. had already shown his patterns. He'd stayed in the camps they'd made, at the trailhead and at the lake; he'd liked stalking them that way, sleeping where they'd slept, drawing energy from their presence. He'd be in the clearing where they'd fallen asleep yesterday morning. Protected by the house-sized rocks.

Once Todd thought this, he knew it was true. He would find A.J. where they had slept themselves, enjoying being where they'd been, waiting until first light when he could see well enough to follow. A.J. hadn't needed to finish them off right away; he liked knowing they were waiting, afraid. He was like the neighbor's cat, who sometimes, since the passing of Roger, came into their yard to hunt. Tossing a defenseless mouse up in the air and batting it around, letting it scamper away for a couple of feet before catching it and sinking his teeth in. Yes, he would be in the clearing, waiting for light. As soon as Todd knew this, he could feel him there, breathing.

Todd made his way slowly to the left of where they'd

been that morning. He would circle around and approach the clearing from the opposite side, which would give him a clear view between the rocks. It was painstakingly slow movement, step by agonizing step, as he tried not to make a sound when he walked. Once the butt of the rifle bounced against a tree, and Todd cursed under his breath. It was dark—consuming, lonely dark—and by the time he saw the massive shape of the boulders, an hour had passed since he had entered the woods.

He kept a distance of about fifty feet from the boulders and circled around to the left. He got to an area on the opposite side and stayed there, not approaching the boulders or the gap between. He'd wait here out of sight until the sky began to lighten. He shielded his watch so that no light would be visible and then pressed a button. The illuminated face said 2:37.

He sat down and leaned back against a tree. Now that he'd stopped moving, he felt cold; he burrowed into his jacket. Images passed before them—Gwen lying down on the riverbank their first day out, the view back toward the lake when they'd reached their first pass. A.J. tied up at the pot garden, and José lying dead on the ledge. Then other things, home things: sitting at the kitchen table with the Sunday paper, Kelly sunning in the garden, Joey hitting a baseball, Brooke playing with her dolls. He saw Rachel from work, and remembered the Colsons. How distant it all felt now.

If he didn't get out of here alive, he thought, he'd had a good life. More success than he'd ever imagined. A beautiful family, two great kids. If it turned out badly in the morning and A.J. killed him, at least he'd left things in order for his family. At least he would have died trying to save other people, instead of falling to a heart attack or cancer. He'd be remembered as a guy who'd been brave enough to take on a killer. He'd be remembered not as an even-tempered corporate lawyer, but as a guy who took things into his own hands, who died fighting, like a man.

He startled awake. What time was it? 4:47. He'd dozed off, damnit, but it was probably all right; the sky was still dark. Dark, but he could make out the shapes of the trees now. Just a few more minutes and he should go.

He shook his head, trying to wake up, and then extended his legs, which were stiff. Holding on to the tree for stability, he slowly stood up, moving by inches so as not to make noise. The dark shapes of the big boulders were clearly visible. He waited five minutes, ten, until he could make out individual branches, and then he slowly moved over behind one of the boulders. He felt the surface of the granite and this shocked him awake; he pressed his cheek against its cold roughness. This is surreal, he thought. It can't really be happening. But it was. He touched his forehead to the granite and said a short prayer. Then he moved slowly to the right, close-hugging the rock, until he could look into the clearing.

Someone was there, sitting back against a tree, his head falling forward. There was a cap on his head, covering his face. Todd felt a jolt of adrenaline go through him; his heart beat so loudly he was sure it was audible. It was too dark still to make out anything else—the color of the clothes, any features. But it was definitely a man, sleeping with a rifle across his knees. A man who had tried to kill them.

Todd stepped clear of the boulder and slowly lifted his rifle, raising the butt to his shoulder. He was exposed, but he didn't feel any fear. His target was asleep and laid out perfectly. I am about to kill a man, he thought. There was no question that he had to do it. He lifted the rifle and set his eyes to the sight. He put the capped head in the cross-bars. Lord Jesus, help me hold steady, and please forgive me, he prayed. Then he held the rifle still and pulled the trigger.

Chapter Sixteen
Gwen

Gwen jumped when she heard the gunshot, even though she'd been expecting it for hours. She looked at Tracy, supporting Oscar from the downhill side. Oscar himself didn't react.

"That sounds like Todd's rifle," Tracy said.

"Are you sure?"

"Pretty sure. It's the same sound as when A.J. used it."

"I hope you're right," said Gwen. "But we haven't heard the signal."

They stood quietly, staring down into the valley, toward the lake and the woods, which were starting to reveal themselves in the light. The dog stopped and looked too, ears erect, sniffing the air. If it wasn't Todd who'd fired the weapon, they'd be in a bad spot—caught out on the slope with no tree or rock cover, still well below the pass. They'd expected to be up and over it by now, and on their way to safety. But it had been slow going with Oscar. They'd left not long after Todd had, moving in a chain, Tracy on the downhill side, Oscar in middle, Gwen above them both. She was glad to be moving, doing something, and it kept them from being cold; the temperature had dropped with the coming of dark. They'd ditched Oscar's pack, Tracy taking on his few items of clothing and food. But everything about their movement was awkward.

The loose rock beneath their feet kept giving way; Gwen would lose hold of Oscar or else fall into him, causing him to cry out in pain. Twice Gwen tripped and fell; once all three of them stumbled. Both she and Tracy had use of a pole, which stabilized their chain. She hadn't been able to see Oscar's face in the dark—they hadn't turned on their headlamps—and she was glad for this, glad not to witness his pain, although she heard it in every grunt and moan and felt it in his staggering movements.

Several minutes passed and Gwen feared that something was wrong. But then they heard it—two more shots in quick succession, the sound welling up out of the canyon, filling and overflowing it like fog.

"Thank you, Jesus," Gwen said. She thought of all the gunshots she'd heard in her life, some of them far too close. She'd never thought that she would welcome the sound.

"Way to go, Todd!" Tracy said. She pumped her fist in the air, pole dangling off it by the strap. "Oscar, did you hear that? Todd got A.J.! Just a little bit farther and we'll be over the pass. Then down the other side, and we're out!"

Oscar nodded—or was it a nod? Gwen couldn't tell. He was having a hard time standing, and Gwen's eyes filled as she looked at his scraped, sallow face, his ripped and bloody shirt. He only had shorts on and he was shivering, the jacket draped over his good shoulder not enough against the cold. She didn't know if he could make it.

"Let's rest for a minute," Gwen said. "I need some water and some calories and Oscar could probably use some too."

"Okay," Tracy said. "But not for too long. We need to get out of sight. On the off chance that it wasn't Todd just now."

They slowly turned to face downhill and positioned themselves on the slope, like children in a single-file line. They dug in footholds so they wouldn't slip as they sat. Tracy was on the downhill side, ready to stop Oscar or Gwen should either one slide. Oscar was still in the middle, resting his feet in the footholds that Tracy had kicked for him. Gwen was uphill, the tallest for once, looking down at the others and beyond. The dog sat at her side, front paws lower than her bottom as she balanced on the slope.

Gwen drank from her water bottle, which was only a third full, but they'd be over the pass soon, and Tracy said there were streams on the eastern side. She ate half of a protein bar—they'd finished the last of their dinners overnight, crouched behind the rocks. She offered part of the bar to Oscar, but he didn't respond.

"You've got to," she said. "Eat it, Oscar. Even if you're not hungry."

The dog sat up and reached for the food, and Gwen pulled it back. She moved closer to Oscar and fed him while Tracy held Timber by her collar. The dog's eyes watched every movement; two long strings of saliva hung from her mouth. Gwen felt for her, but there was so little food. Still, she broke off a bite and gave it to her.

"What should we do?" she asked. "Should we wait for Todd here? Should we at least hang around until we see him?"

Tracy shook her head. "No. We're too exposed. We need to get over the pass. Besides, he'll catch up. He's only a couple hours behind."

Gwen knew she was right—and on top of all that, there was also the unstated but obvious: Oscar had lost a lot of blood, and it wasn't clear how long he'd stay conscious.

"Okay," said Gwen. It felt so good to sit down. Her feet were sore and swollen, but she told herself to ignore the pain. They hadn't slept since their extended nap yesterday morning, and she was tired to the bone. But looking up, she saw that the pass now seemed within reach. It formed an edge against the light blue sky. A mile away at most. They could do it, she thought, gunshot victim or not. They were so close, so close to heading home.

There was a faint sound coming up from the canyon now, like someone chopping wood.

"What is that?" Gwen asked.

"I don't know."

They listened and it continued for a few seconds more. Gwen wasn't sure what it was or what it meant, but it made her uneasy.

"Let's get moving," Tracy said, and so slowly, reluctantly, Gwen pulled herself up, using her pole to brace herself so she wouldn't slip. She and Tracy removed their jackets and then helped Oscar get to his feet. They walked on in the same formation. The terrain was suddenly steeper here, thirty-five or forty degrees, and they'd only gone a hundred feet or so when the ground gave way beneath Tracy's feet.

Gwen heard her yell "Whoa!" and just like that she was gone, sliding feetfirst down the slope on her belly. She reached out frantically to grab something but there was nothing to hold; it was as if she was sliding down a ski jump. She wasn't moving especially fast; she just couldn't stop herself, and there was a particular horror in the mundaneness of her predicament. Gwen saw that Tracy might slide all the way to the canyon floor, more than a thousand feet below. She might have no skin left when she stopped.

Then her foot hit some kind of protuberance and she flipped onto her back. Her pack came off but she managed to grab or dig at something so she at least turned sideways, picking up speed as she continued to slide.

Then abruptly she hit a boulder. It caught her violently in the midsection and her body wrapped around it, limp as a rag doll. Her pole tumbled past her. For a moment she didn't move, and Gwen's heart seized with dread and disbelief.

"Tracy!" she yelled, and her voice echoed through the canyon; she hoped it was Todd down there and not A.J. "Tracy, are you all right?"

For a moment Gwen thought she was dead. But then Tracy's legs twitched and she moved an arm. She twisted her body and embraced the boulder, as if holding onto a rock in a river while the current tried to sweep her downstream. Then she lowered her head. Gwen had to look away for a moment, and so she gazed out over the valley, which was suffused with morning light, the ridge across from them basked in orange and gold. It took her breath away. How beautiful—how unbelievably, dramatically beautiful. And totally indifferent to their struggles.

"Shit," Oscar said, and Gwen realized that she was still holding him up. He'd seen what happened and was looking down the slope.

"Let's get to a safer spot," Gwen said, redoubling her grip. "We need to stop and figure out what to do." There was a rock shelf just ahead of them, and so they shuffled over to it, Gwen digging in her pole to avoid sliding herself, ignoring the pain of the popped blisters on her hand.

Once she got Oscar seated she looked back down the slope. Tracy was struggling to get herself upright. Her legs were moving but she was only using one arm. Her clothes were torn and Gwen could see several streaks of blood on her arms.

"I'm coming down!" she yelled, even though she had no idea how she would.

Tracy shook her head. "Don't!" she yelled weakly. "It's too dangerous."

"Are you all right?" Gwen yelled again, but Tracy didn't answer. She started to move up the slope, though her movements were disjointed; she was laboring, one hand kept grabbing her side, and her face was wrenched with pain. But her legs were both working; at least there was that. She slipped once, twice, but managed to catch herself.

Oscar, watching through bleary eyes, said, "I don't think she can make it."

The dog had been lifting her front paws up and down and whining. Now she nudged Gwen's hand and gave her hoarse bark.

"What?" Gwen asked.

Timber looked at Tracy and then back at Gwen. Then she launched herself down the slope. Gwen yelled, "Hey!" She was afraid that the dog would slide helplessly too, or kick up rocks that might hit Tracy. But Timber moved expertly, somehow in control, like a surfer riding a wave. She started a little avalanche to the right of the boulder where Tracy had crashed; when she got close, she jumped off the rock slide as if turning off a wave and happily ran over to Tracy. She licked and nuzzled Tracy as if she hadn't seen her in days. What did the dog think she was going to do? Herd Tracy up the slope?

Then Gwen got it. Timber darted up the slope ten or fifteen feet, then came back down, barking, ran up again.

She was leading Tracy up, and she could, with her four feet, better manage the terrain; she'd gone down the slope to retrieve her. Tracy grabbed onto her collar and struggled up a few feet. The dog charged ahead again, struggling with the weight, tongue lolling and completely engaged. Tracy stepped and skidded and sometimes crawled behind her, reaching out for the collar with one arm while the other held her side. It wasn't the same as a horse or a mule pulling her up, or even a Saint Bernard. But it was enough, that bit of energy and help, the upward momentum, the strength of a young creature who was born to work.

It took twenty minutes to get up the two hundred feet she'd fallen, with several breaks along the way. First she stopped to retrieve her pack. Forty feet later she paused to pick up something else—the bear spray—and reattached it to her belt. A little farther on she picked up the gun. Slowly they made their way to the spot where Gwen and Oscar waited; when they got close, Gwen stood and pulled both dog and human onto the small ledge. Once Tracy had gained the level rock, she collapsed onto her back. She reached out to pet Timber. "Good dog," she said. "Good dog."

Now Gwen could see the extent of the damage. Tracy's hiking pants were in shreds at the knees. There were several tears in her shirt and her bare arms were scraped badly, streaked with blood. Her hands had cuts and gashes from grabbing onto the rocks as she slid; there was also a gash on her jaw, and dark bruises were forming on her arm.

"We should clean those up," Gwen said. "You've probably got dirt in them."

Tracy shook her head. "They're not serious. They're just scrapes. Let's get over the pass first. What I'm really worried about anyway is my ribs. I think I broke a couple when I hit the rock."

Gwen tried to remember what she knew about broken ribs and came up empty. "Can you breathe okay?"

Tracy shrugged. "I don't know. I think so." She closed her eyes and a wave of pain passed over her face.

Gwen tried to stifle her worry. Of all the things she'd imagined going wrong on this trip, and with all the un-imaginable ways that things had actually gone wrong, the thought of Tracy being hurt or weakened had never oc-curred to her.

"We're almost at the pass," she said.

Tracy nodded. She looked over at Oscar, whose eyes were open, but glazed. "How you doing, buddy?"

He nodded slowly. "I'm here."

"I wonder where Todd is," Gwen said.

"Maybe we can see him by now," said Tracy, and they scanned the floor of the valley—the lake, the stream, the stand of woods where they'd slept, and where the shot had come from earlier.

"Is that him?" Gwen asked, pointing. There was a human figure, small but moving, just outside the edge of the woods.

"I think so," Tracy said. "Wave!"

And because she was the only one who was in the shape to do so, because she was the only one who could lift her arms above her head, Gwen stood and waved, extending her arms as far as she could, hoping that her movements would make her visible against the rock, even with the sun behind her. The figure in the valley stopped for a moment; then it, too, began to wave.

"That's him!" Gwen said excitedly. "He's okay!" She felt a huge surge of relief.

Then the figure started gesturing, pointing toward the opposite slope, crossing his arms in front of him as if to signal a missed field goal.

"What's he saying?" Gwen asked.

"I don't know," Tracy said.

He seemed to be trying to communicate something, but what could it be? That A.J. was gone? What Gwen did know was that he was alive, and so were they. She waved at him one last time and pointed toward the pass. She was ready to get moving again. And now there were *two* injured people to deal with.

"Are you okay to keep going?" she asked Tracy.

"I'm ready. More than ready. Let's get out of here."

They stood and assembled themselves, Tracy grimacing in pain. Gwen had to help her get her pack on, since she couldn't twist to one side. And then Gwen helped Oscar up. They determined that it might be easier to go straight up the slope now, making sure they had footholds before transferring their weight. They went single file, Tracy first, then Oscar, with a little help from Gwen, who brought up the rear. Timber scrambled up and down the slope, finding ledges for them to rest on, easier routes up through the scree and between patches of snow. The top of the ridge was sharp against the clear blue sky; it looked like the edge of the world. Gwen imagined the moment when they crested the range. They'd be able to see all the way into the Owens Valley; they'd be able to see highways and towns. Just a little farther, she thought. Just a little bit farther and we'll be there.

They kicked and hiked for almost an hour and finally the top was in sight. Gwen could hardly contain herself—she loved the moment of reaching the top, when the land on the other side was revealed. The expansiveness of the view would make her feel expansive too; that welling up of joy and wonder was exactly why she hiked. And here, reaching the pass meant more than just a pretty view. It meant the path to their salvation.

They got closer, closer, and the sky seemed closer too. Another fifty feet, another twenty, and then Tracy was there, standing on top like a bighorn sheep, gazing into the distance. Her posture didn't exude the joy or relief that Gwen was already starting to feel. But maybe she was just too tired. Then Oscar gained the top, his shoulders slumped, and he fell to his knees. And when Gwen reached the top, she saw why.

There was a whole new canyon in front of them, another range on the other side. They were not at the easternmost part of the mountains, as they'd thought, but instead on a crest in the middle. The range they'd just climbed was so tall that it had obscured the view of everything beyond, and what was beyond was an even more imposing set of peaks. Looking down into this large new canyon, Gwen wondered if she was losing her mind. It was barren, at least a mile or two wide, with stretches of tundra but mostly hard gray rock. Here and there along the mountain walls were patches of snow. The small lake at the bottom was turquoise, a color she'd never seen before in nature. A third of it was covered with ice. The whole basin looked like a moonscape, a grayscale negative of the lush valley where they'd just been. She must be imagining this; she must have lost her mind.

But looking at her companions' faces, she knew she wasn't seeing things. Oscar covered his face with his good arm and rocked back and forth. Tracy shook her head, an-

gry and speechless. And Gwen looked out at the stark unexpected view and felt despair rise up like a flood. She
took off her pack and dropped to one knee, staring off into
the distance. This close, she thought. We'd been this close.
But they hadn't been close at all. Walking out of this new
canyon would take at least another day—and that would
be with everyone at full strength, with adequate food and
water. There was no way they could all make it down another slope, through a wide, exposed basin, and over the
even sharper, more unwelcoming peaks on the other side.
Her despair began to tighten into fear, into panic. Her eyes
welled and she started to cry.

Chapter Seventeen
Oscar

He couldn't escape the light; even when he closed his eyes, it reached behind his eyelids. Sometimes a solid screen of white, and sometimes spots, moving and swirling in front of him. He'd always loved the sun, but now, on the other side of the pass, it was punishing, relentless, as focused and hot as a laser beam. And there was nothing to temper it, no shade to protect them. But at least his clothes were dry now—even hot to the touch. Two miles closer to the sun than usual, he might be baked alive.

They had stayed at the pass for twenty minutes, resting, trying to figure out what to do. Or Tracy and Gwen had tried; he had stayed silent. It was taking all his energy just to stay upright, to not give way to pain; it was so big in him that he couldn't remember being without it. Vaguely he'd followed the conversation. Should they light a fire and make smoke for rescuers to see? Should they all keep going? Should Gwen, who wasn't hurt, continue on by herself? But they had nothing to burn and no rescuers were in sight and Gwen didn't want to leave them. There was really no choice but to go.

He didn't care what they decided. He was thinking of Lily, her huge grin whenever he bent to pick her up, the way he felt when he carried her on his back. Of his mother, when he was growing up, coming home from a long day's work, but never too tired to make him a meal or help him with his homework. He could sit here with these thoughts until he drifted off to nothing. He did not want to move anymore.

"Hey, wake up!" There was a nudge to his calf. "We need to get going. Do you think you can keep walking?"

He shook his head no. No, he wanted to stay here.

"Oscar." This was Gwen, a gentler voice. "We've got to keep moving. If you could make it down to the lake, we could get you some water."

He said nothing.

"Oscar, how does your shoulder feel?"

He tried to shrug but then felt a shooting pain and cried out. Someone was standing behind him. "Let me look."

His bandage was being lifted away. He could feel them hovering. Was Todd there? No, he wasn't. Oscar couldn't recall where he'd gone.

"How is it?" he heard Tracy ask.

"It's starting to look green. Bleeding stopped, but it's getting infected."

He imagined little creatures, millions of them, feasting on his flesh, then moving on to colonize other parts of his body. Hearty, mountain-infecting agents, different from those in the city. This made him laugh, and he heard the others' silence. He laughed more, and Gwen said, "We've got to get him out of here."

Then they were going down the slope. It was easier walking than what they'd just done. The ground was more solid here, less scree, and they were headed downhill. Someone had his arms—he couldn't tell who—and his legs still seemed to work. He looked down at his feet, his scuffed boots and dirt-streaked legs. Are those mine? he thought.

They're moving so well. As if someone else is controlling them.

It was scorching hot, even at eight in the morning, the sun sending waves of heat that reflected off the ground, so the heat also came up from under them. His clothes stuck to him, soaked with sweat and blood. Was that his own odor he smelled? Maybe it was the flesh of his gunshot wound, rotting. The organisms killing him bit by bit.

He was vaguely aware of the canyon itself, the bigger peaks beyond. There was so much beauty here, so much wilderness. It had been arrogant to think he could handle it. But if he was to stop and rest here and never wake up, this wasn't a bad place to die.

He didn't know how long they walked or how far down they went. He knew only that the sun beating down on him was just that, a beating, punishing and brutal and harsh. The skin of his face was so burned it was starting to flake off; his lips and the underside of his nose were scorched too. He was thirsty, so thirsty, and so very dry; his tongue felt like a pillow in his mouth. He'd long ago lost his sunglasses and his vision faded in and out; sometimes he saw the canyon and mountains, sometimes nothing. They headed left, his right leg straight and his left one bent as he walked downhill. Just when his muscles started to clench, they reversed themselves and headed to the right.

He had no sense of time passing, whether they'd walked one hour or several. But then they were at the bottom of the canyon and there was a bit of green again, patches of tundra, and small, sturdy vine-like plants with tiny pink flowers. And a stream, coming out of the bottom of the lake—the others set him down carefully and rushed to the edge, drinking handfuls of the water and dunking their heads in. With the sun reflecting off it, the stream looked like a river of light. The dog wandered out into the middle and drank. Gwen filled a bottle and brought it to Oscar, holding it to his lips. He tilted his head backward and gulped, water spilling over his face and running down his chin. It felt shockingly cold and good. He gestured to his head, and Gwen poured some on his hair, and he opened his eyes for a moment. He saw Gwen, her face streaked with dirt but alert and determined. He saw Tracy, sitting at the side of the stream, body curled in pain. Gwen left him and poured water over Tracy's head too, tried to wash out her wounds. Then she went to the edge of the water and splashed her own face and arms, finally peeling off her shirt, stepping into the stream, and sitting down in it.

"I wish we had more food," Tracy said.

"I'm going to eat two hamburgers when we get out of here," said Gwen.

"I'm going to eat two *cows*."

Just then a succession of quick staccato sounds cut through the air—not close, but not far, either.

"What was that?" Gwen said.

"Sounded like gunshots."

"And what do five shots mean?"

"I'm not sure, but probably nothing good."

"Well, let's get moving then."

"Yes, let's go."

The sound of clothes adjusted, zippers zipped, packs being lifted back on. Oscar just kept his eyes closed. The sound of the running water was soothing, and he was happy here now. He wasn't thirsty anymore. The cold water on his skin felt delicious, especially when a breeze blew through. Let the others figure out the things like water and food and how to escape from men with guns. He wished he could tell Lily and Claudia, and his mother too, that he wasn't in pain anymore. This was a good place to rest, and he needed to rest. He leaned to his left, easing himself down with his good arm. As soon as his head was against the ground, he fell back asleep.

CHAPTER EIGHTEEN
TODD

When he saw them reach the pass, he stopped for a moment and exhaled in relief. Three figures silhouetted by the light of the morning sun. Visible, moving slowly, and then gone behind the ridge, on the eastern side, and on their way to safety. He had spotted them when he'd come out of the woods; he'd watched Tracy's fall; he'd seen the dog help her up the slope. He knew they weren't out of danger yet—now two of them were hurt, with miles to go before they reached a trail. But they were safer on the other side, out of sight from this valley. Or at least he hoped they were.

As they were stopped on the rocks, after Tracy's fall, he'd gestured to them. He'd tried to communicate that it was no good, no good; that there might still be danger coming. All they knew was that he'd fired twice, which meant he was okay. But they hadn't worked out a signal for what had actually happened. They were continuing on and over the pass with no more worries, believing there was no one else behind them.

His shot had been perfect. It hit his target, and the head jerked right before taking the upper body with it; the figure rolled over, backward and onto the ground. But when Todd rushed into the clearing and over to the body, the face beneath the cap wasn't A.J.'s. It belonged to someone

Todd had never seen. A Latino man, maybe Todd's age. Beside him was a high-powered rifle. A small backpack and a satellite phone. An associate of José's? He must have been. Why else would he be out here, trying to pick off members of their group? Why else would he have needed to kill? And if he was the one who had followed them, if he was the one who'd fired the shot, then where the hell was A.J.?

He stepped back into the center of the clearing, still confused. But he had promised to signal to the others that he was all right, and so he fired two shots into the sky.

Then he returned to the body. As the darkness eased and more light entered the woods, Todd examined the man for clues. He was wearing a khaki-colored work shirt, olive pants. His skin was sun-darkened, dirty at the hands. Todd knelt and unzipped the man's pack, which held only water, a bag of sunflower seeds, some foil-wrapped food. An extra box of ammunition.

Controlling his feeling of revulsion, not looking at the corpse's bloody face, he patted down its pockets. In one pants pocket, a set of keys, including the key to a Chevy. In another, a crumpled wad of small bills and a gas receipt from Fresno. No wallet, no identification. But in the pocket of his shirt—especially hard to reach up there, close to the face—he found a slightly bent snapshot of a girl, maybe seven or eight, looking up from a table and laughing. She was wearing a white party dress and her hair was tied back with a pink bow. A birthday party, maybe? Todd felt a twinge of sadness looking at this picture, for the loss the girl did not yet know she'd suffered. He'd killed a man, maybe a father. He'd orphaned this little girl. Yet this man had tried to kill them, and would still be trying if he were alive. Todd hadn't had any choice but to do what he'd done.

He wondered how this man had followed them without being seen. They'd kept looking behind them, all the way across the valley and up the other side—but the man knew these mountains better than they did. Maybe he'd come in by some alternate route. Maybe he'd just avoided detection. If he'd gone to the pot grow looking for José, surely he would have seen A.J. Maybe A.J. had blamed José's death on them. Maybe he was dead now too.

But what if this man *hadn't* gone to the grow? What if he'd come from someplace else entirely? What if he was totally unrelated to all of it, to José and A.J. and the marijuana garden, their desperate attempt to get out? What if he was just a random psychopath, killing people in the mountains? It happened. And yet Todd, beneath his exhaustion and fear, knew he was being delirious, knew that this man was tied to everything else; that father or not, little girl or not, he was tied to the garden and likely to a drug cartel; that he was bad news and had to be dealt with.

But what if the man *hadn't* killed A.J.? After all, they'd left him a little ways from the camp, and maybe this man hadn't bothered to look. Todd had planned to ditch his rifle here, or someplace close by, so that whoever found this man—who he'd thought would be A.J.—would find his rifle with him. But he wasn't sure now what had happened to A.J., and so he needed to keep the rifle. And if A.J. did show up here, he didn't want him taking the dead man's weapon, so he picked it up and removed the ammunition and then smashed it against a rock. The pounding reverberated through the trees and up out of the forest; he could hear the echo come back from the canyon walls. But the steel barrel wouldn't break, would not even dent, so he went off a hundred yards away and buried the rifle beneath a log. The man himself he left out, propped against the tree. He tucked the girl's picture back into his front shirt pocket.

Todd stood and said a short prayer over the body, asking forgiveness of the man, his daughter, and God, praying that the man's soul rest in peace. Then he made his way out of the woods. It was bright now on the valley floor, the sun almost directly in his eyes, but he walked on into the open air, over to the stream, where he released the man's bullets like silver fish into the water. It was then that he caught sight of the others moving up the mountain. That he'd watched Tracy slide down the slope. That he'd tried to give the message too complex for hand signals. Tracy had gotten back up, and they'd continued toward the pass, and now it was just him. Just him in the canyon, or so he hoped.

He wasn't sure if A.J. was alive or dead. But he did not feel safe moving in daylight, expecting a shot every second as he knelt and splashed water on his face. He knew the safest thing to do would be to wait until dark again, to move up the slope when no one could see him. But he couldn't wait, he did not want to be here, alone in this vast canyon, or even worse, *not* alone. Either way he was overwhelmed by the size of it, the silence. There was an ominous feeling, caused by the knowledge of the dead man and the fear that there might still be a living one.

Then he remembered something—they'd destroyed A.J.'s glasses. They'd crushed the lenses into the ground, stomped the glass into hundreds of pieces. Unless he carried an extra pair or his brother brought him one, A.J.'s vision would be limited. He probably couldn't have found his way over the ridge and into the valley. Even if he could have, there was no way he could line up a shot. And he didn't have his rifle anymore.

All of this gave Todd the bit of confidence he needed. He'd move forward even in daylight. He decided to take one last drink and wet his cap again, and as he knelt and bent over the stream, he caught sight of his reflection. His beard had grown in blond and gray, and his unloosed hair was shaggy. He looked like a mountain man, and the sight pleased him. The firmness of his legs and shoulders pleased him too. Even with a sore knee, and in need of food and sleep, he felt better in his body than he ever did at home. After checking to make sure his water bottle was full and the rifle's safety back on, he set off across the floor of the valley. He wasn't totally at ease—not completely sure that A.J. wasn't out there somewhere. And if they had already been tracked by an unknown man, who else might they encounter? But still, he felt more comfortable. He was headed in the right direction. And he'd killed their most immediate threat.

At the foot of the slope, he looked up and assessed the range again. Their path of yesterday had been more challenging than he had expected—lots of loose rock and unstable ground. He'd start to the right of where they'd gone yesterday, and head as straight as he could up the slope. There were large boulders strewn here and there, the same ones that had protected him from the moonlight. He could duck behind these if there were shots.

The hiking was not any easier. Like yesterday, he'd take a step and then slip back again, working to keep his balance. But going nearly straight up, he was gaining the ridge faster. He labored forty-five minutes, an hour, before he took a break—just in time to watch the others go over the pass. When he stopped, the sweat was streaming down his face. His clothes were soaked. It was only eight a.m., but the sun was harsh at this high elevation, and he was hiking right into it. He drank from his bottle and wiped the sweat off his forehead. When was the last time he'd bathed? When was the last time he'd actually slept, or eaten something other than a Clif Bar? He couldn't remember anymore, and everything about his other life seemed far away, unreal. There was only here and now, himself and the mountains. Just this range to get over, and he was free.

He hiked for another hour or so, making slow progress, stopping more often than he would have liked to catch his breath. When the hell would he get to the top of this thing? He looked up to pick out the lowest saddle. He scanned the range from the left, where the others had gone over, to the middle, all the way to the right. There were a couple of gaps in this direction that looked closer than the area where he'd last seen the others. He decided to head to a saddle that was slightly to his right, so that he wouldn't cross too far from where they had.

Then he saw something moving near the top of the ridge. It was a person, traversing up the slope toward the same gap Todd had spotted. He was moving surprisingly fast. The figure was too far away to make out much detail, but Todd thought he recognized the jeans and white shirt. A.J. The man was up near the top, and soon he'd be on the other side. He had gotten loose somehow, and must have gone through the valley by a different route, or moved across it at night, when Todd and the others were preoccupied with who they thought was A.J., in the woods. Now, he was fifteen or twenty minutes from cresting the ridge within range of the others, who had no idea that he

was still alive. They'd be caught unaware, completely surprised. Picking them off would be child's play.

Todd had to warn them. He had to let them know that
something was wrong. And he had only one way to do it.
If he used his ammunition now, he might not have what he
needed later—for killing game or defending himself. But
he didn't have a choice. He stepped behind a large boulder,
just in case. Then he pointed his rifle toward the sky and
fired and fired and fired.

Chapter Nineteen
Gwen

They walked like drunks or wounded soldiers, arm in arm and weaving. They would take a few steps and then stagger, stop, collect themselves again. Gwen, who was in the middle, yanked them up to keep them from falling. The midmorning sun was direct and powerful, and although they'd had their fill at the river, she was still parched with thirst. Even the dog was tired, trotting along with her head down and her tongue lolling out. Gwen looked up at the granite walls ahead of them and they started to blend and swim. Was this heat exposure? Exhaustion? Delirium? Suddenly she pictured her bed, the welcoming softness of it, the clean sheets, the luxurious new comforter she'd bought. She closed her eyes and almost fell into the image of it. With great effort, she pulled herself back to where she was—trying to get her friends across this moonlike landscape and out of the mountains.

They crossed a particularly swept-clean bit of ground. Fifty feet later, in a kind of gulley, they reached a cluster of scraggly, wind-blown trees. They stepped beneath the spindly branches until they found a spot of shade. Never had Gwen been more grateful for shade—she had longed for it like water. Several of the trees were tangled together at their tops, barely above their heads; there was a fallen, dried-out log to one side. They unlinked arms and all sat down behind the log, Gwen helping ease Tracy and Oscar to the ground before collapsing herself. She sat with her knees bent, arms curled around her legs, the dog sprawling out at her feet.

They didn't speak for several minutes. Then Tracy said, "You'll have to go on by yourself."

Gwen forced herself to lift her head. "What?"

"You're going to have to leave us and go on by yourself. There's no way Oscar and I can make it over this range." Tracy was lying on her back now, one arm holding her ribs, the other hiding her face.

Gwen felt a welling up of fear. "Maybe someone's looking for us. Maybe someone's coming soon."

"No one's coming," said Tracy, and the fear in Gwen's chest curdled and turned. She tried to remember how long they'd been out. Three days? Four? It was still within the time they were supposed to be out. Tracy was right. No one was coming for them.

"I can't leave you," Gwen said, feeling sick to her stomach.

"You have to."

"But I don't know where to go."

"Just find the easiest way up and aim for one of the gaps between the peaks."

"I can't do this, Tracy. You could, but I can't."

"Yes, you can. You've been doing it already."

Gwen glanced up at the slope—it looked steep and unscalable. She'd barely been able to make it this far.

"I'd *love* to be the one to go," Tracy said, struggling to sit up. "But my ribs are killing me and I can't really breathe. It's got to be you, Gwen. You can make it. Everything you've been doing has been leading up to this."

She looked at Gwen directly now, and there was a nakedness that Gwen had never seen before. Her cheek was scraped and her eyes were dull, her hair as dry as straw. Gwen knew that Tracy was right. She *had* known it, had known it for hours, ever since Tracy had fallen. Then Tracy turned away, and the moment was gone.

"What do you think is the best way?" Gwen asked.

Tracy took a few seconds to answer, and Gwen realized with alarm that she was trying to gather enough breath to speak. "I think the lowest part is pretty much straight above us," she said finally. "I was looking from the stream. There's that peak to the left, but there's a lower, less jagged section there in the middle." She paused and took several labored breaths. "Then once you're over, you can figure out what to do. Maybe start a fire for smoke. Or you can just head straight down toward the Owens Valley. It's probably ten or fifteen miles."

Gwen wasn't so sure—this is exactly what Tracy had said before. Maybe there was yet another canyon beyond these peaks. Maybe the mountains went on forever. But what she said was, "And what are *you* going to do?"

Tracy shrugged, or tried to; every movement brought a grimace. "Stay here in the shade with Oscar. Get more water at the stream if we need it. And keep an eye out for Todd." She managed a pained smile. "This has been great, Gwen. The best trip ever. It's just like I always imagined."

Tracy was losing it. Or maybe she had lost it a long time ago. But the thought of Todd catching up to them eased Gwen's mind a bit—their one other unhurt member.

"Should we all just wait for Todd?" Gwen asked. How far behind was he? Two hours? Three? But there was no way to know which way he'd cross the canyon—he might miss them altogether. Then she looked at Oscar, curled on the ground, the dried blood dark on his shirt. He didn't move and she stared for ten, twenty seconds before she saw that he was breathing. There wasn't a minute to waste.

"All right," she said finally. "I'll go." She struggled to get up and then swung her pack on. There wasn't much weight to it anymore. But even if there had been, even if it was full, she had a feeling she'd be able to handle it.

"Good," Tracy said. "And take the gun." She reached for her waistband.

"No, I don't want it."

"You need it, Gwen. You don't know who you might run into."

"I don't know what to do with it, Tracy."

"What do you mean? Just use it if you have to."

"No way. I'd probably hurt myself."

Tracy paused. "Then at least take the bear spray. Or you'll be totally defenseless."

Gwen stood for a moment, considering. Finally she reached over to take the canister that Tracy held out and stuffed it into the lid of her pack. When she was ready to go, she looked down at Tracy and Oscar. Tracy was huddled over again, Oscar was on his side, both lost in their private worlds of pain. Gwen's eyes filled with tears. Would they get out of this alive? "I'll see you in the Owens Valley," she said.

She left the trees and walked back into the open, using her single pole. She was now at the base of a slope even steeper than the one they'd climbed that morning. It appeared to be solid granite and as she looked back and forth, she thought, No way. She felt alone, more alone than she'd ever been—even the dog, after taking a few tentative steps, had turned back and stayed with the others. But as she studied the wall she realized it wasn't really vertical. Steep, yes, but with rock steps and little plateaus; if she picked her way carefully, she could climb it.

She started south, the wall of mountain to her left, the canyon to the right. She stepped onto granite ledges as big as truck beds, as patios, and onto narrow flats of dirt and rock between them. There were stretches of twenty or thirty feet where she was able to walk level, scanning the rocks above her for an entry. Then she'd step onto the next shelf, or pull herself up, finding footholds or cracks that she could squeeze between, broken-off bits of rock to use as stairs. At first she was conscious of how big this all was. She had always been with Tracy or Devon when she'd ventured outdoors, had never gone for a hike by herself. And now here she was, completely alone, deep in the Sierras, trying to scale a slope whose top she couldn't see, with the lives of her friends in her hands. It was ridiculous, unthinkable. She'd never be able to do it.

But as she slowly gained elevation, moving left and right, she began to forget their predicament, the lack of food and water, even the men who'd been after them with guns. She was absorbed in the challenge of what she was doing, solving puzzles, gaining five feet by moving up between two rocks, ten by walking diagonally across a broken slab of granite. Once she reached a huge boulder that had been split right down the middle. It looked like a Venus flytrap or two clamshell halves, which might lure her in and then clamp shut. She walked around it and moved on. At times she'd have to reach up and grab onto a bit of rock, and she was surprised by how her arms looked, dirt-streaked and darker and lined with muscles that hadn't been there a week before. When she looked behind her, she was amazed to see how much height she had gained, the basin now well below her, the trees like scrubby bushes on the ground. This gave her confidence—if she'd gained this much elevation in so short a time, maybe she could make it to the top. She stopped and breathed deeply and was surprised to find she wasn't tired. There was new energy coursing through her, her veins seemed filled with fresh blood; her lungs took in greater gulps of air. Standing there, staring out over the canyon, she had an image of what she looked like—ragged and dirty, yes. But solid and strong. A human being at the height of her physical strength, working with and not against her surroundings.

She moved northeast now, taking what the mountain gave her. Fifteen minutes later she reached a dead end. A sheer vertical cliff, unscalable, angling out so she couldn't get around it. She looked left, no way around. Right was no better. It was like a door had slammed down, closing off any forward path. She tilted her head back and peered up, shading her eyes with her hand. The cliff was more than fifty feet high, dirt and rock, no obvious footholds. A set of roots dangled out the side of it, like the frayed ends of a wire. She cursed herself for not taking the rock-climbing class that Tracy had told her about, for not learning how to read this cliff face like a sheet of music. Just looking up at the top of it sent a shiver through her body. She would have to retrace her steps.

Shaking her head, cursing, she headed back the other way, moving over ground she'd already covered. Then she reached the place where she'd chosen the route that led to the wall. She remembered why—the other way did not look promising. A steep rock face she'd have to shimmy across in order to gain the next ledge. She surveyed the scene in front of her: Directly up was another vertical wall. Down and around might get her to a better vantage point—or lead her all the way back to the canyon floor. Going right seemed like the best bet, but it did not look very inviting. Rock outcroppings, like bulbous growths on the side of the mountain, brown and red, maybe volcanic. It looked like a giant pile of porridge, and about that stable too. There were places to step, sure—it was not a flat wall—but only small ones, with a sheer drop of a hundred feet. And her toes were so swollen and painful she didn't trust them to hold her. If she fell or got hurt and couldn't go on, they might all be lost. Gwen could see, though, that if she could get beyond the outcroppings, there was solid granite shelving above.

She collapsed her one pole and stuck it into her pack. She closed her eyes and said a silent prayer. Then she took one step off the flat rock and onto a three-inch ledge. It held. With her hand she grabbed onto a piece of jutting rock and slowly brought her left foot over. She shuffled sideways, stepping carefully with her right foot and putting her weight down, then reaching out with her right hand, repeating the movement with her left. She ventured out ten feet, twenty. Her fingers were raw from the popped blisters but she ignored the pain. Then a rock broke off in her right hand and pulled away from the wall, and she gripped tight with her left and held. The rock bounced off the wall just past her foot; she heard it falling down the side of the cliff. She glanced down despite herself and saw open space; the rock finally crashed to a stop somewhere below. She found a solid hold with her right hand and hugged the rock face, breathing hard; her heart beat so violently she thought the force of it might push her off the wall. This was a bad idea, she thought. Maybe I should go back. But when she looked left she couldn't remember exactly how she'd gotten to where she was; it was as if the holds had made themselves visible only for the moment that she'd needed them, and had since been reabsorbed into the rock. She looked above and found an overhang; no passage there. She looked to her right and saw some possible holds—but after her near fall, how could she trust them? She closed her eyes for a moment and felt the panic welling up in her chest. Hold it together, she thought. Hold it together. You've made it this far, you've got to trust yourself.

She looked left again, then above and right. There was no clear way. But she had to move, for the sake of progress and to quell her own panic. So she took a tentative step to the right, finding a two-inch ledge and stepping down on it, first with a little weight, and then with more. It held. She reached out with her right hand and found a protruding piece of rock. She pulled, and it stayed firmly in place. She found small ledges for her left foot and hand and moved onto them; they were solid. Slowly, carefully, she made her way across the rock face, looking up at the granite landing every once in a while to make sure it was really there. She felt alternatingly terrified and powerful— amazed to be doing what she was doing, and then disbelieving. Never, never could she have imagined herself like this.

Just then an image of Robert came up in her mind, from the last time she had seen him. He'd visited her office and sat slumped in a chair, a strange, wry smile on his face. Later she understood that he had come to say goodbye. She'd been so sad this last year, but now she knew how much she still had to fight for. She wanted—she wanted very much—to live.

Gwen's feet were throbbing, her hands hurt, and her arms and legs were burning. But she was confident now that she'd make it. She'd learned to bend her legs to lower her center of gravity, and that helped her keep her balance. After the near fall she knew not to look down. She looked only where she was going and then at the granite slab again. Just a bit farther, she told herself. Just a bit more and I'll be safe.

Suddenly it was as if a path had opened up and the rest of the way was clear. She knew which way to go, she followed it, and then she was lying facedown on the slab, holding onto the warm rock with outstretched arms and limp with relief and exhaustion. She pulled herself up and peered back over the edge at the cliff face. It was steep, nearly vertical, rugged and unstable. There was no way she could have made it. But she did.

She retrieved her bottle of water and drank several large gulps, then looked out over the landscape. What a view, she thought. What a view! The whole basin, which had seemed barren from the other side, was beautiful and grand. An amphitheater of jagged granite, with a gleaming blue ribbon of water winding through it. On the other side she could make out the peaks they'd crossed earlier, which they had thought made up the eastern crest. Two sharp peaks, one gray and one volcanic red, curled toward each other like mirror images, like yin and yang, partners in a graceful millennial dance. Another mountain was shaped like a sail—the top and bottom corners held in place, the body blown taut and triangular. And everywhere, the mountains were half-draped with snow, housing three or four small pockets of ice that she realized were glaciers. The sight of them took her breath away. This glorious landscape, forged by the forces of geology, by the movements of earth, by God, was its own justification, perfect in itself.

She glanced back, up to the top of the ridge, and saw open sky beyond it. She knew now that the top was within her reach. Tracy had been right—she could do this. There was so much she hadn't known she could do.

She rested for ten minutes and ate part of a protein bar. Then she stood up, took out and adjusted her pole, and started walking again. The mountain was giving her a route to the south, so that was where she headed, picking her way up through the rocky slope again. The rocks were full of color—how wrong she'd been to think the landscape was colorless!—dark blue, orange, metamorphic red, purple, pink, sage green. Some rocks were primarily one color and shot through by another; others were as mixed as bouquets. As she passed an intricate pile of boulders, a small gray creature with a rabbitlike head ran in front of her, squeaked, and then scurried away.

She was approaching a jutting-out wall of rock, a corner of the mountain. If she went around it she'd be out of sight of Tracy and Oscar, but it appeared to be the easiest way to go. She held onto the rock with both hands and shuffled around the corner, onto a ledge that looked out at another canyon. She took a few steps farther out and her heart skipped. There was a sheer drop-off of at least two hundred feet and it was windier here; she'd stay close to the wall until she got to safer ground. Ahead of her, another slope, with a large field of snow. Below her in the distance, at the bottom of the canyon, she saw a faint line across the ground. A trail? She remembered the smooth area they'd crossed just before they reached the trees—they might have walked right over it. If it was a trail, maybe someone would come along and find Tracy and Oscar. Someone who could help.

It was colder here because of the wind, so she dropped her pack to pull out her jacket. When she stood up again, A.J. was standing in front of her.

"Funny meeting *you* here," he said.

Her heart leapt into her throat and she let out a gasp. How the hell did A.J. get here? His cheek was cut and swollen and there was a smirk on his face; his voice sounded intimate and mean. He held a gun in his right hand, and it was pointed at her chest. This can't be real, Gwen thought. This cannot be happening. She turned and pressed her back against the rock and a small sound of terror escaped her.

"You guys left without saying goodbye. It hurt my feelings. I thought we were friends."

Gwen stood straight and tried to back up farther. But there was no give, just the warm hard rock. She looked at the gun in his hand, the glasses on his face.

"I'll bet you're wondering where I got this stuff," he said, as if reading her mind. "You really think I'd come out here with only one pair of glasses? I had a pack with me, remember? I left it at the camp. Once I got loose from your amateur little tie job, I just went and found it."

"You . . . you got loose by yourself?"

A.J. grinned and a kind of spasm went through his shoulders; he seemed to be enjoying himself. His face was burned red and his hair was wild, as if it had been whipped by the storm.

"Yep, all by myself. Don't get me wrong, it took a minute. I had to find something sharp enough to cut the rope. But there was a nice little stub sticking out of the tree, and once I twisted around and found that, I just rubbed until the ropes cut. But I got a bit of my arm too. See?"

He held his left arm out toward her and she saw the scrape mark just above the wrist, where you'd hit a volleyball. She also saw again the swastika tattoo embedded on a red and black flag. Despite the heat, she started to shiver.

"Then I had to figure out where you guys went. At first I thought you'd finish the loop, but I have to give it to you, you were smart. No telling who was waiting at the trailhead. Or what happened to your Volvo. Nice car." He grinned, and there was a strange maniacal light in his eyes. Behind him, ridge after ridge of mountains extended into the distance, gorgeous and impersonal. Is this where she would die? she wondered.

"I saw your footprints up the ridge from the trail," he continued. "All that loose scree held the tracks like snow. So I went up to the top, and there you were, plain as day, making your way through the valley. With that damn ungrateful dog. After all I've done for her, she follows *you*! The little traitor! Fuck border collies. Next time I'm getting an Australian shepherd." He screwed up his eyes and jerked his shoulder, as if trying to shake something off. "I just headed to the south of you, parallel the whole way. It was pretty easy to track you, I have to say. But even I was surprised when your friend got shot. It wasn't me, I swear, and it wasn't my brother. Maybe it was one of the kid's friends. And hey, if that's what happened, it's kind of perfect, don't you think? Their Mexican got your Mexican!"

He laughed again, eyes wild, and kept pointing the gun at her chest. She felt the heat of the rock against her back and could not think what to do. If she rushed him he would shoot her. But if she did nothing he might shoot anyway. She was frozen with fear and helplessness. At least on the cliff face her fate had been in her hands. Here there was nothing to do.

"Look, why don't you let me go? We won't tell anyone what you're doing back here, and we won't say a word about the kid."

A.J. shook his head exaggeratedly, like a young child hearing an answer he didn't like. "No, no, no, Gwen. That! Won't! Work! You've seen too much, you know too much, you all have to go. First you, 'cause you're the leader now. Then your friends."

Gwen realized with horror how helpless Tracy and Oscar were. And they believed that A.J. was dead.

"I'm impressed you made it this far by yourself," he said. "I wouldn't have picked you to be the one to hold it together. But maybe you're the toughest after all." And now he had a different kind of smile, and a chill went up Gwen's spine. "I sure did enjoy watching you in the river."

She thought of their rest at the edge of the creek, how good it felt to wash off several days' worth of dirt and sweat. Now, knowing that A.J. had been watching, she felt violated, naked. Instinctively she crossed her arms over her chest.

"Why don't you take off your clothes for me?" he said, voice rough and low. "I'd sure like to see you up close."

Gwen shook her head no and squeezed her arms tighter.

"Come on." He stepped forward and touched the gun to her chest; she could feel the hard metal probing through her clothes. "Show me what you're good for."

Gwen didn't move. Now lust and anger darkened his

face. He raised the gun to her temple and grabbed her breast. His hand went under the fabric and pinched her nipple hard, then moved up and squeezed her throat. She felt the roughness of his hairy arm scraping her chest. "Undo your pants," he said, "or I'll undo them for you."

Suddenly he jerked away and cried out in pain. There was a flash of white fur. He was dragged back a couple of steps and the gun fell from his hand. The dog had sunken her teeth deep into his calf, and she was whipping her head back and forth, growling, tearing through the flesh. The blood splattered on her muzzle and onto the rocks.

"Get the fuck off me!" A.J. cried. He jerked and flailed, pounding the dog's back and head, and as he spun with her, he kicked the gun and it flew off over the ledge. Timber yanked and twisted and he fell to the ground. Gwen had moved to grab the gun but now it was gone; then she remembered the bear spray. She unzipped the lid of her pack and pulled out the canister and removed the plastic safety. She stepped over and expelled a quick powerful blast right in A.J.'s face. His forehead, cheeks, nose, and hair turned a bright, sickly orange. He cried out—an awful, gargled sound—and his hands went up to his face. "I can't breathe! I can't see!" he gasped. "What the fuck did you do?" Then: "Jesus Christ, I'm burning!"

The orange spray swirled back toward her. She felt the heat on her face and her eyes began to sting. She stumbled back a few feet, reaching out to grab the rock wall; her lungs were burning as if she'd swallowed fire. She could barely open her eyes but when she did, she saw that A.J. was writhing on the ground on his hands and knees, scratching at his face as if trying to rip off the burning skin. He was gasping, hyperventilating, crying in pain.

"You blinded me, you fucking bitch! I can't breathe!"

The dog was standing a few feet back from him and sneezing. A.J. was wriggling closer to the edge. Gwen stumbled back over to him, waving her hands in front of her as if to clear away smoke. He was gagging now, grasping blindly at the dirt. She put her foot against his hip and shoved hard; he fell over onto his back, right at the edge of the cliff.

"I'm going to kill you, you bitch!" he rasped, reaching blindly, but she stepped up and pushed him again with her foot; he didn't realize what was happening until he started to fall. He grabbed at the rock but there was nothing to hold and he tipped out over the edge and was gone. A horrible scream came out of him and echoed through the canyon. He tumbled down the cliff face, screaming all the way, until he crashed on a rocky ledge two hundred feet below. His head hit a rock and split apart like a melon. His body lay broken and still.

Gwen could only keep her burning eyes open for a few seconds at a time, but she looked down anyway to make sure he was dead. Then she turned to look at Timber. The dog was sitting back three feet from the edge, tongue lolling out, gazing at the mountains, as if enjoying the beautiful view. How had she gotten up here? Had she found another way? She must have, that crazy dog; she must have left soon after Gwen did. Her muzzle was soaked with blood and her teeth were red; there were speckles on her chest and sides. She kept sneezing, big events that made her whole body shake. But other than that, she seemed unharmed.

"Thank you," Gwen said. "Good girl." She wanted to pet the dog's head but when she touched her own skin, a new burning would begin, like spot fires. Her face felt as if it might burn off. Just beyond the ledge there was a patch of snow the size of a swimming pool, and she picked up her pack and stumbled over to it. When she got to the snow she fell to her knees, scooped it up in handfuls, and pressed it to her burning face. She remembered something she'd read about pepper spray—was bear spray the same thing?—and pulled out her water bottles, rinsing out one eye and then the other. Holding her eyes open made them burn even more but she didn't know what else to do. When the water was gone she buried her face and hands directly in the snow. Finally, the pain began to subside. She sat back on her heels, noticing that her pants were soaked through at the knees. The dog stepped up and tentatively licked her face. She jumped back and her tongue flashed out and she curled her lips, trying to get rid of the terrible taste.

"Sorry, girl." If it had been this bad from a backdraft, she couldn't imagine how A.J. had felt. Thank God Tracy had made her bring the bear spray. But it wouldn't have made a difference if the dog hadn't come.

Once the burning sensation eased a little, she sat and collected herself. What to do now? How to signal to the others? She couldn't go back—she'd never make it across the cliff face again—and she needed to press forward. It seemed like she should let them know that A.J. had reappeared. But maybe not. He was dead, he was gone, and that knowledge wouldn't necessarily help; his brother might still be out there. As for the other guys, José's friends, she didn't know.

She looked up and to her left, and a whole new part of the range was visible now. There was a gap she hadn't been able to see before, maybe half a mile away. Two small, sharp peaks like the spires of a castle, with a windswept cirque between them. The top of the cirque, between the peaks, was lower than the other gaps she'd seen. She could walk straight up. But there was snow—a field of untouched snow stretching at least a hundred yards down from the top. Maybe that was a good thing; maybe her shoes would sink in, and that might help her footing. Or maybe, if it was hard, she'd slide backward. Damn, she thought. I wish I could ask Tracy. She felt another surge of nervousness. But then she thought of what had just happened, of A.J.'s body lying broken, and she knew that she could handle it.

"What do you think, pup?"

Timber smiled at her, tongue hanging out the side of her mouth. Gwen felt slightly frightened by the knowledge of what the dog could do. But Timber had saved her, given her the few seconds she needed to get to her pack. And besides, she was glad for the company.

She took a moment to loosen her shoes and readjust her bunched socks, and then laced up again. They walked parallel to the top of the ridge, following a narrow ledge. As she got farther from the place where she'd come around the corner, she could see how much easier the terrain was on this side, how quickly A.J. could have caught up with them. In another few minutes, she found herself at the bottom of the cirque.

The bowl of snow looked more daunting from here. A football field–sized expanse of white, framed by the towering spires. But there was the top, within sight, and she knew, she *felt*, that this really was the eastern crest this time. All she had to do was get to the top. From there, she could walk to the Owens Valley.

She stepped onto the snow and it held her, the uneven surface bending her foot sideways. She took another step and the same thing happened. The snow was solid, frozen, like waves on a petrified ocean. And slippery, half-formed into ice. She used her hiking pole to stabilize herself and took one slow step at a time; Timber picked her way carefully, stepping into depressions, and moved more easily up the slope. Then Gwen put her foot down and broke through the crust, sinking in up to her knee. "Shit!" she said aloud, pulling her leg out and brushing snow from the top of her shoe. She got back on the surface again and walked tentatively, breaking through every ten or fifteen feet, getting progressively more tired, and colder.

The going was very slow, and she didn't know what was worse, the crusty ankle-twisting surface or the plunging through. The tops of her feet were burning, and she realized she'd gotten spray on them when she'd loosened her shoes, so now, despite the snow, every time she took a step it felt like she was lifting her feet through fire. The bright glare of the snow was hurting her eyes, and here, at what must have been over twelve thousand feet, she was struggling to breathe. But she kept going. At one point she stopped and ate several handfuls of snow, then rubbed some on Timber's face to wash off the blood. The dog tolerated this and bent down and bit off a frozen chunk, crunching on it loudly. Then she took off and charged up the slope, legs working wildly, tail waving like a flag to lead the way.

As they neared the top the slope steepened, and Gwen paused, looking around to consider her options. There were really only two. Head straight up, or traverse, and she chose to traverse, moving diagonally to the left, then the right. But when she looked down and saw how steep the slope was now; when she slipped and barely caught herself with the pole; when she saw that if she did fall, there was nothing to hold onto, nothing to keep her from skidding all the way past the end of the cirque and farther down the mountain, she decided it was better not to look. She remembered stories Tracy had told her of climbers on Shasta and Rainier, sliding all the way down sheer gullies like this to injury or death. That won't happen to me, she decided.

She hiked straight up, kicking steps into the snow. Moving like this, with her pole to support her, she made slow but steady progress. Twice, three times a foot slid out beneath her, but she dug the pole in and caught herself. When they were within striking distance the dog ran ahead, all the way to the top. She stood there, looking east, striking a proud and happy pose, and Gwen knew that they had made it.

And then she was there herself. And a new world opened before her. A small plateau just below that held another teal lake. Beyond that, her eye traveled over gradually lessening ridges and peaks, back down into gullies and forests. She saw the great Owens Valley off in the distance, high brown desert, flat and unarable. She saw a range of red mountains behind it, stark and plain, as if mere shadows of the range on which she stood. She saw a tiny ribbon of highway bisecting the plain, light gray against the red-brown earth. And in the center of the valley, a cluster of buildings, metal roofs reflecting the sun. She stopped and dropped her pack and sat down heavily. A town, she thought, tears rising up. And people.

She stared at the reflecting lights, which flickered and wavered like a mirage. In the midday sun, a distant river gleamed. Once she was sure that this vision was real, she turned and looked back where she'd come from. Layer upon layer of mountains rose off to the west, with dozens of sharp peaks cut through by deep canyons, and marked with stubborn pockets of snow. Up here, at this pass, she stood above them all—there was nothing between her and the sky. She had *crossed* those mountains, she told herself. It didn't seem possible, and yet it was true. Turning to look at the valley and town again, she felt herself at a border, a tipping point between wilderness and civilization. Were these worlds separate or related? she wondered. Could she carry one back to the other?

She rested just long enough to eat a bit of snow she'd put into her water bottle and to give another handful to the dog. She needed to keep moving. Tracy had told her that there were trails on this side, not more than a few miles apart. The descent looked easy here—not so steep, and she could zigzag through the scree. She started down, trying to be cautious, but looking up too, hoping to see a hiker or even a copter, anyone who could help her get out of here.

It took her twenty minutes to traverse down to the edge of the lake. Feathers of ice floated gently on the surface. Both she and the dog drank thirstily from the frigid water, and she refilled her bottles. They kept on. After another twenty minutes a few scraggly bushes appeared, then occasional windswept trees. She was tired, very tired, and it was hard to keep moving; all her energy and will had been focused on reaching the pass, and she'd somehow forgotten or put out of her mind that she still had miles to go. The sun seemed to penetrate the material of her clothes and she felt seared, dried out, and depleted. Tears filled her eyes. As she descended, the Owens Valley became less visible, disappeared from sight; it was obscured by sub-peaks and canyon walls. But she knew it was there, and that kept her going, even as she stumbled several times, too tired to watch where she was placing her feet. Each time she managed to catch herself—with the pole, or by grabbing a rock. Timber came over and touched her occasionally, providing encouragement.

They made it back down to the tree line and Gwen was glad for the cover; she stopped and drank half a bottle of water. She closed her eyes, but she couldn't let herself fall asleep—she had to keep moving. And she couldn't be distracted by the growling in her stomach, the hunger that was starting to eat her away from inside.

She hiked methodically through the forest, between tall shading pines and scattered rocks. She leaned more heavily on the pole now and reached out for trees to help keep her balance. A few more miles, she kept telling herself. A few more miles and I'll be safe. She had never known she could do something like this, but now she was sure she would make it. And as she moved down the mountain, it occurred to her that she came from a long line of women who walked. She thought of her great-aunt Emmaline, who had trudged for hours each day through all kinds of weather in order to provide for her family. For the first time Gwen understood how exhausting this had been, how heavy the mail bag must have felt on her shoulder. She thought even further back, to Phillis, her grandmother's grandmother, who'd braved the hilly forests of Tennessee and Kentucky on her long trek north to freedom. Now Gwen could feel the sharpness of the rocks under Phillis's bare feet, the terror as she fled men pursuing with ropes and guns. Those women had pushed forward, despite exhaustion and discouragement and menace and fear, to reach the promise of safety. If they could press on, then she could too.

She rounded a large boulder and almost walked into a bear. It was coming up the slope straight toward her. Cinnamon-colored, huge, with tremendous rippling muscles in its shoulders and back, it had paws the size of dinner plates and sharp curved claws. He swung his great head back and forth, looking up at trees or the steep mountain walls, entirely at home in his world.

Gwen froze—he was ten feet away and she had nowhere to go. An involuntary sound came out of her, and at this the bear turned and saw her. She was so terrified she could not move; the dog pressed against her and growled. The bear's big, wet nose twitched and its ears perked up and then lay back against its head. He raised himself up halfway on his back legs as if to confirm what he had seen. Then he turned and galloped off into the forest.

Gwen tried to walk but she was shaking so much she couldn't control her legs. Timber let out a few tentative barks; all the hair on her nape was standing up.

"Oh my God," Gwen said, leaning against a tree. "Oh my God." The bear, for all its fearsomeness, was the most magnificent creature she'd ever seen. But what would it do now? Would it come back? For all she knew it had climbed a tree and was waiting to ambush them. She managed to calm herself and started walking downhill, the dog sticking close by. Her legs wobbled and her heart raced; she was trying not to gasp. She looked everywhere as they walked, whipping around completely one time when she thought she heard something behind them. Then she noticed something moving off to the left. There was a clump of thick bushes maybe forty feet away. They were quivering, and between them she could make out a bit of brown. It was obviously the bear—was he gearing up for an attack? Gwen held her breath and prayed. For ten, fifteen seconds nothing happened. And then she realized something both unbelievable and comforting. She understood that the bear was hiding. From *her*.

She felt a surge of relief and adrenaline, and this helped power her down the mountain. For the first mile or so after she'd seen the bear, she kept looking back over her shoulder, but she knew that it was not coming after them. They moved slowly and carefully downhill, and soon Gwen was feeling groggy again—the lack of sleep and food catching up with her and dragging down her limbs. Twice, she stumbled over rocks and fell; the second time she twisted her knee. But she kept on, despite her growing exhaustion. She hadn't made it this far to give up now.

Then suddenly they came upon a worn groove in the earth. A trail. She stared at it in disbelief, not trusting her eyes. But Timber seemed to know what it was and she began to run down it, as if this had been their planned route all along. They followed the trail left and downhill for a hundred feet, two hundred—it was real. Gwen could hardly keep her eyes open, but she knew the trail would lead them to safety.

She rounded a bend, and saw that she was at the top of some switchbacks that twisted down through the forest. Then movement between the trees—another bear? No— there was color, orange and green. She stopped and squinted and made out two figures—people. Carrying backpacks. Walking up the switchbacks, walking toward her.

"Hey!" she yelled weakly, her voice half its normal volume. She called out several more times but they didn't hear. So she steadied herself against a rock and waited until they were closer. "Hey!" she yelled again. They seemed to be taking forever. Now Timber caught sight of them too, and she gave a muffled bark. She ran straight down the slope, hackles up, white tail raised and flashing. Finally the people looked up. They stopped for a moment, turned toward one another, and continued up the switchbacks, faster. When Gwen saw that they were coming, she collapsed to her knees and gave a prayer of thanks and broke into gasping sobs.

It took them another five minutes to reach her. They were a young couple in their twenties. He was tall and blond; she was dark-haired and petite. They both carried well-worn packs and were dressed in hiking shorts and long-sleeved shirts. When they got within sight she could see the worry on their faces, and it was because of this that she understood how bad she looked. The dog barked at them protectively, but Gwen called her back. "It's okay."

"Hey," the boy said when they were closer. "Are you all right?"

"I'm okay," she managed. "But I have three friends back there, and they need help." She gestured behind her, toward the pass.

"You're the missing backpackers!" the girl exclaimed. "They were talking about you at the ranger station yesterday!"

"We're missing?" Gwen said, confused. She didn't know what day it was; she didn't know how long they'd been gone.

"They found your car burned up at some remote trailhead," the boy explained. "They've been searching for you—didn't you hear the helicopters?"

Gwen shook her head.

"You need some water," the girl said. "You look dehydrated. And when was the last time you ate?" She'd already set her pack down and was rifling through it.

"I don't know. Could you please get help? Two of my friends are hurt, and one of them's been shot."

The couple looked at each other.

"They both need medical care right away. Can one of you go back down and get someone?"

"That'll take too long," said the boy. "But I've got my safety beacon, and I can signal for help. Hopefully a rescue crew's not too far away. They've been looking over toward the west side of the mountains."

"Where are we now?"

"Near Eitan Pass," the boy said.

Suddenly Gwen started to shiver. Her pants and feet were still wet from the snow, and the sun had gone down over the ridge.

"Let's get you warmed up," the girl said. She took a down jacket out of her pack and wrapped it around Gwen's shoulders. Then she pulled off Gwen's shoes and socks and gave her a pair of dry socks. The dog lay down beside her.

The boy took a canister stove out of his pack and handed it to the girl, who set it up to make some hot water. And then he got out his safety beacon—an oval black plastic device the size of a wallet—found a clearing in the trees, and pressed the button to call for help.

Chapter Twenty
Oscar

A sound, a rumbling, like a huge truck coming, or an earthquake rattling a house. He felt it before he heard it, the ground suddenly unstable, but he was too weak to move or to cover himself. It grew closer, bigger, seemed to settle overhead. Tracy must have felt it too—where was she? The vibrations in the ground were strangely comforting, interesting, except that they jostled his shoulder. Would he bleed more? He didn't know. He didn't think that there was any blood left.

After some time—he didn't know how much—there were voices. Someone making their way across the rocks.

"Over here!"

Was that Tracy? He couldn't tell. No one had talked in hours.

Then the sounds were closer. "Here," the same voice said again. "He hasn't spoken for a while."

"Any movement?" This was a new voice, female, not Gwen's. Where was Gwen?

"No. But I've checked his pulse a few times. Just to make sure."

A hand on his forehead, fingertips on his neck, direct and strong and intimate. He tried to pull away; they were disturbing his quiet.

"There's a pulse. Faint, but there," the new voice said. "We need to get him out of here."

Someone handled him firmly by the shoulders, the legs. Leave me alone, he thought. Don't bother me. A yank on his shoulder sent a jolt of pain through him and he screamed.

"Sorry, sorry," the new voice said.

"At least we know he's alive."

They picked him up and moved him, set him down on something else. It was cold, hard, just bigger than his body. Had they put him in a coffin? He felt himself being lifted. It was warm, uncomfortably warm, and he knew they were back in the sun. The whooshing sound was even louder now, something huge and heavy cutting the sky. They set him down and he heard yelling. "Over here! Easy!" Some other things he couldn't make out. Maybe they were trying to make him more comfortable. Then hands moving over him and sounds of things being tightened, cinched; something was holding him down.

"Pull 'er up!" someone yelled, and he felt himself leave the ground, swing in the open air. He felt but didn't see the earth give way beneath him, he was moving up into the sky. Was he dying? Was he already dead? And going up to heaven? He didn't know, but as he swayed in the wind, he cried out. He didn't want to fall back to earth. He opened his eyes and saw a huge white underbelly, an umbilical cord leading up to a massive body. Nothing but sky around it. Around him. If he turned over, he would roll into the air. He did not want to be taken in, he did not want to die. But try as he might, he couldn't move. The air, the ground, the underbelly—what did it matter anyway? He was dying or dead. Maybe the rope would snap and it would really be over. But it didn't, and then there was no more sky, and firm hands pulled him over, and in.

"Let's get him fluids!" a male voice shouted over the sound of the machine.

"Is he alive?" came another voice, familiar.

"Barely. He's lost a lot of blood. And he's fried to a crisp."

"Rope going back down!" someone yelled.

Hands were all over him, cutting his clothes, poking him. In a few minutes the sense that whatever they were in had taken on more weight.

"There's one more down there," someone said. It was the same voice he'd heard on the ground.

"There's two," said the familiar voice. "Our other friend was behind us."

"We'll have to come back for them—we don't have room. And we need to get this guy to the hospital."

And then more words and more prodding that Oscar didn't hear or feel. A swooping turn of the helicopter, then speed. He tried to tell himself he was headed out and home. He could let go now. And even with the noise, the movement, the voices and hands, he reached a place of quiet and still.

CHAPTER TWENTY-ONE
TODD

Todd watched the helicopter disappear over the ridge. At first, it had hovered on the other side of the pass, so he hadn't seen what happened. Then, on this side, well north of his location, he'd watched a rescue litter with a person attached let down on a rope; he'd seen the litter pulled back up with someone in it. Oscar, he guessed, since his injury was worst. He was sure it had picked up Gwen before. So now it was just Tracy and him, and then they'd be out, and this ordeal would finally be over.

He did not know what had happened, but he was fairly sure that A.J. was dead. Several hours before, after he'd crested what he'd thought was the final pass and discovered a new canyon below him, he'd heard a faint, male, unmistakable scream, someone crying out in mortal anguish. It hadn't sounded like Oscar, and anyway, Oscar was too far gone to muster such energy. There had been no gunshot, though—had A.J. fallen? Been attacked by a mountain lion? Run into someone else from the cartel? And did that mean there was still somebody dangerous on the loose? He didn't know, but he thought A.J. was dead. He felt it, the removal of something malevolent from the world. And with him gone, the others would have a better chance to make it. Led by Gwen, the last one he would have expected. Gwen, who had toughed it out, and who was now someplace hopefully down in the valley, safe, waiting for the rest of them.

When the copter was out of sight, he rested for a moment. The land was barren here, treeless. The lake where he'd stopped was a kind of blue he'd never seen before—teal, dramatic and beautiful. To the left he heard a disturbance of rock and saw a lone startled deer; he raised his rifle reflexively but did not shoot. He was hungry, and he'd thought of eating bugs or silver-blue mountain butterflies. But the helicopter would be back for him soon; there were still a few hours of daylight. He'd make his way to a place where he'd be easy to spot, and then he'd be flown to town, where he could eat at a table and sleep in a proper bed.

He closed his eyes for a moment. A meal, a shower, a bed—how wonderful. He would call Kelly to let her know that he was all right; he would talk to both his kids.

And yet there was something bittersweet about the thought of all that. He had been somewhere else, and it had changed him. Or maybe it had stripped away some unessential layer and he was left with who he truly was. With a twinge he imagined the moment when he could hug Joey and Brooke; they were the only things in his daily world that really mattered. He realized with a surprising clarity that right now, at this moment, he felt satisfied. Even happy. Yet on top of his relief that the end of their ordeal was near, he felt hollowed by loss. He thought of the life he was about to return to, and knew he didn't want to go back.

Chapter Twenty-Two
Gwen

Gwen struggled to wake up. Everything was heavy; it felt like there were sandbags on her body. When the room finally came into focus, a young woman she'd never seen before was sitting in the corner. She was wearing a ranger uniform, olive pants and khaki shirt. A wide-brimmed hat sat on a table behind her; a walkie-talkie and gun were attached to her belt. She had long dark hair that was pulled back into a ponytail, and smooth olive skin, and she looked too young to be a ranger—especially when she saw that Gwen was awake and her face broke into a smile, which carved two perfect dimples into her cheeks.

"Well, hello," she said, sitting up straight. She sounded young too, collegiate even.

"Where am I?" Gwen's own voice sounded strange to her, like she was talking through cotton. Had she seen this woman before?

"You're in Mercy Hospital, Inyo County," the ranger answered, pulling her chair up to the side of the bed. "You've been asleep for about three days."

"Three days!" Gwen looked past the woman at the beige walls, the heavy institutional door. "What day is it?"

"July 5. A Thursday."

Gwen took this in. Thursday. They'd been gone for a week. Somehow it felt more like a year.

"You were pretty out of it in the helicopter," the ranger said. "Unconscious by the time we got here. It was mostly heat exhaustion, dehydration, so they've been pumping you with fluids. And now here you are, back with us again."

"You were in the helicopter with me?" Gwen vaguely remembered swinging through space and being pulled into the copter. She remembered this same voice, urgent and full of authority. The same too-young-looking face.

"I was there. I'm Jessica Montez, by the way. I'm a National Park Service ranger—Law Enforcement and Search and Rescue." She held her hand out and Gwen lifted her own to shake it. Her arm felt weak, and for the first time she noticed the tube that fed into it, attached to bag of fluids at the side of the bed.

"Were we still in the park? I thought we had left it."

"You did, but we were the closest rescue unit. Inyo County Search and Rescue was farther north, and the CHP helicopter out of Fresno was looking over on the western side. We were just to the south of you when the call came in, and so we flew right up. Plus, there were some other elements that made this case relevant to us."

Gwen took this all in. If she hadn't been so out of sorts, she would have been impressed.

Ranger Montez got up and went to the door, where she gestured to someone out in the hallway. A middle-aged male ranger came in, thick through the middle, with slightly burned cheeks and deep wrinkles. His face was kind, though, and the wrinkles around his eyes and mouth looked like they'd been caused by laughter.

"I'm Ranger Perry," he said, holding out a beefy hand. "Glad to see you're awake. You're in good hands here with Ranger Montez."

"Nice to meet you," Gwen said, shaking his hand. She didn't know what else to say. "I can't believe I've been asleep for three days."

"You've been in and out," said Ranger Montez, returning to her seat. "And you were tossing around quite a bit, especially the first day. Talking about A.J. and needing food. And someone named Robert. You kept saying that you had to get moving."

Gwen closed her eyes for a moment; she wasn't ready to think about where she'd been. But the image of A.J.'s face appeared unbidden—his smirk, his touch, the confusion and horror on his face as he went sideways over the cliff.

"We were able to reach your mother," Ranger Montez said. "She was very relieved to hear you're okay."

So relieved that she rushed right up here to see me, Gwen thought. "Are my friends here too?" she asked, and Ranger Montez nodded. She exchanged a glance with her colleague.

"Todd Harris is in good shape," Ranger Perry said, pulling up a chair. "He was checked over and given fluids and then discharged. Oscar Barajas is critical but stable. He lost quite a bit of blood and he's been fighting an infection. But he's over the worst of it. Tomorrow they're taking him by ambulance back to LA."

Gwen closed her eyes again. "Thank God. And Tracy?"

Ranger Montez tilted her chin a bit. "We're not sure where she is. She was there when we took Oscar up in the rescue litter—we gave her something for her pain and wrapped her up. But when we went back to get her, she was gone."

"What do you mean, gone?"

"I mean, she wasn't there. We did pick up Todd, of course, a couple of miles to the south. But he hadn't seen her, either. Inyo SAR's still searching the area."

Gwen tried to digest this. Tracy was gone. She still had the gun when Gwen left her—had she tried to go after the men tied to A.J. or José? Had someone connected to one of them found her and killed her? Had she wandered off in pain and confusion? Or had she simply disappeared?

"We did find three bodies, though," Ranger Perry said, leaning forward, and Gwen was alert again. "Two men associated with the Mexican drug trade. And a known domestic criminal, Arthur James Miles."

Gwen glanced around the room, avoiding his eyes. There was a TV on the wall, muted, playing an afternoon talk show. Her heart was beating out of her chest. She felt the eyes of both rangers watching her steadily.

"Do you want to tell us about them?" the ranger asked softly. His voice was deep and soothing.

She did not know where to start. She did not know how all their actions looked now, in the light of day, when they were out of the mountains.

"A.J. shot a young Mexican kid. We accidentally stumbled onto a marijuana garden the kid was protecting."

Ranger Montez nodded as if Gwen had answered a test question correctly. "This is part of why we're involved, because of the grows in the national parks and national forests. We found it and finished eradicating it the day after we rescued you."

"The second guy, I don't know," Gwen said. They'd never seen a second guy—had A.J. killed him too? Or—and now she felt a chill of realization—had that been who Todd shot?

"Someone was shooting at us," she continued. "I thought it was A.J."

"But then?"

"But then I saw A.J. the last day we were up there. I was totally surprised. I thought—" She was about to say she thought he was dead, she thought that Todd had shot him. But it occurred to her that she didn't know what Todd had told them.

Ranger Montez waited to see if Gwen would finish the sentence. When she didn't, the ranger asked, "And what happened to A.J.?"

Gwen's heart felt like it was coming up in her throat. In a moment she'd change from someone who'd been fleeing a pursuer to someone who'd caused a person to die. She looked at Ranger Montez, then Ranger Perry, straight in their eyes.

"He attacked me. He'd captured us back at the pot garden but we fought him and tied him up. But he got loose and followed us, and then he caught up with me and began to assault me. Then the dog—it had been his dog, but she'd come along with us—she bit him, and I grabbed my bear spray and sprayed him in the face."

Ranger Montez nodded. "That would explain the residual bear spray on your hands and clothes. And then he fell over the edge?"

Gwen kept her voice steady. "I pushed him."

The rangers exchanged a look again, and now Ranger Perry pulled his chair up closer. His face was grim. "We appreciate your honesty, Miss Foster. But we're going to pretend we never heard that."

"What?"

"Arthur Miles fell over the cliff on his own. I told your friend Todd to forget what he told me too—that he shot the other individual, a Mexican national. The gun that killed the second man was the same one that killed the first. It was Arthur Miles's gun, and as far as we're concerned, Arthur Miles was responsible for both deaths."

Gwen stared at him, confused. *Todd* had shot the second guy? And that was who had shot Oscar? And this ranger was making up a different story? And this other baby-faced ranger, this girl who'd saved their asses, was going along with it?

"I'm perfectly happy to take responsibility for what I did. And it sounds like Todd is too."

"That's honorable of you," Ranger Perry said. "It is. But you take the blame for this publicly, and you'll put your lives at risk. Your lives, and the lives of your loved ones."

Ranger Montez pushed her chair closer to the bed, the legs squeaking on the linoleum. "You stumbled into a drug war, Miss Foster," she said. Her eyes were bright and intense, and for the first time, she seemed older. "A drug war, and a race war. Those people aren't messing around. They're fighting over where to grow their crops and how to distribute them, and they each cut into what the other one thinks is their territory. There are millions of dollars at stake here. Tens of millions of dollars. And it's all intensified by the racial angle, since Miles was part of an antigovernment white supremacist group."

"I got that."

"Part of why they got into the drug trade in the first place was to fund their other activities—conferences, concerts, printed materials, websites that preach hate. They want to do battle with the cartels for economic *and* racial reasons. And then all of you show up, and it's like fuel on the fire."

"He was terrifying," Gwen said, her voice shaking. She remembered the look on his face when he pressed up against her, the rough hands on her breasts and stomach. Thank God for Timber, she thought. Thank God for that damned crazy dog.

"Yes," Ranger Perry said. "He is. Or he was. He's one of the most notorious leaders in the California white supremacy movement. And he's under suspicion for two other murders, which is probably just the tip of the iceberg. There's no question that you did the right thing, Miss Foster. He would have killed you without a second thought."

Gwen's skin prickled with revulsion and fear. He was gone, she told herself. He was gone, and yet she could still see him clearly.

Ranger Montez reached out and covered her hand. The warmth of her touch brought tears to Gwen's eyes.

"I'm sorry," the ranger said. She took her hand away, and after a moment she spoke again. "The Mexican growers are just as bad. They kill anyone who gets in their way. Three innocent people who wandered into grow areas, like you did, have been murdered just this year—all on national forest and National Park Service lands. Not to mention what they do to their own. The young guys who guard the fields—some of them are captured in Mexico and forced to do this work, or the cartels threaten to murder their families."

Gwen thought about José, his youth and his fear. She thought about Oscar, falling forward, the torn and bloody flesh. "That second guy was trying to kill us too."

Ranger Perry nodded. "And they will *keep* trying if they think you had anything to do with their garden being destroyed, or with their men getting killed. Better they believe that Arthur did all of it. And A.J.'s associates can believe that he was killed by one of them—or that he just fell over a cliff."

"And the cycle will continue," Gwen remarked. "Each side blaming the other."

"Better they blame each other than you," the ranger said. Now he leaned forward again. "Look, I know you want to do the right thing. But in this case the right thing is making sure that you stay safe. You and your families."

Gwen heard the implication loud and clear, and heeded it. She looked at the two rangers' sober, concerned faces and could not believe she was really having this conversation. "And this is the story you're putting out there?" she asked.

"We've already put it out there," said Ranger Perry. "You and your friends were on a backpacking trip and happened to get lost. And separately, in another part of the mountains, a bunch of bad guys had a conflict over drugs and several of them were killed."

Gwen was silent for a moment. She knew it made sense—and it would save her from having to talk about what happened.

"What you did . . ." Ranger Montez began. "What you did took a whole lot of guts. You hiked almost fifty miles, over two major passes, in what, three days?—with no shelter and I'm sure no sleep."

Gwen thought about this. Fifty miles. It seemed so long. And in that distance everything had changed.

"You were attacked by a murderer," the ranger continued, "and you fought him off with your bare hands and killed him. It's pretty great." She shook her head. "It's pretty unbelievable."

For the first time Gwen felt the truth of this—relief,

and amazement, and pride. "Well, me and the dog," she said. "Hey, where's the dog?"

"With your friend Todd."

She was relieved. "He took her home to LA?"

"He took her, but he isn't in LA. He's here."

"I thought you said he'd been discharged."

"He was." And now the ranger broke into a big smile. "He stuck around to wait for you."

The next morning, Gwen woke up in time to see Oscar loaded into the transport ambulance. She hadn't realized how tiny the hospital was until she went outside—smaller than her office building at work, the size of a bus station in a lonely country town. Oscar was in a travel gurney, swaddled in blankets, with two IVs attached to his arm. His shoulder was bandaged, and there were dark circles beneath his eyes. He was groggy from pain or drugs, but when he saw Gwen, he smiled.

"I'm glad you're okay," she said. He was just about to be lifted through the ambulance door.

"I don't feel so hot," he replied slowly. "They're taking me to Huntington Hospital, to be closer to home."

"That's good. Claudia and your mother can take care of you."

He lifted his hand toward her, and she grasped it. "Thank you," he said, eyes bright and intense. "Thank you for saving me."

When Oscar was gone she thought about calling Todd, but she realized she didn't have his number. Then she remembered that it wouldn't have mattered anyway, since he didn't have his phone. She'd seen Ranger Montez again that morning—the ranger had been there when Gwen woke up, and had made sure she'd eaten breakfast—but Gwen had forgotten to ask what hotel Todd was in. They'd avoided speaking of what had happened and talked instead about other things. Gwen told Ranger Montez about her job and learned that she was from Southern California too; she'd grown up in San Diego and had fallen in love with the outdoors through trips with the Boys & Girls Club. Ranger Montez entertained Gwen with stories of life with the National Park Service, silly tourist and animal encounters—like the man who ran naked and screaming through a campground after finding a bear in the shower; like the partying hikers on Mount Whitney she'd convinced to stop drinking with the promise of a bar at the summit.

Gwen found herself laughing for the first time in days. But she was ready, more than ready, to go home. The ranger had said that Todd would pick her up at noon, and since she had a couple of hours, she decided to go out and buy some clothes. The hospital staff had brought her a pair of jeans, a shirt, sneakers—but they were all too big, and she didn't like to think about where they'd come from. The rangers had taken her hiking clothes and pack, which was fine with her; she didn't want to see any of it, anyway. But they'd brought back her ID holder with her credit card and cash. So she put on the ill-fitting hospital clothes and ventured into the town.

Her legs and back were sore and she felt a little wobbly, but otherwise, she was uninjured and grateful. What an amazing thing to be in a town! It was a small place, three stoplights, and half the storefronts on the main strip were empty. The town appeared to be blue-collar white, with a few Natives here and there. There was a Ben Franklin, a hardware store, a shop that sold fishing supplies, all in old brick buildings that made the place feel like Main Street from the 1950s. And yet walking down the block, past the American flags and red, white, and blue streamers left over from the Fourth of July, Gwen was overcome with joy. She was out of danger, back among the living.

She found a small general store and chose the simplest things she could: jeans that fit, a polo shirt, some no-name sneakers. Not the cutest stuff for sure, but it would have to do. And even in this simple outfit, she felt infinitely better—clean, and ready to reenter her life.

She returned to the hospital along quiet backstreets, moving for the sake of moving and not trying to outrun anything. The whole town was dwarfed by the mountains behind it, which loomed like a wave about to break. She stopped and looked at them, this range that had stood for tens of thousands of years before her and would continue to stand long after she was gone. Deep in those mountains three men had died. And somewhere, maybe, Tracy still wandered. Where was she? And how was it that Tracy was the one who hadn't made it out, when Gwen was here, in one piece, and alive? For a moment she remembered the intense, wild fear, the sense that she might die at any moment. It was over, she was safe, and about to head home. She offered up a silent prayer of thanks.

When she got back to the hospital, Ranger Montez had returned. Gwen filled out a few forms related to the rescue, and then a few more for the hospital. She handed them back and then the ranger reached out and grasped her hand. "I've got to go," the ranger said. "But it was really a pleasure to meet you." She held Gwen's hand just a second longer than she needed to, the dimples coming back as she smiled.

"Thank you, Ranger Montez," Gwen said, meaning it, sorry to take her hand away. What an impressive person, she thought. What a wonderful calming thing it had been, just to be able to look at this woman.

"It's Jessica. And feel free to call if you remember anything else." She paused and smiled as if she wanted to say something more, but then decided against it. "I hope you come back up to the Sierras sometime," she said finally. "You should give them another chance."

It was almost an hour before Todd was due, so after checking with the front desk, Gwen returned to her room. She was tired, completely worn down. The bed was made up already so she lay down on top of it. Three days she had slept, the rangers said. She could easily sleep three more.

She was awakened by someone yelling, "Timber, wait!" And then a flurry of wriggling fur, muffled yelps of joy, and wet kisses.

"Well, hi there!" Gwen said to the dog, who nuzzled her in return.

Timber was trailing a new leash, Todd nowhere to be seen. She panted and smiled, her fur white and clean, her long tail thumping the bed. She snuck in another kiss and rested her head on Gwen's chest, and Gwen closed her eyes, laughing, and held her tight.

EPILOGUE
ONE YEAR LATER

The scholarship presentation was set to start in half an hour, but Gwen couldn't keep her eyes off the sky. The clouds were gorgeous, stretched thinly across the top of the mountains. When she'd arrived at the park at six thirty that morning, they were lit pink on the bottoms, and that—along with the balloons on the fences, the neat rows of white chairs, the stage that was already draped with colorful banners—had convinced her it would be a lovely day. Now, at nine thirty, families were already lining up outside the rope barrier. There were a few more signs to put up, certificates to get in order, the AV system to check. She would be introducing all the kids today—thirty of her students who'd just graduated from high school and were headed off to college in the fall.

"Are you reserving seats for the graduates?" Todd asked.

"Yes, the first two rows."

"Okay." He stretched masking tape between the first and second rows, and set *Reserved* cards on each of the chairs.

Gwen smiled. It was still strange to see Todd in a button-down shirt and tie, but she was getting used to it. He had been volunteering for much of the last year—helping review contracts, sponsoring a field trip, coming to talk to a group of youth on Career Day. His firm had made a donation to provide all the graduates with $2,500 scholarships, and he was here to see them presented. At first Gwen had been unsure about his interest in helping—and some of her colleagues, like Devon, had been downright resistant—but now she was glad he was there. He seemed genuinely pleased to be involved, and it probably gave him something to do—which was especially important since he and his wife had separated.

By nine forty-five, over a hundred people were waiting. Some of Gwen's colleagues monitored the line but all the families were patient—maybe it was pride on behalf of the students; maybe it was the pleasure of being outdoors on such a beautiful morning. The park—which used to be so overrun by gangs that people avoided it even in daylight—had been completely redone the previous year, and had recently reopened with new baseball fields, a soccer field, playgrounds and pools, exercise stations for the runners who circled the park, and vast amounts of grassy, tree-lined, unstructured space, one area of which they were using for the day's event. Watts had not had a space like this in all the years that Gwen had worked there, and for many more years before that. Arriving this morning, under that colorful sky, and seeing all the early-morning joggers and cyclists, Gwen had been filled with happiness, and pride.

At ten, Gwen's colleagues unhooked one end of the barrier. Families streamed in and took their seats, and there was a chatty hubbub of excitement. Gwen noted happily that the Latino and African American families intermingled, did not sit in different sections. People were talking to one another, kids playing with kids, mothers laughing and comparing stories, men shaking hands and clapping each other on the back. These families had made sacrifices, she knew—creating quiet zones in overcrowded apartments so that their kids could do their homework; working multiple jobs; pushing school officials and social service agencies and churches and clinics to ensure their kids got what they needed. All of this even though most of them lacked formal educations themselves, and many had language barriers. Gwen moved among them and greeted the parents she knew, hugged the beaming kids. Ricardo Flores, who'd graduated from Jordan, was attending USC. Darius Colson, from Locke, would be attending Cal State Northridge. Katrina Johnson and Maria Villalobos from Alliance were going to UCLA, and Pedro and Juanita Gonzalez, twins from King-Drew Medical Magnet, would be going to UC Riverside. LeHenry Stevens, who'd grown up in Nickerson Gardens, had gotten a full ride to Stanford, and Charise Tolliver, from Jordan Downs, was going to Howard. Sylvia Morales, Lupita Gomez, and Dawn Stanton, the girls from Lincoln, were going to Berkeley, Cal State Long Beach, and UC San Diego. And Sandra Gutierrez, the girl she'd worried about so much, had received a scholarship to UC Santa Cruz.

"Thank you," said Mrs. Gutierrez, hugging Gwen tight. That was all she could manage through her tears. They had plenty to celebrate, Sandra and her mom, and fewer things to be scared of. Sandra's stepfather was in prison now, and would be there for at least eight years.

Mixed in with the families were other guests—the principals from the various high schools that the students had come from, teachers, coaches, pastors, representatives from partner agencies; the deputy from the mayor's office who'd come to present a proclamation from the city. In one of the back rows sat Oscar and Claudia, and Oscar's daughter Lily; they'd come in and taken their seats, waving at Gwen across the crowd.

Finally everyone was assembled and Dr. Morrison, the head of Gwen's agency, took the stage. She began with a short prayer, and then thanked everyone for attending. She congratulated all the graduates, and thanked Harrington & Fletcher, Todd's law firm, for awarding the scholarships, as well as several of the corporate partners who had donated a "college care package"—school supplies, backpacks, gift certificates for books—for each of the graduates. She thanked God for imbuing the children and families with strength and determination, and for blessing them with such a beautiful day. Then she turned the mic over to Gwen.

When Gwen stepped to the podium, she gazed out at the audience—the proud faces of the students and their families. She looked past them at the rest of the park—the kids starting to gather for baseball; the booths at the farmer's market; the two police cars stationed fifty yards beyond their event, unobtrusive but present, just in case.

"I want to tell each and every one of you how proud we are," she began. Beside her, with another mic, her colleague Julio translated her words into Spanish. "You have succeeded despite facing challenges and barriers that others can't even imagine. You've succeeded despite the assumptions of many people outside the community, and some inside too, that there's no hope for the youth here in Watts."

"Viva Watts!" someone yelled from the audience.

"That's right!" agreed another.

"You will need every bit of your optimism, your hard

work, your determination, your faith to keep on with your success as you enter this next stage of your lives," Gwen continued. "But you've already shown that you have all those things. And let me tell you something: you have them *because* of where you grew up, not in spite of it. All the difficulties you've faced have made you stronger, more compassionate. They've made you who you are."

She thanked the principals, the teachers, her coworkers, the families. And then, one by one, she called the students up and introduced them, announced which school they'd just graduated from and what college they'd be attending. When she called Sandra up, and then the three girls from Lincoln, she had to clench her fists to keep her voice from shaking. Dr. Morrison handed them each a certificate—and a check for $2,500. It wasn't much—not enough to cover tuition or rent—but for many of them, it would pay for them to travel to campus. It would enable them to buy clothes, or a laptop, or a desk and chair, or glasses. Each student posed with Gwen and Dr. Morrison as a photographer took a picture. It was time-consuming, but the families couldn't get enough—they erupted in cheers and applause for every student.

As Gwen spoke the words about experience and strength, she knew that they applied to her too. Before last summer she wouldn't have been able to stand up and speak in front of a crowd. Before last summer she couldn't have said these words and meant them. But since she'd returned from her trip to the Sierras, everything had taken on a different light. It hadn't happened right away. For weeks she'd called the Forest Service every few days, hoping for word about Tracy. For months she'd checked and double-checked her windows and doors; she'd dreamt of A.J. and José and gunfire, and constantly thought there was someone behind her. But A.J. was dead, and none of their names had come out in the media. She carried the burden, as did Todd, of having taken a life, but it was a burden that was never made public. All that was reported—just like the rangers had promised—was that members of two rival groups, a white supremacist group and a faction of a Mexican drug cartel—had killed each other, and that law enforcement had eradicated their gardens. There was no mention of Gwen and the others at all.

Because of this, no one outside of Oscar and Todd were aware of what had happened. As far as her family and colleagues knew, they'd gotten lost and had to be helped out of the mountains. One of them, Tracy, had never come back; there had never been any word of her. She'd just vanished, and Gwen felt the loss of her, despite her lingering confusion, even anger. It was just like Tracy to disappear so that the story didn't have to end. Maybe she was still in the mountains, outrunning threats, whether real or imagined. Maybe she was trying to settle a score with A.J.'s brother, or José's men. Maybe she'd gotten out and gone somewhere else, come up with a new name and started over. Or maybe she'd gone deeper into the mountains to forge a new life, just like she'd said she wanted to do.

But Gwen suspected it was none of these, suspected her friend was gone; that she'd wandered off and fallen or hurt herself and hadn't made it out. She was saddened by the reckless way that Tracy had handled her life—maybe if you courted danger the way she did, you could only beat it for so long. Tracy's house stood unchanged, and Oscar said her family didn't want to touch it, just in case she did come back. If it hadn't been for Tracy's disappearance, it would have been hard to believe their trip had really happened.

Once Gwen had recovered physically and gone back to work, the slightest things gave her pleasure—her banter with the receptionist, her first sessions with the next crop of kids in the new school year, even the damned boring management meetings that took up half of each Tuesday. She was grateful to be able to do these things, grateful to be alive. And after what she'd been through, she found that she wasn't inclined to keep quiet anymore if she had an opinion. She proposed several adjustments to their programs and Dr. Morrison, after being surprised at her assertiveness, took her suggestions. It wasn't long before she was promoted. Now she not only ran her own youth groups, she supervised all the other staff who ran groups too.

"You keep this up," Dr. Morrison warned, "and you might be running this place someday."

The promotion had led to a raise that made another change possible—six months before, with Oscar's help, she'd bought a condo in Baldwin Hills. Yes, she'd needed to borrow some money from her mother and stepfather to cover the down payment, but she would pay this back as quickly as she could. She didn't have much furniture yet, and there was nothing on the walls. But there was a decent-sized grassy area where Timber could run, ringed by a small garden of native plants. She couldn't be happier about her condo-in-progress. She finally had a place of her own.

As the last of the students stepped off the stage, Gwen felt her eyes welling with tears. A year ago, her sense of purpose and faith had been wavering; she'd despaired over whether she could really make a difference. She didn't feel that way anymore. Not every kid they helped was going to make it, she knew. But many of them did.

As she looked out at the boys—jostling and kidding with each other, accepting the hearty handshakes from men and cooing from the women—she thought for a moment of Robert. He'd been gone for two years now. She still grieved for him, but the pain was more manageable these days. She knew that he was still with her, and always would be. And the best way she could honor his life, she realized, was to fully live her own.

From his seat in the fifth row, Todd watched Gwen and smiled so much his face began to hurt. She looked lovely up there, and happy. It wasn't just that she was wearing a bright, patterned dress and that her hair was flowing over her shoulders. Something exuded from her, a confidence and self-possession. He could see the other men checking her out, and felt pride and amusement. Gwen seemed oblivious to the attention; she didn't even get why her colleague Devon had wanted to hike with her, and had gotten his hackles up when Todd appeared.

Todd was glad to be here today, glad to have something to do on a Saturday morning. Several months ago, Kelly had asked him to leave, and so now he was renting a one-bedroom condo off of Beverly Glen and getting used to being single again. Things had been tense when he returned from his trip—she knew there was something he wasn't telling her. And she wasn't pleased by the sudden crashing of their household by Timber—who was wild, and wrestled with leashes, nipped and herded the children; who jumped on tables with all four feet and ate straight off the dinner plates. But Todd couldn't keep up the charade anymore. Things had changed. *He* had changed. And he was surprised by how much he'd been shaken up by

Tracy's disappearance. For all her gung-ho craziness, she'd brought something out in him, in all of them, and it was strange to think that her vibrancy, her life, might now be gone from the world.

Not that the separation from Kelly had been easy. Even though he knew it was over between them, it had still been a tough few months. He missed his wife, he missed what they once had been. And he missed his children terribly. Right now they were spending every Sunday with him and a couple of nights during the week; otherwise, the condo felt horribly empty. Dogs weren't allowed in his complex, and Timber was most attached to Gwen anyway, so as soon as she had closed on her place with the yard, Timber joined her in Baldwin Hills. He made the best of the time he had with his kids and tried to keep things cordial with Kelly. He'd heard from a colleague that she was dating an heir to one of the city's old oil families.

Because of the divorce and upcoming custody battle, it wasn't practical to leave his job. He didn't like it any better than he had before. But volunteering with Gwen's agency had given him a new sense of purpose. Like today— although he didn't admit it to Gwen, he'd been nervous about coming to Watts, to an event in an open-air venue that had apparently been a gang stronghold. Even this morning he'd felt exposed and self-conscious—he was the only person, including the cops, who wasn't black or Latino. But the park had been surprisingly nice, and the event was clearly a success, with no hint of trouble. And as he saw the parents hugging and crying over their kids, the kids who were so thrilled just to have money for clothes, he felt both shame and pride. He had come to take so much for granted. He was impressed by the park too—he would never have believed there was such a pretty place in Watts. But there was beauty everywhere, he realized, everywhere around, if you just knew where to look.

From his spot in the last row, Oscar was smiling at Gwen too. She was doing well up there with her speaking, better than he would have imagined. Seeing her in her element, and driving through the surrounding neighborhoods to get to the park, he had a greater appreciation for what she did.

"She's like to faint up there in this heat," a mother said from the row in front of him.

"She'll be all right," Oscar told her. And he knew that she would be. She'd handled a hell of lot tougher than this.

Beside him, Lily was wiggling impatiently—just a little bit longer, he told her. On her other side sat Claudia. He'd seen a couple of the other men watching her and had felt not the angry possessiveness he might have a year ago, but pride. He knew that if they looked down at her hand, they'd see the simple diamond engagement ring. They were to be married at the end of summer. And then they'd start working on a brother or sister for Lily.

It had taken Oscar three weeks to fight off the infection from the bullet wound, another couple of months for the shoulder itself to heal. He'd undergone surgery to sew his shoulder together, and now it was fine, except for the dark raised scar the size of a cigar that bisected his lion tattoo, and the pain he sometimes felt when he lifted his arm. He'd even started working out again, although he didn't go to SportZone—it was too strange being there, with Tracy gone. He hadn't missed much in terms of work, since there wasn't much to miss, but when he went back in the fall, he represented a few more buyers—including

Gwen—before going to work for his uncle David. Now he spent his days visiting the same neighborhoods he had as a realtor. He'd downsized and simplified—traded the BMW in for a Kia, bought tidy, more casual clothes. Although there were aspects of the old job he missed, there were also things he gained—the satisfaction of working steadily and hard, and seeing tangible results. Getting a paycheck every other week. When they were done here, they were going shopping for a new sofa and table; before she moved in, before they were married, Claudia wanted to replace his bachelor belongings.

Gwen stepped down off the stage to receive a flurry of thank yous and hugs from the families. Oscar and Claudia approached, and she thanked them for coming. Todd, who'd reappeared, gave Lily a hug and congratulated Claudia on her engagement. He and Oscar shook hands and clapped each other wordlessly on the back.

After Oscar and Claudia left and the crowd dispersed, Todd helped with the cleanup, folding chairs and picking up fallen streamers and untaping signs from posts. When everything was in order, he came back, looking sweaty and a bit sunburned.

"So, now that the school year's over, do you have any summer plans?" he asked.

"Actually," said Gwen, "remember Ranger Montez? She called me a couple of weeks ago and invited me on a hike she'd leading up in Mineral King."

"Oh really?"

"I think she feels bad about what happened last year," Gwen said, blushing. "She said she wants to show me another side of the Sierras."

"She didn't ask Oscar and me if *we* wanted to see another side of the Sierras." He smiled. Awkward as this was,
he didn't begrudge it. Sure, he'd wondered if there might
be something between Gwen and him—despite their dif-
ferences, despite his sadness about the end of his marriage.
But they were good as friends too, and he'd be fine with
that. She was meant to be in his life, no matter what.

Gwen smiled and looked away. What could she say?
She wasn't sure what Jessica's invitation meant either, but
she'd been glad for it. She had thought about the ranger
often in the months she'd been back. She felt a bit nervous
about going to the Sierras again, but this—a day hike, no
camping out, in the company of a ranger—seemed like to
good way to do it. And she would be happy to see Ranger
Montez again, whatever it meant. Jessica was a good one.

So was Todd. She was aware of this as they stopped by
the potluck reception that the parents had put on, and ate
plates full of tamales and fried chicken, mac and cheese
and chilaquiles, carnitas and cornbread, flan and bean
pies. She watched him interact with the families—nodding
and bowing respectfully; shaking the hands of the young
scholars with gravity and tenderness. She and Todd were
so different, and she was aware of that here more than anywhere else, where he looked so out of place. And yet they
were connected, and she did not want that to change. She
wondered, half-smiling, what would piss her mother off
more—if she brought a white man home for Thanksgiving,
or a woman. Neither of them would try to tell her what she
couldn't do. She would never let anyone tell her that again.

After they'd eaten, they walked across the park and
back toward their cars. It was almost one o'clock now, and
the park was full. On two baseball diamonds, Little League

games were underway; boys and girls of about twelve years old wore crisp uniforms and new-looking gloves. The soccer field and basketball courts were teeming with kids. In one corner of the park, the farmer's market was still open—dozens of booths were packed with fresh produce and fruit, home-baked goods, brought by farmers who'd driven in from the Central Valley. Beyond the farmer's market was the playground, where children played on new swings, slides, and seesaws, and dug in sandboxes, while their mothers—and even some fathers—watched from the side. A few hearty souls were still jogging despite the midday heat, and a group of senior citizens were using the leg press machines. They passed a large stage and sound system set up for an afternoon concert; people of all ages were already beginning to gather.

"I had no idea this was here," Todd said.

"These people have always been here. There just hasn't been a place for them to come."

Things weren't perfect, Gwen knew, not by a long shot. Here in this oasis, with its fresh grass and new sports facilities and large shading trees, it was lively and safe—thanks to overdue county funding and community-minded—finally!— police and stubborn residents who demanded the right to enjoy their own neighborhood. But there were families in the housing project just across the street who were still afraid, because of gang boundaries, to come to the park. And in the other housing projects and other neighborhoods, just out of sight, the despair, drugs, and violence continued. Beyond this area of green, beyond the sight of the police, there was trouble still, trouble not easily fixed, trouble as old as the city itself.

But Gwen didn't want to think about that now. She

was proud of the kids whose success she'd been a part of, proud of the families, schools, and community that produced them. She felt comfortable in the presence of this man, who—whatever he was to her—did not question what she could do or who she could be. Tonight, she'd go for a jog with Timber around her new neighborhood. She'd come home and drink a glass of wine on her upstairs patio, and look out over the city she loved.

As they headed toward the edge of the park, past the trees, the mountains came back into view. There, in those mountains, she'd started to hike and first learned to trust her body. There, she was with Robert on what might have been the last happy day of his life.

"They are beautiful, aren't they?" Todd said.

They both stopped and looked. Even from where they stood, they could see the folds of small canyons, the lines of a trail, the antennas on top of Mount Wilson. A few more clouds had drifted in over the range, and it was dappled now in shadow and light. She loved these mountains, despite everything—these, and the San Bernardinos to the east, and the grand, untamed Sierra. They would stay there at the edge of her city, her life, to return to whenever she needed.

"Yes, they are," she answered. She smiled at Todd with an understanding that didn't need to be spoken, and they turned and walked out of the park.

Acknowledgments

I am deeply grateful to the following for their help with this book.

Thanks to Jennifer Gilmore and Kyoko Uchida for their early and insightful readings.

Thanks to Johnny Temple, Johanna Ingalls, Ibrahim Ahmad, Aaron Petrovich, and everyone else at Akashic Books for taking on another of my novels.

Thanks to Richard Parks, Monica Valencia, and Hugh Evans for their specific and expert help.

Thanks to the friends who've accompanied me on trips into the wilderness. And love to two big-spirited men who've been called home to the mountains.

Thanks to the dogs: Russell, the English springer spaniel, for his spirit and companionship; and Ariat, the border collie, for choosing our cabin.

And finally, my love and gratitude to Felicia Luna Lemus— for her caring attention to this book and our lives, and for always walking beside me.